Kindling Flames

Stolen Fire

Julie Wetzel

Crimson Tree Publishing

THIS book is a work of fiction. Names, characters, places and incidents are the product of the authors' imagination or are used factiously. Any resemblance to actual persons, living or dead, business establishments, events or locales is entirely coincidental.

Kindling Flames

ISBN: 978-1-63422-068-2
Cover Design by: Marya Heiman
Typography by: Courtney Nuckels
Editing by: Cynthia Shepp

This is dedicated to my father.
I love you, Daddy.

Prologue

HAPPY SHOPPERS BUSTLED ALONG THE BUSY STREET WITHOUT NOTING THE darkness leaning in the shallow doorway. A snicker slithered out, cutting through the frosty air. They had no idea what was hiding among them.

Taking a deep breath of cold, winter air, the shadow picked out a lone woman walking past. The form of a man slipped into the crowd unseen and followed the woman down the street. Sharp, canine teeth lengthened as he stalked his unsuspecting prey. His heart leaped for joy as the girl turned into the entranceway of a parking garage. This would make taking his prize so much easier.

He hadn't been a vampire for very long, but he was really starting to like it. The power fresh blood gave him was exhilarating, even though his transformation wasn't finished. There were still days when his strength waned, but those were getting rarer. Soon, it would be complete. Those winged creatures he'd captured had promised him the revenge he so desired, but he hadn't expected this.

Following his prey deeper into the privacy of the garage, the vampire slipped his arms around the woman, catching her by surprise. His thin fingers muffled her screams as he pinned her against his chest. Sinking his fangs into her neck to drain her lifeblood, he thought of the one responsible for his misfortune.

Just you wait, Darien Ritter, your turn will be soon.

1

The sound of the elevator opening pulled Vicky's attention from the stack of files she'd been transferring to the computer. She wasn't surprised that company was dropping in unannounced. Recently, most of her evenings had been spent entertaining members of Darien's new menagerie.

The number of people now in Darien's care had surprised Vicky. She hadn't realized that Darien's claims on Christian and Lillian's people would bring so many new people into their lives. With the exception of a few, Christian's people had been pretty easy to deal with. It was Lillian's menagerie that was vexing.

Lillian had been very active about turning those she found special, and her kiss had been the largest in the area. Darien had been very reluctant to enter his new menagerie's space after he had been forced to claim their master's life. Lillian's fledglings knew the laws governing vampires demanded her death, but taking steps too aggressively would only lead to harder feelings and resentment. Some of Lillian's people were nearly masters themselves. Elliot had been a key player in the changeover. He had been on good terms with most of Lillian's people and had quickly agreed to help Darien through these trying times.

Darien had been only too happy to accept Elliot's offer. It had been many years since Darien had kept the company of his own kind, and having a menagerie dropped onto his lap had been rather shocking. He had done his best to balance his normal workload with the new demands, but the stress was starting to show.

Closing the folder of financial reports, Vicky looked up from where she sat on the floor at the glass coffee table. She was surprised when only one person walked into the room. "Hello, Elliot," Vicky greeted the familiar vampire. She looked over the casual way the tall man was dressed. He had a classy leather jacket pulled over a dark blue shirt and stonewashed jeans. His long, blond hair was tied back in a neat braid that hung most of the way down his back.

Elliot smiled at her. "What are you doing on the floor?" He perched on the arm of the couch closest to the door. It was one of a pair of blue sofas that matched the loveseat decorating the main living room of Darien's penthouse. Even though Darien's home was elegant, his furniture was simple, comfortable, and functional.

Vicky nodded to the angel stone hearth and the fire crackling softly behind her. "Enjoying the warmth."

Zak snuggled against her legs, purring loudly.

Elliot's hazel eyes twinkled as he chuckled. "I can see that, but what are you working on?" He nodded at the computer on the glass table.

Vicky looked at the machine. "Oh, I'm trying to catch Darien's files up." She patted the stack of papers next to the computer. "These are all of last month's records for his small businesses."

Elliot cocked an eyebrow at her. "Shouldn't he be doing that?"

"Well, yes, but he's been so busy lately that he hasn't had time for them." Vicky sighed. "He hasn't had much time for anything recently. I thought I would get this out of the way so he could relax a bit."

"Does he know what you're doing?" Elliot asked.

Vicky looked away, trying to hide her guilt. "Not really," she said shyly. Turning back to look at Elliot, she gave him a half smile, showing he caught her doing something she really wasn't supposed to do. "He started to work on them when we got home but got a call that upset him. Right now, he's up on the roof, pacing it off." She let out another deep sigh. "He's been doing that a lot lately."

Elliot chuckled again. "You're a good woman." He smiled warmly down at her. "Now that everyone's recognized Darien as their new master, things will start to settle down."

Vicky gave him half a smile. "I hope so. He's been all wound up these last few weeks. I don't know what to do with him. He goes from being very distant to clingy and back without warning. I know he's stressed, I can feel it through his mark, but I don't know what to do about it."

Elliot drew in a long breath and let it out heavily. "Just be there for him. This is something he just has to deal with." He shook his head. "I'm glad to hear that he finally marked you properly."

"Yes." Vicky turned to look down at the pile of work in front of her, slightly embarrassed by where their conversation had gone. "It took some convincing to get him to try it again, but I think it made him happier."

Elliot grinned at the light color creeping up her cheeks. "Oh, I know it made him happier. He hated the fact that Zak had a mark on you and he didn't."

Zak wiggled his tentacles so they wrapped farther around Vicky.

Elliot looked over at the hellhound curled up next to her. "How did Zak take it?" He could just see the fay's beady, little eyes and sharp teeth nestled into the mass of greenish black tentacles.

Vicky smiled and scratched her fingers into the fay's back. "Rather well. He only ate two of Darien's pants that night, but he hasn't really chewed anything else up since."

"He can feel Darien through you," Elliot informed her.

Vicky looked down at the fay thoughtfully. "So, he's being good because he knows Darien's stressed," she stated, looking back up at Elliot.

The little whine Zak made pulled a laugh from Elliot. "Could be," he said as he stood up. "I'll let you get back to work before he eats your files."

Vicky looked down to where Zak's tentacles were pulling the stack of papers off the table. "You've already eaten two of my pens tonight," she huffed, swatting the feelers away from the paper. "These are not for you."

Elliot laughed and turned back out to the elevators. He punched the button for the rooftop terrace so he could find his worried friend.

The cold winter air brushed across Darien's skin as he paced the rooftop terrace. Worry ate at him as his mind churned over the phone call he'd received. One of the new members of his menagerie was missing. Mary, one of the few living members of Christian's menagerie that Darien had taken in, had called frantically to report that Erin had run off. Everyone was currently out looking for the traumatized girl.

Darien was at a loss as to what to do with Erin and her sister, Bridget. After claiming the rights to Christian's people, Darien had done his best to clean up the mess Christian had left, but he never dreamed he would find two children locked away in a closet. That man had truly been one sick puppy.

Mary had been working with the girls, trying to get them readjusted to the world. They were slowly making progress, but the sight of Allen feeding had been too much for the younger of the girls. Allen had apologized profusely and insisted that Darien's direct attention to this matter was not needed. They would find Erin well before Darien could make the drive across town.

Darien had let them go with instructions to call him as soon as she was safe. It really pissed him off that anyone could hurt children the way these little girls had been. Children were too precious to be put in such hurtful situations.

Claiming Lillian and Christian's menageries was turning out to be more than Darien had bargained for, but it was something he had to do. Had he abandoned them, Clara would have been forced to deal with the menageries, and that would have been a death sentence for all of them.

Christian's people had crossed too many lines to be allowed to roam free. As it was, Rupert and the wolves had already helped cleanse some of the more colorful characters from their ranks. Darien had released those humans who had been either strong-armed or blackmailed into Christian's service. A clever bit of magic had seen that they would never speak of their experiences to anyone.

Dealing with Lillian's brood would have been harder on everyone. Even though some of Lillian's get were almost masters, they still needed the strength of an older vampire to wake at dusk. Had Darien turned them out, no one would have gone against his decision and attempted to help them. They were rightfully his, to keep or let die as he saw fit.

To Clara's great relief, Darien had gone to them that first evening and called them to life. He had offered himself as their master. Each one had accepted him and tied themselves to him. Now, they were a warm, almost comfortable feeling inside him, like a soft hum just beyond his perception. It was odd being tied to so many, but he was slowly getting used to it again.

The sound of the elevator pulled Darien from his pacing. He turned as his friend stepped out into the night. "Did they find her?"

Elliot stopped at Darien's sudden outburst. "Find whom?" he asked, concerned he missed something.

Darien sighed heavily and rolled his face up to the sky in exasperation. "Erin. Did they find her?"

Elliot cocked his head as he considered Darien's words. "I didn't know she was missing." He pulled out his phone to call

Mary. She answered on the first ring. "Is Erin missing?" Nodding his head, he listened to what happened. "Did you look under the shed?" He paused as Mary ran to check.

Darien looked on with awe as Elliot thanked the woman and hung up the phone. "And?" he asked, worried for the little girl's safety.

Elliot shrugged his shoulders as if it were nothing. "She was under the shed."

"How did you know where she'd be?" Darien asked, flabbergasted.

"Bridget told me that she and her sister saw a cat hiding under the shed yesterday." Elliot explained. "It makes sense that Erin would hide in a place where she thought things were safe."

Relief washed through Darien. "I don't know what I'd do without you, Elliot. You have no idea how valuable you've been over these last few weeks."

"Well, I knew you wouldn't be able to handle everything on your own." Elliot shrugged again. "With your business and the needs of the new kiss, you have way too much on your plate."

Darien let out another long breath. "You're right. I had no idea things would be this stressful." He found one of the benches around the many planters and sat down. "So, who did you bring today?"

Elliot joined him on the bench. "No one." He leaned back, crossed his legs in front of him, and looked up at the dark sky. "You met the last of them yesterday."

Darien looked over at him, surprised. "You mean, that was everyone?"

"Yup." Elliot laced his fingers together over his stomach. "They've all accepted you as their master."

Darien sat quietly, thinking about the multitude of people who had passed through his home in the last weeks. He had absolutely no idea what he was supposed to do with them now. Their link with him would ensure their well-being, but interacting with them personally was a little overwhelming. It had been a long time since he'd had people depending on him outside of a business setting. Elliot was the youngest of his living fledglings, and he hadn't needed anything from Darien in a long time. "What do I do now?" Darien asked, a little bewildered at the situation he found himself in.

Elliot laughed at him. "Well, for starters, you could step back and take a look at those around you."

Darien looked at Elliot, not understanding what he was talking about.

Seeing his confusion, Elliot went on. "You haven't been yourself in a while. Those of us who know you have noticed."

Darien folded his hands together and leaned forward to rest his elbows on his knees. He hung his head and let out a long breath. "I'm sorry, Elliot," Darien apologized. "I know this has been hard on you."

"I don't mind." Elliot looked over at his friend without moving. "And, I'm not the one you should be apologizing to."

Darien turned his green eyes to his friend, confused.

"There is someone closer to you who has been very patient as you've dealt with things."

Darien sat up, surprised, as comprehension dawned on him.

Elliot nodded. "She's downstairs right now, sorting through your paperwork."

Darien closed his eyes and rubbed his hands over his face. "I totally forgot about those files when Mary called." He let out a ragged breath.

"Understandable." Elliot nodded again.

Darien shook his head and leaned back against the bench. "This isn't the first time Victoria has picked up my pieces." He looked up to the sky as he talked. "Somehow, she always has what I need ready for me. Just the other day, she finished going over my expense report and gave me the highlights as we walked to the meeting. I was supposed to have gone over it the night before, but I had completely forgotten about it."

Elliot smiled to himself. "You are really lucky to have her

around. I'm glad to hear that you finally marked her."

Darien sat up and looked at Elliot in surprise. "She told you that?" he asked, completely blown over.

"Only just now." Elliot's smiled widened. "She said she was worried about you. She can feel how upset you are."

Darien chuckled and relaxed back against the bench again. "She is a very quick learner when it comes to those things." Feeling down his link to Vicky, he smiled. It was easy to feel her concern tickling at the edges of mind, but her attention was tuned into her work. "You know, I need to do something extraordinary for her," Darien decided.

"You've already given her your soul." Elliot grinned at him. "What else were you thinking?"

A slow smile crept across Darien's face. "I know just the thing." He stood up from the bench. "Come on."

Elliot popped up from where he was relaxing and followed his friend. "What are you thinking?" he asked.

Darien shot him a mischievous grin.

Elliot looked at him, puzzled, as they got into the elevator to go back downstairs. He didn't know what the older vampire would do, but knowing Darien, it was going to be memorable.

Darien starred down at the blonde furiously typing away on his computer. He loved the way she looked, sitting on the floor in front of the fire. The way the light reflected in the golden curls she had pinned loosely to the back of her head made his heart sing.

When Vicky came to the end of her page, she flipped it over and looked up to the man watching her. "Did you get everything worked out?"

The corner of Darien's mouth turned up in a slight smile. "Yes." He came over and looked down at the work he had left. Picking up the page Vicky had just finished, he scanned over the figures. "What are you doing?" He cocked his eyebrow.

Vicky looked away, embarrassed that she had been caught doing something he preferred to do himself. "Helping out," she said in a small voice.

Darien held his hand for her.

Vicky took it and let him lift her to her feet.

Darien pulled her against him. "Thank you." He wrapped her in a warm embrace.

Vicky let out a long, contented sigh and leaned into him.

"I've asked so much of you these last few weeks."

"It's just a little paperwork." Vicky smiled.

"No." Darien kissed her on the top of the head. "It's so much more than that." He held her against him for a moment longer before going on. "Marry me."

Vicky pushed back so she could look up at his odd request. "I already said I would." Affection filled her face.

Darien shook his head slightly. "No, I mean now."

Vicky was slightly surprised by the sudden request. "Like, 'now' as in *now*?"

Darien nodded his head.

Vicky pushed back a little more. "My mom would kill me if we ran off and got married without her. Oh, and Vanessa would be furious; she's already put so much effort into planning my wedding."

Darien cocked an eyebrow at her. "Since when has Vanessa been planning our wedding?"

"Since college."

Darien raised both eyebrows in surprise.

Vicky let out a deep breath. "It's a long story." Vanessa had started planning Vicky and Tim's wedding before things went south for them. She had kept all the ideas, knowing her friend would find a better man later.

Darien shook his head, amused. "Well, since your friend has put in so much work already, do you think she would want to make the rest of the arrangements?"

Vicky stared at his suggestion, openmouthed. Vanessa would be beside herself with joy over this offer.

"Of course, there would have to be some adjustments to her plans." Darien looked back at his friend leaning against the wall, watching them. "How would you like to be my best man, Elliot?"

Elliot tilted his head to his friend, accepting the position. "I would be honored."

Vicky blinked at them, stunned. "Will that be okay?"

"Why not?" Darien responded. "I would say he knows me better than anyone else."

"No, no." Vicky chuckled at the misunderstanding. "I mean, letting Vanessa plan our wedding. She has some very grand ideas."

Darien tipped his head back and laughed. He drew in a deep breath before going on. "Of course. I think my pocketbook can handle her."

Vicky gave him a doubtful look that drew another laugh from him.

"And I think Elliot can rein her in where she needs it." He looked over to his smirking friend. "So, are you up to the challenge?"

Elliot pushed away from the wall, laughing. "It will be an intriguing challenge." Walking over, he placed a hand on each of their shoulders. "Let me be the first to congratulate you. So, when is the wedding going to be?"

Vicky turned questioning eyes up to Darien.

"As soon as possible," Darien added.

"Well, with Thanksgiving just passed and Christmas coming up, it would probably be best if we waited until after the first of the year," Vicky pointed out.

"January is going to be busy at work. With the start of the new year, there is always a lot of paperwork." Darien pondered the timing. "If we plan for the end of January, we could take time off in February for our honeymoon."

"That would also allow for time to make all the arrangements," Vicky agreed.

"Perfect." Darien pulled her in for another embrace as Elliot stepped back. "Then you had better go see if Vanessa can do it."

"Oh my!" Vicky exclaimed as she stepped out of Darien's arms. She turned surprised eyes up at him. "With everything that's happened, I forgot to tell the girls about our engagement. They are going to be so furious with me!"

Darien laughed as Vicky went to call her friends.

"You really do have a special one, there." Elliot patted his friend on the arm. "Do you think you can handle getting married?"

Darien took a deep breath and let it out in a heavy sigh. "I think so." He looked down at the computer and the neat stack of folders waiting for his attention. "It will definitely be more fun than some of my other long-term partners." This drew another laugh from Elliot as Darien settled to the floor to pick up where Vicky had left off.

2

"SO WHAT IS THIS ALL ABOUT?" VANESSA ASKED.

Vicky just smiled and wiggled excitedly in her seat. She shook her head at her best friend. "We have to wait for Maggie and Beth to get here." Looking around the dance floor of Alchemy, she searched for her missing friends. "I want you all here for this." Turning back to her best friend, she studied her for a moment. Vanessa had managed to pull her long, red hair up into a messy bun that gave the beautiful woman an elegant edge. It matched the tight, black dress she had somehow squeezed her ample chest into.

"Come on, Vicks." Vanessa prodded her friend. "I couldn't believe you would call us out here on a Tuesday night. This had got to be big. What is it?"

Vicky just grinned into her drink and shook her head.

Vanessa studied her friend. "Oh my God, you're not pregnant, are you?"

"No!" Vicky gasped at the idea. "Why would I invite you out to a club if I were pregnant?"

Vanessa giggled at the shocked look on Vicky's face. "He asked you, didn't he?" The grin on her face widened.

Vicky couldn't contain the blush that rose in her cheeks.

"Oh, girl, you had better show me the ring."

Vicky giggled to herself and held out her hand so Vanessa

could see the emerald and diamond band wrapped around her finger.

Vanessa marveled at the ring for a moment before letting Vicky's hand go. "Details, girl!" she demanded.

"What details?" Beth's voice cut through the pulsating music as she and Maggie came up to the table.

"Lover boy proposed," Vanessa informed the rest of Vicky's friends.

"Really!" Maggie squealed in excitement.

Vicky smiled and nodded as the short brunette dropped to give her a hug.

"That's magnificent!" Maggie said. When she turned Vicky loose, Beth gave Vicky a hug to rival the first excited girl's.

"Let's see it," Beth demanded as she forced Vicky to slide over in the booth. Maggie joined Vanessa on the other bench.

Vicky held her hand out for her friends to inspect the ring.

"It's not a diamond," Maggie protested.

"It's got some diamonds in it," Vicky defended as she looked over her engagement band. A large emerald held the crowning spot as a row of smaller emeralds marched down the sides of the band. Two lines of diamonds bracketed the colored stones, making the ring sparkle in the twinkling lights of the club. "It's platinum," she explained. This brought an appreciative noise from the girls.

"It's beautiful." Vanessa grinned. "But, what's this?" She touched the green line set into Vicky's skin.

Vicky pulled her hand back and rubbed the line, embarrassed.

Beth pulled Vicky's hand up so she could look at the band stretching across her hand and around her wrist. "Did you get a tattoo?" she asked as she inspected the mark.

Vicky pulled her hand back from her friend and hid it under the table. "It's not what you think." Her mind worked furiously to come up with an explanation for the strange mark. How was she supposed to tell her friends that the fay had set the hand-fasting ribbon into her and Darien's skin? She had expected the line to fade, but it was still as bright as the ribbon Dakine had used on Halloween. Vicky looked at the questioning faces around her and knew she would have to give them something. "A couple of Darien's associates didn't like the fact that we were living together unmarried," she said shyly. "They insisted that we get engaged. This," Vicky held her hand up so they could see the green band, "was part of that. It's temporary," she assured her friends, hoping it was true. Pity shone in her friends' eyes.

"He asked you to marry him to save face?" Maggie said, sounding disgusted.

"No, no!" Vicky shook her head for emphasis. "It's not like that. The handfasting was to make his friends happy. *This* was to make us happy." The soft look in Vicky's eyes as she caressed the ring was enough to settle her friends' ruffled feathers.

"So, have you talked about a date?" Beth asked.

Vicky nodded her head. "The end of January."

"That's fast," Maggie said, shocked.

"Darien wanted to elope, but my mother would kill me if we did that," Vicky informed her friends.

"Wow!" Vanessa exclaimed as she picked up her drink to take a sip. "So, do you have any ideas on what you want?"

Vicky nodded again. "We were actually hoping that you'd be willing to help plan the wedding." The look on Vanessa's face was priceless as Beth and Maggie squealed in delight.

"I would be honored." Vanessa's voice was breathy with shock and joy.

"We can go over the details later." Vicky took her best friend's hand and squeezed it. "Right now, let's go dance to celebrate." The girls agreed and slipped out of the booth, heading towards the dance floor. Vicky paused for a moment to make sure her bag was tucked securely into the booth before following her friends.

A strange feeling tingled up Vicky's spine, and she stopped to look around. A man stood at the far end of the bar, watching her intently. She studied him for a moment. His lean frame wasn't very tall, quite average by most people's standards. His chocolate brown hair stood up in loose spikes, overshadowing an almost hawk-like face. He was fairly handsome in a nondescript sort of way, but it was the look in his eyes that gave Vicky chills.

"Come on," Vanessa called to her stalled friend.

Vicky glanced at Vanessa, and then back to the bar, but the man was gone. She blinked in confusion before turning her attention to her beckoning friends. Shaking the shiver from her spine, she slipped onto the dance floor. Since Darien had taken her in, there had been a lot of people watching her. This was probably nothing to worry about.

Vicky's worries were brushed away when she stepped onto the dance floor and found herself in the arms of a familiar man. She had only been properly introduced to him a few days ago, but she had seen him several times in the club. Looking around, she couldn't find his identical copy. "Where's your brother?"

The twin chuckled at her and spun her around so she could see his duplicate. "He's found something interesting."

Vicky laughed as her eyes located the matching man dancing with Vanessa. "So which one are you?" She knew he was either Jakob or Josh, but the trouble came in trying to tell which was which.

A sweet smile slipped across the vampire's face. "That's Jakob." He nodded towards his brother. "I'm Josh."

Smiling, Vicky caught the hint of untruth and called him on the lie. "Somehow, I can tell when you're lying to me, Jakob."

Jakob chuckled lightly. "I can see our master has marked you well, My Lady."

"How can you tell?" Vicky asked, surprised.

Jakob laid his fingers gently on her chest. "I can feel him in you."

A soft ripple of powers caressed the inside of her skin. It felt like cool silk. Vicky could feel the question from Darien as the echo of Jakob's power rippled across their connection. Smiling, she sent reassuring thoughts across their invisible link.

She could feel Darien relax back to whatever he had been doing.

Surprised at how strong the link was, Jakob withdrew his power. "Forgive me. I didn't mean to disturb our master." He bowed his head to her slightly as they danced. "I did not realize your link was so strong."

She brushed the error away. "It's all right." Something odd hit her as she processed his words. "I thought Darien had marked you, too."

"Yes." Jakob nodded. "We are all bound to Master Darien, but my bond is much thinner than yours. It's just enough to ensure our safety."

Vicky could hear a hint of envy in his voice.

Jakob let out a sad sigh. "Lillian had us bound so tightly to her. It's odd to not have her presence in my mind."

Vicky looked away from the hurt she could feel in him. "I'm sorry." There was really nothing she could say to make it better. "Darien really is a good man."

Jakob grinned weakly. "I know. Lillian didn't give him any choice. It's just taking time to get used to the changes."

Vicky looked up at her dance partner. "And are you getting used to it?" She was truly worried about the people Darien had taken in.

Jakob smiled at her. "It was strange for a while," he admitted. "Master Darien's connection fluctuated at first, and we were worried that he didn't have enough strength to support us all. There were stories about how powerful Darien was, but those first weeks made us all question them. Then he marked you." Jakob's eyes warmed as he spoke. "Somehow, that stabilized our connections. It no longer took any effort to keep the link with our master."

"And is he as powerful as the stories say?" Vicky asked curiously. She had felt Darien's power, but she had nothing with which to compare it.

"That and so much more," Jakob said softly. "Lillian's power was a solid weight, almost tangible when you reached for it, but

Darien's is something else completely. It's light and airy, and when you reach for it, it's a pulsating radiance that threatens to engulf you." Jakob had closed his eyes and stilled as he spoke about the power supporting him.

Vicky paused in her dancing in response to the vampire in front of her.

Jakob's eyes popped back open, and he grinned apologetically. "Sorry." He took Vicky's hand and spun her around to get her moving again. Rolling her in his arms so her back was against his chest, he slipped back into the beat of the music. "Thank you, My Lady. My brother and I are at your service if you should ever need anything." Vicky's eyes widened as she looked over to the twin she could see. The nod of Josh's head and the look in his eyes echoed the sentiments of his brother.

"Thank you," Vicky answered as soon as she got over the surprise. "And let your brother know I appreciate it."

Jakob laughed behind her. "He already knows." There was a note of mischief in the vampire's voice. "My brother and I are connected."

Vicky considered this for a moment. "So, he knows everything you do?"

"And I know everything he does," Jakob confirmed. "In fact, your friend there has invited us both over for the evening."

Vicky bit her lower lip, trying to keep the surprise from slipping out as a giggle. She turned in her partner's arms to face him again. "Don't let me stop you." She worked to keep her embarrassment from showing.

Jakob raised his hand to Vicky's cheek and caressed it gently. "It's almost a shame our master protects you the way he does," he said softly. "I'm sure you would be magnificent." He ran his finger over her lower lip in a very suggestive way.

Vicky's eyes widened in surprise as the blush she'd been fighting bloomed in her cheeks.

Jakob's eyes darted to something over Vicky's shoulder, and he released her. He bowed himself away from her and went to join his brother.

Turning around, Vicky found Elliot standing behind her, watching the younger vampire fall into step with Vanessa. "Elliot!" Vicky's voice squeaked a little and she cleared her throat, trying to recover. "What are you doing here?"

Elliot shifted her to a new position on the dance floor, and they fell into step with the rhythm of the music. "Darien called and asked if I could check on you," he explained. "He felt the wash of power from our friend there and was worried."

"He was... um..." Vicky didn't know how to explain it.

"Checking you out," Elliot finished for her. "You and Darien are still an enigma. I'm sure there will be many boundaries pushed before things fully settle down." He looked up to the twins wrapped around Vicky's best friend. "Those two are natural-born troublemakers. Keep an eye out for them and their shenanigans."

Vicky nodded her head and filed this information away for later thought. She was definitely going to have to have a long talk with Darien. There was too much she still didn't know about dealing with vampires. For the moment, she relaxed, knowing Elliot would see her through the rest of the night.

3

Vicky paused as the door from the foyer swung shut. She shook her head at the sight that was becoming more common. The first rays of the morning sun were slipping through the windows of the breakfast nook to dance on the white marble of the shotgun kitchen. Darien sat at the iron scrollwork table, picking over Vicky's breakfast.

"Maybe Odette should start making you a plate, too," Vicky teased as she went over to see how much of her food was still there. He had eaten her toast and most of the eggs.

Darien gave her a guilty grin as he vacated the chair so she could sit down. "It just looked so good this morning."

Vicky took her seat and looked at her breakfast. There was still plenty left. Darien's fay housekeeper and cook had been slowly increasing the amount of food she prepared in the morning. Apparently, she has taken into account Zak's begging and Darien's increased appetite for solid food. "At least I know I won't get fat with you two around," Vicky teased, and she pulled out Zak's sausage and bacon to drop to the little horror wiggling on the floor by her feet.

Darien snickered at her as he pulled down the blue tumbler for his normal breakfast of blood from the crisper drawer.

Vicky glanced back at him moving through the kitchen. "Isn't it odd that you're craving solid food?"

Darien paused in his task to think about it. "Maybe a little," he admitted, "but it could be the new menagerie. They draw more energy than I'm used to."

Vicky gave him a dubious look. "But shouldn't you be craving more blood? I didn't think you got energy from food."

Darien shrugged at this thought and changed the subject. "Did Vanessa agree to plan our wedding?"

Vicky gave him a pointed look but switched to the new topic. "She was thrilled." She turned her attention to her breakfast as she spoke. "Vanessa will be over after work today to get started on the plans. I talked with Elliot last night, and he'll be stopping by as well. I want to get those two working together as soon as possible." Vicky shook her head softly. She had told Darien all of this last night when she had gotten home from the club. He was becoming even more of a scatterbrain as things piled up in his life. A strange thought popped into her head as she watched Darien finish his blood and rinse the cup out. "Do you think it'll be all right for Elliot to work with Vanessa?"

Darien gave her a surprised look.

"He *is* a vampire."

"I think Elliot's old enough to control his bloodlust," Darien said, slightly offended. "He's not going to attack her."

Vicky snickered at the misunderstanding. "That's not what I meant. Vanessa is sharp. Won't she notice something's off about Elliot?"

Darien came over and raised his hand to Vicky's face. "You didn't notice anything off about me." He caressed her cheek.

Vicky smiled and leaned into his soft touch. "Point." She conceded to his logic.

"Besides, Elliot's better at memory manipulation than I am. If something happens, he can handle it." Darien leaned over and kissed her softly. "Stop worrying about it, and finish your breakfast so we can go."

Vicky chuckled and turned back to her food as Darien left to finish getting ready for work.

Vicky looked up from her desk as the door to the office swung open. A large bouquet of flowers struggled its way into the room.

"Delivery for Miss Victoria Westernly," the voice of the deliveryman called from behind the foliage.

Vicky stood up from her desk to give the man a hand.

Handing her a clipboard to sign, he set two dozen red roses on the middle of her desk.

There was only one person Vicky could think of that would send such a present. "They're beautiful." Vicky smiled as she went into Darien's office. "Thank you."

Darien looked up from his computer, confused. "What's beautiful?"

Vicky's smiled slipped slightly. "The flowers."

"What flowers?"

Vicky pointed towards her office. "The ones you sent me."

Darien stood up to go see what Vicky had gotten. "I didn't send you flowers."

Confused, Vicky followed him from the room. "If you didn't send them, who did?"

Darien shook his head at the question. He looked over the gift and found a small card among the blooms. 'Congratulations' was written across it in block letters. The card was otherwise unsigned. "I'm not sure." He showed the card to Vicky. "Maybe someone's heard about our engagement."

Vicky smiled as she turned the vase around to get a better view of the roses. "Well, whoever they are, I like their style."

Darien chuckled at her and patted her back gently. "Since you're already interrupted, could you go get me some coffee?" He turned to go back into his office.

Vicky looked up at the clock, it was almost five, and they would be leaving soon. "This late in the day?"

"Please. We've had such a long day that I'm having trouble concentrating on these files," Darien explained.

Vicky grinned as she picked up her bag. They'd spent the morning running around and had missed their normal coffee break. "All right," she agreed and moved the flowers from her desk to a little end table between the chairs in her office. Darien thanked her and disappeared back into his office. Vicky couldn't help but laugh at Darien and his passion for his coffees. Any other vampire would be sick on the stuff, but he had to have at least one cup in the afternoon to get through the rest of the day.

Pondering over who could have sent the flowers, Vicky rode the elevator down to the fifth floor café. Her mind was still turning the question over when she stepped up to the counter and was met by a face she didn't know.

"How can I help you?" the young man asked.

"Where's Sue?" Vicky asked, shocked that the spunky werewolf wasn't there.

"She took the day off, My Lady," Sue's replacement answered.

With the addition of the 'My Lady', Vicky knew that this had to be one of Rupert's wolves. She considered what looked to be a teenage boy with floppy, brown hair. "Do you know what Mr. Ritter's usual is?" Vicky asked.

"Carmel macchiato," the boy answered, and turned to get the coffee. "By the way, I'm Derrick."

Vicky smiled at him. "Is Sue okay?" She had never known the woman to take time off.

"As far as I know." Derrick set the finished drink on the counter. "Will there be anything else?"

"No, thank you." Vicky took the drink and stepped away from the counter. It felt weird not having Sue there.

"Have a nice day, My Lady." Derrick waved and went to clean the machines.

Vicky's mind spun on this new development. She didn't like having someone else in the café. It just felt wrong. She thought about it all the way back to her office.

"Here's your coffee," Vicky said, setting the coffee on Darien's desk.

He nodded his head in acknowledgement.

She started to go out but stopped. Having Derrick in the coffee shop bugged her. "Did you know that Sue wasn't in the café today?"

Darien looked up from his work. He could hear the concerned note in Vicky's voice.

"There was a guy named Derrick there."

"Derrick fills in when Rupert needs Sue for something," Darien explained. "That's not a problem."

Nodding, Vicky went back out to her desk. It still didn't feel right, but she let it go. Now, if she could just find her place again, she could get these numbers entered before the end of the day, and Darien wouldn't have to worry about his small business status reports again until next month.

Vicky looked up from her files when she heard Darien come out of his office. She had been trying to get back into the groove to finish the project, but it just wasn't working. Stretching in her chair, she slipped the folders into her desk drawer for tomorrow.

"You okay?" Darien asked as he waited for Vicky to get moving. Usually she was fairly quick about getting out of work.

"Yeah." Vicky pulled her bag up and slipped it over her shoulder. "I don't think I got enough sleep last night," she admitted sheepishly. A sluggish feeling had plagued her all day. A case of the flu was going around in the office, and she hoped she hadn't caught it.

Darien chuckled at her. "Come on." He pulled her into his side. "We still have to plan our wedding tonight."

Vicky smiled and started to let him pull her towards the door, but she stopped when the roses caught her eye. "Can I take the flowers home?"

Darien considered the enormous bouquet. It was much too large to fit into the XKR-5 Jaguar he had been driving since someone helped to total his Aston Martin DB9. "Sure." He kissed the side of Vicky's head and turned her loose to pick up the flowers. "It's starting to get a little too cold to drive a convertible, anyway."

Vicky grinned and went to hold the door for him. She had complained about the temperature every morning since the start of December. Hopefully, Charlie could find something with a nice heater for the rest of winter.

"Do you think Elliot will know who sent the flowers?" Vicky asked as Darien maneuvered the arrangement into the elevator. Slipping in behind him, she hit the button for the basement garage, where Darien kept his car collection.

"Perhaps," Darien answered from behind the flowers.

Vicky grinned, trying not to laugh at the sight. She helped Darien off the elevator and led the way to the small shack where the keeper of Darien's cars could always be found.

"Good evening, Mr. Ritter. Lovely flowers," the sweet old man said as he opened the door to greet his boss. "Good evening, My Lady."

"Good evening, Charlie," Vicky greeted him. She hadn't figured out exactly what Charlie was, but she was sure he wasn't human.

"I need transportation." Darien set the heavy vase down. "Something I can haul this in."

Charlie looked over the vase and smiled. "I have just the thing." Slipping into his shack, he came out with a little, black box and handed it over to Darien. "It's in forty-five."

Darien pushed a button on the box, and a key popped out.

"It's new, so be careful with her."

Darien smiled at the warning. "Thank you." He picked up the flowers and turned towards the parking places containing his cars. Darien loved old cars and kept a vast collection of them squirreled away in numbered bays lining the walls of the expansive, underground garage. Vicky had seen quite a few of them in her time as his personal assistant. He liked to take them out and show them off from time to time.

Vicky couldn't help but wonder what Charlie had chosen for them this time. Her eyes scanned up and down the rows of cars as they walked. Most of the ones sitting out were new. There was everything from small, sporty cars to large vans. There was even one unmarked box truck. She paused as her eyes caught a flash of gold between two cars. "Darien," Vicky called to get his attention.

He paused and looked back to where Vicky had stopped a few steps behind him. "Yes?"

"There's something there," Vicky whispered to him. Her mind flashed to the headlines of the morning paper. A woman and been killed not far from here two nights ago. Her throat had been ripped out, and her blood drained.

Darien stepped back to where Vicky was looking into the darkness between the vehicles. "Come out," he demanded of the dark shape hiding there. A tawny wolf slunk out into the light. Darien relaxed as he recognized the werewolf cowering before him. "What are you doing here, Sue?"

Sue whined a little and limped over to huddle against Vicky's leg.

Shock filled Vicky as her eyes found dark patches of blood in Sue's orangish fur. "Darien!" Vicky gasped, bending to look for the source of the blood. There was a nasty bite mark on Sue's hindquarter. "What have you been up to?" Vicky asked the wolf.

Sue whined and shivered in the cool air of the garage.

Darien looked down at the wounded wolf. "Come on. Let's get her home, and I'll call Rupert."

Sue whined again and leaned on Vicky as Darien led the way to a metallic-red Range Rover.

Pushing the button to pop the back hatch, he stuck the flowers inside. "Come on, girl." Darien reached down to pick Sue up into the car. He staggered under her weight, and Vicky grabbed him to keep them both from going over. Sue whimpered as Darien manhandled her into the back, where she curled up and looked out at them.

"Can you do something for her?" Vicky asked, worried about her friend.

Darien reached his hand out to touch the wound, and Sue snarled at him, hunching up away from him. He quickly pulled his hand back from her.

"It's all right, Sue. He won't hurt you," Vicky said, trying to calm her.

Sue growled a little and laid her head down.

Darien sighed deeply. "I don't think she wants me to help. Let's just get her home. It's won't take much time for her to heal that, anyway." He shut the hatch down and ushered Vicky around to the passenger's side.

She nodded and got into the SUV. She couldn't help but wonder how her friend had come to be here in that condition.

Darien shut her door and made his way back to the driver's side. He looked down at his hands, thinking. What was going on? Sue couldn't have weighed more than two hundred pounds. That should have been easy. He'd never had a problem lifting anything in the past, why did he now? His mind left that problem and slipped to another. What had happened to Sue? If she was hurt, shouldn't she have gone home to Rupert? Darien took a deep breath and let it out before sliding into the driver's seat of the unfamiliar SUV. He was going to need most of his concentration to get the much-larger vehicle safely through the streets of the city.

4

Letting out a long sigh, Darien slipped the key out of the ignition of his new Range Rover. The drive through city traffic had been grueling this evening. An ambulance and several police cars near the city center had slowed the normally heavy traffic to a crawl, making the already-long day longer. Darien just wanted to go inside and lie down for a while. Glancing at the wolf curled up next to the roses in the back of the SUV, he drew another deep breath before getting out. He still had to call Rupert before he could rest.

By the time Darien reached the back of the car, Vicky had the hatch open. Sue slipped from the vehicle with ease. Her fur may have been coated in drying blood, but the oozing wound had nearly healed. Retrieving the flowers, Darien led the way into the building.

Ethan greeted them with his normal, warm welcome but raised an eyebrow at Sue. He had gotten used to some of Darien's eccentric ways, but the large wolf leaning against Vicky's leg was definitely noteworthy. "Excuse me, Mr. Ritter." Ethan pinned an awkward smile to his face. "You really need to have that animal on a leash."

Darien shot Ethan a piqued glance. "It's okay." He pushed the suggestion out to the concierge and turned his attention back to where he was going.

"Pardon me, sir, but it's not okay," Ethan reprimanded. "I know I haven't enforced the rules for your Shih Tzu, I mean, how much damage can such a cute thing do?" A stifled laugh from Vicky drew Ethan's attention for a moment. He looked at her curiously before turning his attention back to Darien. "But, you *are* required to have pets on a leash in the common areas."

Darien just stared at Ethan, confused. Why hadn't Ethan bent under the suggestion? The man had had his will bent so many times that it shouldn't have taken anything to bend it again.

Vicky stepped in when she sensed Darien's confusion. "We're sorry." She sunk her fingers into the thick hair at the back of Sue's neck. "We hadn't expected to bring her home with us." Vicky gave Ethan her warmest smile as she went on to explain. "See, she belongs to a friend of ours, and when we found her injured, we couldn't just leave her."

The mention of an injury drew Ethan's eyes to the dark bloodstains on Sue's coat.

"Could you find it in your heart to forgive us just this once?" Vicky pleaded with him.

Ethan's eyes narrowed a little as he considered his options.

"Please?" Vicky added for good measure.

Ethan let out a deep breath and nodded his head. "Sure, but just this once." He held up his hand with one finger up as he spoke. "But, please make sure your dog is on a leash from now on."

"Thank you." Vicky nodded her head and reached up to push Darien back into motion.

Still in shock, Darien let Vicky push him to the elevator doors, where she punched the button and hurried them out of the lobby. "What just happened?" he asked, trying to process the events. He was sure that he had pushed enough power into his words to command the young man.

Vicky chuckled. "We got yelled at." She patted Darien's arm and smiled to herself. "I didn't know there was a leash law in the building."

Darien looked at her, confused. He shook his head, trying to clear the fatigue from it. "Yeah," he answered as the rules of the building ran through his mind. "Pets are supposed to be on a leash at all times in the common areas."

Vicky laughed at the idea of trying to put the wiggly ball of tentacles on a lead. "Oh, I'm sure Zak will *love* that."

Darien couldn't help but smile at that image as the door to his penthouse opened up. Sue leaned into Vicky as they led the way out of the elevator.

He pushed the failed suggestion to the back of his mind for the moment. Right now, he had an injured werewolf to look after. "Come on." Leading the way into the kitchen, Darien set the large vase of flowers on the breakfast nook table. "We need to find Sue something to eat." He stripped off his overcoat and folded it over the back of one of the iron chairs.

Vicky looked down at the blood drying on Sue's fur and back up to Darien pulling off his suit coat. "But, shouldn't we get her cleaned up first?"

Darien looked at the werewolf sitting by Vicky's feet. "Healing such a wound takes a lot of energy," he explained as he took the cutting board from its home. "It's best that we feed her first." Adding a large knife to the board, he turned to the cabinets on the wall opposite the sink.

Vicky considered this as she scrubbed her fingers into the fur at the back of Sue's neck. "Is there anything I can do to help?" She stepped away from the patiently waiting werewolf. Dropping her bag onto the iron chair, she laid her coat over Darien's.

Retrieving two metal mixing bowls from the cabinet, Darien added them to the growing pile of supplies. "Can you fill one of these with water?" He turned to the refrigerator, leaving the bowls for Vicky.

"Sure." Vicky pulled the smaller of the two bowls to the sink and ran cool water in it.

Darien retrieved several paper-wrapped packages from the

meat drawer. He placed these on the table with the cutting board and broke the tape. Rolling a roast out on the cutting board, he started reducing the meat to bite-sized chunks with the large knife.

Sue shifted when the smell of the meat hit her, but she stayed seated where Vicky had left her.

Taking the bowl of water over to where Sue waited, Vicky set it down in front of her friend. "Here."

Sue sniffed at the water but turned her attention back to Darien dumping his work into the second bowl. He opened the second package of stew meat and added this to the first pile of chunks. Sue fidgeted more as Darien picked up the bowl and turned to her.

"Aren't you going to cook that?" Vicky asked, horrified that Darien intended to feed her friend raw meat.

Darien paused and looked at Vicky, then Sue, and then the bowl.

Sue had stood up and was staring at the bowl intently.

He held it down for the wolf to see. "Do you want me to cook it?"

Sue gripped the bowl in her teeth and pulled it down.

Darien set it on the floor, and the hungry werewolf dug in with relish.

Vicky's stomach flipped a little at the thought of eating raw meat, and she turned away.

Darien caught her eye and smiled as he went to clean up the counter. "Don't worry," he reassured her. "She's a werewolf. She prefers it that way."

Vicky looked back to her friend and nodded her head. It really did look as if Sue were enjoying the raw slivers of flesh.

Darien finished washing up and turned to look at the werewolf then up to Vicky. "Keep an eye on her. I'm going to go call Rupert."

Vicky nodded as Darien left through the door to the foyer. Letting out a deep sigh, she turned to the coats stacked on the iron chair. "I'm going to put these up," she informed Sue, picking up the pile of clothing and heading out to the closet. Hanging Darien's suit coat on the end of the banister, she dropped her bag on the floor next to it.

Once the rest of the outerwear was stashed in the hall closet, Vicky returned to the kitchen. The growl from her friend made Vicky stop just inside the door. Her eyes came to rest on the tense scene in front of her. Zak had wiggled in from the living room and was gurgling while staring at Sue's bowl.

"Zak!" Vicky reprimanded the small horror.

Zak looked up at her and chirped.

Vicky scooped him up and away from where Sue was eating. "That's not for you."

Zak wiggled intently towards the raw meat.

"If you're hungry, I can get you something." Taking the little fay over to the refrigerator, Vicky pulled the door open. She took out a package of sliced turkey and ripped it open.

Zak's wiggling ends were into the package and shifting the thin slices of meat into his sharp teeth before Vicky could set him back onto the floor. He consumed the entire stack of meat and started chewing on the plastic.

"Bottomless pit," Vicky grumbled as she found some more treats for the hungry fay. She dumped a packet of sausages out, and he nabbed them up before they could hit the ground.

Sue watched from her bowl as Vicky passed bits of food to the hellhound.

After a while, Vicky shut the door to the refrigerator. "You have had enough," she complained, taking the many empty packages away from the little horror.

Sue snickered and nosed her mostly empty bowl towards Zak.

The little fay turned at the sound. Gurgling his appreciation, he wobbled over and buried his face into the remains of Sue's dinner.

Vicky just laughed at him. "Thank you, Sue." Reaching down,

she tugged on a few of Zak's writhing feelers.

The small fay gurgled his pleasure and licked the blood from the bowl.

"Let's go get you cleaned up." Vicky held open the kitchen door so Sue could lead the way out and up the steps to the bathroom. Snagging her bag on the way past, Vicky dropped it in her room before following them in to the bathroom. "Would you like a bath or a shower?" Vicky asked the wolf.

Sue hopped over the edge of the tub and sat down at the end away from the faucet.

Vicky looked at her, confused. "Do you want to shift back, so you can relax?"

Sue shook her head.

Cocking her head in confusion, Vicky started the water running. In a few moments it was hot, so she plugged up the drain. "Bubbles?" Vicky offered the rose-scented soap to her friend.

Sue let out a strange noise that sounded like laughter and shook her head.

To Vicky's surprise, Zak wobbled into the room, right over the edge of the tub, and into the water. She hadn't expected him to come in and help. Darien tended to yell at the hellhound for joining her in the bath. "Okay." Vicky said, confused. When Zak grabbed the brush she used on him and started running it over the bloody area on Sue's back, Vicky figured out what was going on. "Let me get changed, and I'll be right back to help." She left Sue in Zak's care as she went to change. Obviously, Sue was not in the mood to shift, and it would be much easier to help her friend wash away the blood if she didn't have to worry about getting her work clothing wet.

Darien lay back on his couch and studied the drifts of clouds painted on his ceiling. The phone call to Rupert had not gone as

Darien had expected. Instead of being happy to hear his sister was all right, Rupert had been very abrupt. Darien could tell that his friend was pissed about something, but the alpha wolf didn't stay on the line long enough to tell Darien anything other than he was on his way. Darien closed his eyes and let his mind drift over the day.

Something still bothered him about the bouquet of roses that Vicky had received. It wasn't Elliot's style to send that type of present, but the younger vampire was really the only person who knew about the wedding arrangements other than Vicky's friends. If the flowers had come from either of them, they would have signed the card.

Pushing that from his mind, Darien next contemplated how his suggestion to Ethan had failed. Sure, he was bad with memory manipulation, but he had always been able to bend people to his will. What was happening to him?

Darien let out a long breath, relaxing a bit more. He was bone-tired and somewhat achy. The feeling of his menagerie pressing on the edges of his mind gave him a moment of thought. Maybe they were straining him more then he realized. He had almost dropped Sue when he lifted her into the car. Could the additional load on his powers be stressing him that much? It had been a long time since he had last supported a group as large as this, but he didn't remember his fledglings ever being this hard on him before.

Lillian had never shown any signs of fatigue. Darien had always considered himself powerful, but he really wasn't feeling it at the moment. Could Lillian have been that much more powerful than he was? Darien's mind brushed over each one of the vampires linked to him as he checked to make sure they were okay. They all seemed to be fine, but Darien was still worried. Maybe he should get Elliot to join his menagerie and help support the load. The last thing Darien wanted was to fail those depending on him for their continued existence.

The sound of Vicky's voice pulled Darien from his thoughts.

He blinked a few times, trying to make sense of what she'd said, but his brain wouldn't process it. His eyes followed her around the room as she moved about, talking to him. Shaking his head, he realized that he had nearly fallen asleep on the couch.

"What?" Darien's voice cracked a little as he spoke.

Vicky smiled at him and laid his coat over the end of the couch near his feet. "I said I've gotten Sue cleaned up, but she won't shift back."

Darien processed this for a moment before nodding. "Rupert is on his way to take care of her."

"That's fine, but don't forget—Vanessa and Elliot should be here shortly to talk about the wedding arrangements." Vicky turned back to the bed were she had dropped her bag. Darien let out a loud groan that made her turn towards him with an amused grin on her face. "You forgot, didn't you?"

Darien drew in a deep breath and pulled himself to sit up on the couch. "Yes," he admitted as he kicked out of his work shoes. "I should probably get changed, then."

Vicky laughed at his reluctance. "It really isn't going to be that bad." Coming over, she slipped into his lap.

Darien wrapped his arms around her and shifted his head into her warmth. Pulling her with him, he leaned back into the couch. He liked the way she felt against him.

After a moment, Vicky tilted his head back so she could kiss him softly. She could feel how tired he was. "Do you want me to call and see if we can reschedule?"

Darien considered this for a moment. "No. It'll be fine." He really needed to talk to Elliot about joining the menagerie. The sooner he could get someone to share the load, the sooner he would be back to his old self again.

Vicky kissed him softly again and unfurled herself from his lap. "Then get up and get changed." She pulled on his hands until he stood up. "They'll be here soon."

Darien nodded and released Vicky's hands so she could go get things ready for their upcoming guests. Turning to his bed, he found that Vicky had been kind enough to lay out something comfortable, yet presentable, for him to wear. He sighed his happiness with her. She did some of the most thoughtful things.

Vicky, Vanessa, and Elliot sat in a group at one end of the glass table in Darien's living room. Vanessa had brought over a file box filled with her ideas for Vicky's wedding. They had spread the items across the glass table and were trying to fit them into Vicky's idea of the perfect wedding. Vanessa wanted to go for a huge church wedding on a Saturday afternoon. Elliot had shaken his head and suggested they have a small ceremony at the local country club where Darien was a member. Vicky had sat back and let the two argue over the details, enjoying the way they played off each other. Darien had been right in choosing Elliot to help with the planning. He had a way of undercutting Vanessa's ideas so far that she had to scale back her plans to find some middle point between the two. They were just starting to haggle over the number of guests when Vicky heard noises from the foyer.

"Where is she?" Rupert's voice boomed through the penthouse as he stomped into the living room.

Sue looked up from where she was curled up with Zak in front of the fire.

Rupert's eyes ran across the people in the room and stopped when he found his sister in wolf form.

Vicky pushed herself up from the floor, trying to draw the alpha werewolf's attention. "Good evening, Rupert. This is my friend, Vanessa." She pointed out her human friend, trying to get him to realize that this was not the time to go into supernatural issues.

Rupert just grunted without looking away from Sue.

Darien stepped through the door from the kitchen and looked over the scene.

Elliot met his eyes for a moment of silent communication. "Why don't we go out and check on dinner?" The younger vampire touched Vanessa's shoulder, breaking her from the tension building in the room.

She looked up at him. "But, Darien's cooking," Vanessa protested. She wasn't sure what was going to happen, but it didn't take a genius to know that something was going to go down.

"I'm sure he needs a female's touch." Elliot pushed his will into the words, and Vanessa stood up.

"Of course." She bent under the suggestion, and Elliot drew her out of the room to the kitchen.

"Thank you," Darien breathed as they passed. Elliot nodded his head and kept his concentration on the woman he was guiding from the room. Now that the human was out of the room, the tension peaked as the two werewolves glared at each other.

"What the hell happened?" Rupert hissed at his sister.

Whining a little, Sue laid her head back down on the rug.

"Don't give me that," he growled. "You nearly killed Bernie's lieutenant."

Sue snarled at the mention of the injured wolf.

"You know how important these talks are! Why the hell did you attack him?"

She growled again.

"Are you going to shift back so we can talk?" Rupert was trying to keep a level head, but it was easy to see he was very upset.

Sue whined again without moving from the rug.

"Damn it, Sue! Bernie wants your blood, and if you don't shift back and explain yourself, I'm going to have to give it to him."

She squirmed and whined again, but she didn't shift.

"Fine," Rupert growled. "If you won't do it, I'll just make you." He lunged at his sister, intending to grab her.

Sue must have known what he was going to do because

she was up and out of his reach before he could catch her. Zak gurgled warningly at the mad alpha as Sue rounded the couch and stared at her brother.

"Get back here!" he demanded and made as if he would chase her down.

Turning, Sue slammed into Vicky, knocking her back to the loveseat. She buried her face into her friend's chest and whined loudly.

Thrown by the off behavior, Vicky wrapped her arms around her friend's head.

When Rupert went to grab the wolf away from Vicky, Zak dropped his dog impression, roaring in anger. He yanked the riled-up alpha back and placed himself in front of Vicky and Sue.

"*Wait*," Darien cried as he threw himself into the middle of the chaos erupting in his living room.

"Stay out of this, vampire!" Rupert growled, regaining his footing. "It is none of your concern."

Sue pressed her head harder into Vicky's chest and whined.

Darien grabbed Rupert by the arm and forced him to look at him. "It became my concern when Sue went to Vicky for protection."

Rupert glared at the man but couldn't argue with him. He was in Darien's bailiwick.

"Have you considered that there might be a reason she's acting this way?" Darien tried to reason with the upset man.

Rupert relaxed in Darien's grip slightly. "Then why won't she just tell me?" he groaned, exasperated. "I've got a very mad alpha demanding an explanation and nothing to tell him."

Sue whined and rubbed her head on Vicky again.

Vicky scratched her reassuringly. "Maybe we should all just calm down for a minute," she said, trying to comfort Sue. She could tell that there was something bothering her friend. "I don't think Sue would have done something so rash without a reason."

Rupert laughed wryly. "Then why won't she explain it?" he growled at her. "I've got to do something soon, or all hell is going to break loose."

Sue whined again and fidgeted in Vicky's arms.

"There's got to be a reason." Vicky thought for a moment. "Maybe Karl knows what's wrong."

Sue growled, and Rupert went very still at this suggestion.

"Sue and Karl had some kind of fight last week, and she refuses to talk to him," Rupert explained. "Karl keeps coming over to see her, but he won't tell me what happened."

Vicky could feel the rumble of anger issuing from Sue.

Darien took a deep breath and let it out loudly to break the silence that fell in the room. "Go tell your visiting wolves that I'm dealing with the issue," he finally answered. "If they have a problem with that, send them to see me." Even though he felt weak, he was sure he could pull enough power together to intimidate a few werewolves. "Leave Sue to us. We'll find out what's wrong."

Rupert looked at his sister pressed into Vicky's arms, then to the hellhound writhing protectively in front of them, and back at the vampire. He threw up his hands in defeat. "Fine!" he growled. "You take care of this, but she can't come home 'til this is solved." Rupert turned and stormed out of the room.

Sue pressed her face more firmly under Vicky's arm with another soft whine.

Darien looked at his assistant and followed Rupert from the room.

Vicky scrubbed her fingers into Sue's fur again. "It's okay," she reassured her friend. "You can stay with us as long as you need to."

Zak gurgled an agreement and came over to touch Sue reassuringly.

Whimpering, Sue sat down next to Vicky. She pressed her head hard into her friend, and Vicky gave her what comfort she could.

After a few minutes, Darien came back. "He's going to talk to the other wolves." He came over and scratched Sue's ear. "But this issue won't be solved until we get some answers."

Sue looked up at the vampire.

"Can you tell us what's wrong?"

Sue whined but didn't elaborate on the issue.

Darien sighed. "All right, but he's sending Karl over to talk with you."

Sue growled a little at this.

"Do whatever." Darien turned away from the upset werewolf. "Just don't get blood on my rugs." Shaking his head, he went back into the kitchen where he had been cooking dinner before Rupert had shown up.

"Come on." Vicky pushed Sue back a little so she could stand up. "Let's go see how Vanessa is faring." She let the issue with Sue lie for the moment. If the wolf wouldn't shift back, she couldn't tell them what was wrong. There was no point in pushing. Zak shifted back to his Shih Tzu form and followed the two girls into the kitchen where Elliot had Vanessa laughing at something. It was clear that he had her enthralled; there was no way she could have missed the exchange in the living room unless he had done something to her.

"Is she going to be okay?" Vicky asked as she approached Darien. Vanessa was acting a little more than drunk.

Darien smiled at her as he stirred the stew on the counter. "Yes," he reassured her. "Elliot gave her a glass of wine with a little suggestion." He chuckled. "She's going to wake up tomorrow with a bit of a hangover to go with the hole in her memory."

Shaking her head, Vicky watched her best friend flirt with Elliot. "She's incorrigible," she said with a laugh.

Darien's grin widened as he agreed. "Maybe we should call it an evening." He sighed. "I don't think we'll get anything else done tonight."

Vicky had to agree. She had seen Vanessa drunk on many occasions, but Elliot had done a pristine job on getting her completely soused. He had managed to sit her in one of the iron chairs, but she was leaning her head against his him, humming happily as she petted him affectionately.

"I think I'm going to like your friend." Elliot grinned at Vicky as Vanessa slipped her arm around one of his legs, cuddling him.

Vicky rolled her eyes and came over to her drunken friend. "Vanessa." She tried to get the woman to focus on her.

Vanessa looked up and smiled drunkenly. "Hi, Vicks!" she slurred.

Vicky giggled at her and held out her hands. "Let's get you home."

Nodding, Vanessa slipped her arm out from between Elliot's legs. Lifting her hand up, she cupped his butt, copping a feel as she released him. A goofy grin cut across her face. "He's got a nice ass," she whispered to her friend in a very loud slur. Both Darien and Elliot's smiles widened as they tried not to laugh.

"Come on, Vanessa." Vicky helped her friend up from the chair and pulled her arm over her shoulder.

Elliot moved to help support the wobbly woman. "I'll take her."

Vicky looked up at the tall vampire. "Are you sure?" She didn't want to burden him with her randy friend.

Vanessa was already trying to lean into the man.

"It won't be a problem." Elliot shifted most of her weight to his shoulder. "I'll make sure she gets home uncompromised."

Vicky grinned at him again. "It's *you* I'm worried about," she teased as Vanessa petted his chest.

Elliot chuckled and started to lead Vanessa off.

"Elliot," Darien called before his friend could leave; he still needed to talk to him about the menagerie.

Elliot and Vicky stopped and looked up at him.

"I need your help."

"What do you need?" Elliot offered.

"I know it's been a long time, but do you think we can open our link back up?" Darien gave his friend a pleading look. "I'm afraid that I'm not strong enough to support the new group."

Elliot gave him a very concerned look. "Darien, you're more

powerful than all of us," he reassured his worried friend. "Your people are fine."

"I'm not sure about that," Darien confided in him. "Lately, I've been having some... issues."

"You have nothing to worry about," Elliot tried again. "I can feel your power through my mark. It's sure and steady, but if it will make you feel better, then yes, I'll add my strength to your menagerie."

Darien let out a relieved breath. "You know that I only ask this of you to ensure the young are safe."

Elliot smiled at him. "Of course." Closing his eyes, he focused inward to reopen his connection to Darien.

Vicky could always feel Darien in her mind, but Elliot's cool, green energy washed over her for a second before receding to that point just beyond her consciousness. Her mark had been added after Darien had picked up the other vampires, so it was strange feeling the addition.

"Thank you, my friend." Darien came over and touched Elliot on the shoulder. It was easy to see that this meant a lot to him.

Elliot returned the touch almost lovingly. "You know you can always call on me for anything."

Vicky looked away from what felt like a very intimate moment between the two men.

Elliot dropped his hand away and cleared his throat. "Well, let me see if I can get this one home." He nodded towards Vanessa. She hung, almost asleep, between Vicky and Elliot. He shifted her so he could swing her up into his arms.

Darien led the way to the door and held it open for the group.

"Do you need help?" Vicky asked as she pulled Vanessa's coat out of the closet.

"Nah." Elliot shook his head and helped Vicky pull Vanessa's coat on her before scooping her back up. "I can handle one small female."

Vicky laughed and thanked him as he stepped into the

elevator.

"Have a good night." Elliot shot her a broad smile as the door slid shut.

She turned to look at Darien. His face was carefully devoid of emotion. "Is there something I should know about?" She knew Darien had been having some problems as of late, but he hadn't told her how bad they were.

Darien let out a sigh, and his face showed the fatigue he was feeling. "Maybe. I'm just not used to having someone draw power from me." Wrapping his arm around Vicky, he held her close. "I've just been so tired lately."

Returning his embrace, Vicky guided his head down to rest on her shoulder.

"The menagerie depends on me for their strength, and if I can't cut it, they will be the ones who suffer."

"It will be okay," Vicky soothed him.

Darien held her for a long time, taking comfort in her warmth. Finally, he let out a deep breath and stood up from her. "I know." He turned and led her by the hand back into the kitchen, where the pot of stew was happily bubbling away. "I asked for Elliot's help to ensure that it was."

Vicky nodded. "I felt him join the bond."

Darien smiled. "He was always there," he informed her. "Vampire marks never go away, but they can be closed down when not needed."

Vicky thought about this as she recalled what Jakob had said about feeling Darien add her to the bond. Remembering the encounter, she realized she had felt the twin's power, both through her skin and in her head; only she hadn't comprehended it at the time.

"So, I'm connected to all the vampires in your new group?"

Darien confirmed her thoughts. "Yes, but the bond goes through me, so they can't affect you unless I allow it."

Vicky mulled this over for a moment. Honestly, she was a little bothered that she had such an intimate connection with so many people, but she was glad for her joining with Darien. She pushed the thought from her mind. "How about we get something to eat and go to bed early." Vicky turned to press against Darien.

He gave her a knowing smile and curled his arm around her. "Anything you want, My Lady." True, he was tired, but he was always up for some good, quality time with his love.

5

DARIEN KNEW HE HAD PUSHED HIMSELF TOO FAR THIS TIME. HE ACHED ALL OVER, and the hot water from his shower hadn't done him any good. Pulling on his dress shirt, he forced his shaking fingers to fix his tie. For a moment, he considered having Vicky cancel his day, but what excuse was he going to give her? Vampires didn't get sick. Darien willed himself to be well, and the slight tremble left his hands.

Grabbing up his suit coat from the end of the couch, he slipped it on and looked at himself in the mirror over his dresser. His eyes looked darker than normal, and his skin looked paler. He tried to shake away the odd feeling and convince himself that all he needed was some fresh blood. Drawing himself up to his full height, he turned to face the day.

Vicky looked up at the familiar sound of Darien coming into the kitchen. Usually he was up before she was, but today he had taken a lot longer to get ready. "Morning." She smiled at him.

Zak scampered from where he was trying to steal Sue's breakfast to bump into Darien's legs affectionately.

The impact nearly knocked Darien off his feet, but he caught himself on the counter.

"I've still got some toast left," Vicky offered.

Darien's stomach rolled at the idea of solid food. "No thanks." He pulled down one of the blue tumblers and turned to get his blood. "I don't think I can handle solid food today."

Vicky nodded and turned her attention back to her plate.

Darien poured his blood into his glass and stared at it for a moment. Even this didn't look appetizing. He swallowed the lump that had formed in the back of his throat and raised the glass to his lips to drink. The feel of blood going down had never revolted him before, but today it gagged him. Swallowing hard, he forced himself to drain the glass as quickly as he could. The cold liquid swirled in his stomach, and he gripped onto the edge of the counter as his body disagreed with the offering. He swallowed hard, trying to keep the blood down, but his stomach cramped and brought the liquid back up.

Vicky jerked away from her breakfast when she heard Darien vomit into the sink. It only took her a moment to get over to his bent form gripping the sink with white knuckles. "*Darien!*" Vicky gasped and wrapped her arm around his body to support him as he emptied his stomach. He trembled in her arms as she held him. She could feel the heat radiating from his skin.

When his heaving subsided, she pulled the dishtowel from under the sink and gave it to him to wipe his face. "Come on." She pulled him away from the mess and into one of the breakfast nook chairs. When the smell of her leftover food hit him, he bolted back to the sink to dry heave several more times. Vicky pulled a chair over to Darien and placed him in it. He relaxed in the chair and let his head hang backwards resting it on the high back.

"What's wrong?" Vicky asked as she turned on the water and rinsed the wasted blood and bile from the sink.

Darien just shook his head and breathed shallowly through his mouth. He felt like death warmed over. Vicky laid her wrist across his forehead. He felt cold and clammy, but Vicky's eyes widened as she moved her hand to his cheek and pressed her lips against his forehead.

"You're running a fever!" Her voice was high with surprise.

Zak wiggled against Darien's leg, but it was all the vampire could do to sit in the chair.

"You are *not* going to work like this."

Darien didn't bother arguing with his assistant. He wasn't even sure he would be able to get himself back up from the chair. Groaning his acceptance, he swallowed hard. Just that noise made his stomach roll again.

"Do you need fresh blood?" Vicky offered.

Darien clamped his mouth shut and shook his head slightly trying to suppress the cramps that were instigated from just the suggestion of food.

Vicky shifted from foot to foot, worrying. Darien had all the classic signs of the stomach flu, but she knew it was impossible. He had already informed her that vampires didn't get sick like humans did. Deciding on a course of action, Vicky came over and rubbed Darien on the shoulder reassuringly. She would treat him as if he were sick. "Come on." Pulling on Darien's arm, she urged him up. "You need to go back to bed."

Darien just shook his head, unwilling to move yet.

Vicky released his arm. "At least let me have your coat." She tugged on the sleeve of his jacket. Darien had gotten blood on it when his stomach first heaved, and the stain would be much harder to get out once it dried.

Nodding, he let Vicky pull the sleeve loose. His stomach rolled again as he shifted, but he breathed in short, shallow breaths and was able to calm it.

Peeling the coat the rest of the way off him, Vicky set about rinsing the dark liquid from the material. Once the fabric was clean again, she turned her attention back to Darien. She pulled his tie off and unbuttoned the top two buttons of his shirt. "Come on." Vicky heaved on his arm again, trying to get him up.

Finally, Darien gave in to her insistence, but he found himself too weak to stand on his own.

Vicky slipped under his arm and let him lean on her as she guided him into the foyer and up the steps. His feet moved heavily as she encouraged him on with soft words. In no time, they were back in his bedroom, where Vicky leaned him against the doorframe and stripped him out of the rest of his suit. He didn't protest when she made him lie on the bed and pulled the blankets up around him. He was hot, cold, and trembling, all at once.

Vicky tucked him in and went to get the wastebasket from the bathroom. "How do I get ahold of Dakine?" she asked as she came back and set the trashcan next to the bed.

Darien swallowed again, but his stomach was feeling better. "Magic." He spoke softly, afraid the vibrations from his voice would make his stomach turn again.

Vicky considered her options. Darien was in no condition to show her how to call the elven lord. She patted the covers over top of him. "I'll call Elliot. You just get some rest." Picking up her bag from the couch, she clicked off the light.

Darien wanted to argue with her. He really did have important stuff to do today, but he just couldn't work up the energy. Drawing in as deep of a breath as he dared, he let it out in a frustrated sigh and forced his mind off it. Vicky would handle things for him. That was one of the many reasons he loved her.

Lord Dakine and Elliot both looked over the flushed vampire wrapped in a blanket sitting on the stool in his kitchen. Darien was still very sick, but he no longer felt ready to die. As long as he did not try to put anything in it, his stomach was behaving itself for now.

Dakine rested his fingers on Darien's chest and searched him for the cause of his illness. "I don't know..." The elf shook his head. "I can't find anything magically wrong with you, but..." The word hung in the air as he shifted his hand against Darien.

"But what?" Darien asked. His voice was a little hoarse from the many times he had thrown up throughout the day. Vicky kept plying him with glasses of both blood and water, but everything he tried to drink came back up. She had even tried giving him her own blood, but he couldn't get his fangs to work properly.

Dakine gave him a concerned look.

Darien sighed heavily. "Just tell me."

"Kian, I have never seen anything like this." Dakine dropped his hand away from his friend. "Your energy comes across as human."

Darien stared at him, dumbfounded. *How could that be?* "What?"

"I said—you seem human to me." Dakine shrugged.

Darien looked over at Elliot to see if he had answers.

Elliot reached out and took up Darien's arm. He slowly lifted Darien's wrist to his mouth, making it very clear what he intended to do.

Darien braced for the sting of Elliot's fangs.

Surprise lit the vampire's face as Darien's blood slid across his tongue. He took another hard pull at the wound.

"Elliot!" Vicky's voice broke the silence of the room. She could not believe the scene she had just stepped into.

Elliot released Darien's hand and stepped quickly away from his master. He'd tasted Darien's blood many times before, but this time was something else. It was thick and warm—like melted marshmallows, but not quite as sweet. In fact, he had never tasted anything like it. Refusing to look at Darien, Elliot backed away. He had only meant to taste him, not to drink so deeply. If the older man could see his eyes, he'd find more than just surprise in them. Darien's blood was definitely human, but it held a power in it like nothing Elliot had ever come across before, and he wanted more of it.

Vicky picked up Darien's wrist and applied pressure to the lightly bleeding wound. "What do you think you're doing?" She turned a pointed glare at Elliot. Never had she expected to come back and find Darien with Elliot's fangs sunk in him. She had only stepped out of the room for a moment to check on Sue, who was curled up in the living room with Zak.

"It's okay." Darien patted her arm lovingly. "He was testing a theory." He looked over to his friend. "And?"

Elliot gave him a curt nod as he tried to put down the bloodlust that had swamping him. "Human," he muttered. The ball of energy that was Darien's blood churned in Elliot's stomach, pushing him to take more. If this was the way Darien's blood had tasted when he had been truly human, it was no wonder his sire had prized him so highly. The only question was—what type of control did that man have to not drain Darien at every feeding? Elliot took another step away from his tempting friend.

Vicky looked from Elliot's response and odd reaction to the elven lord. "Human?" she asked, concerned.

Dakine nodded. "Somehow, Kian has managed to turn himself human."

Vicky looked to where Darien sat in thought. "But how can that be?"

Darien looked up to Lord Dakine, hoping he would have an answer.

"I have no idea." Dakine reached out for Darien's injured hand to heal it. Vicky relinquished it reluctantly, but the broken skin was already whole again. Dakine turned Darien's wrist to see past the smears of blood. "Apparently, not all of him is human." He released the wrist and came closer to search Darien again.

Vicky backed up to get a cloth to clean up the spilled blood and give the fay room to work.

After several very frustrating minutes, Dakine dropped his hand away. "I can't find anything that would cause this. It's like you were never turned."

Elliot touched the link he had with Darien. "But I can still feel him."

The cool green of the vampire's power filled Darien's senses. "And I can feel you, too." He tried to push back against Elliot's connection, but it was like he lacked something to push with. "God, what's wrong with me?" Darien surged up from the stool to pace the length of his kitchen. How could he have lost his powers?

"Whatever magic has done this is beyond my knowledge." Dakine shrugged and swept his long, silver hair back over his shoulder. "But my knowledge is limited to mostly fay and high magic. There are other schools out there that might be able to give you answers. Perhaps you should consult your books."

Darien stopped in his tracks and turned surprised eyes towards Dakine. "That's a fantastic idea!" Coming over, he clasped his hands on the elf lord's shoulders. "Thank you for your help." Darien slipped past his friends and out of the kitchen without another word.

Dakine looked over at Elliot in surprise. Apparently, something he'd said sparked a memory in Darien's mind.

Elliot returned the same look of confusion. There was no telling what the ill man had remembered that would give him that type of energy.

"Well," the fay lord turned to Vicky. "I guess I will take my leave of you, now." He bowed to her, swirling his robes about him. "Until next time, My Lady."

"Thank you, Lord Dakine." She escorted the fay to the elevator.

Elliot followed.

"Are you leaving, too?"

Elliot nodded. "I have other things that I need to do tonight." His schedule really wasn't that busy, but he needed to get out of there. That hot feeling from Darien's blood was radiating out, and it was staring to do strange things to him. He needed to get something to dilute it soon.

"All right, then." Vicky reached out to touch Elliot's arm in farewell, but he shifted away from her hand before it reached him. A confused look crossed her face, but she pulled her hand back and weaved her fingers together. "Have a nice night."

Elliot clamped his jaw shut and nodded to her before slipping into the farthest corner of the elevator. He could feel Darien's energy running through Vicky, and he wanted to put as much distance between them as he could.

As soon as the door was shut, Lord Dakine gave the vampire a calculating look. "Are you all right?"

Elliot nodded again. "Yeah." He didn't want to go into his desire to drain Darien right now. "I just need to get something to eat."

Dakine considered him for a moment as they rode to the lobby. Finally, he nodded. "Good hunting, my friend," Dakine bid before he stepped off the elevator.

Elliot wanted to laugh. A good hunt was exactly what he needed right now.

"Darien?" Vicky called as she peeked into his office. She could hear him rummaging around for something. When he didn't respond, she pushed the door open and stepped in. "What are you doing?"

Darien looked up from the dusty tome he was reading. "Looking for something." He snapped the book shut and dropped it to the table. There was already a growing stack of them. Turning back to the shelves, he pulled another one out. "There was something in one of these books about being human." He flipped through some of the pages before closing the book and dropping it on the pile. Another book was soon in his hands.

Vicky came over and put her hand on the precariously stacked books. They had started to shift and were in danger of falling off the desk. "What was it?"

Darien skimmed over the next book before dropping it to the desk. "I don't remember."

Vicky took it and stacked it neatly with the others.

"It had something to do with some type of fay wanting to be human." He flipped through the next volume, only to discard it into Vicky's waiting hands. "There was a love story involved. The fay wanted a girl, but she wouldn't have him as he was." Darien continued to search books as he spoke. "He did something to turn human. It was something horrible, but I can't remember what it was." Vicky continued to catch the discarded books as he dropped them. *"Aha!"*

Darien's cry of discovery startled Vicky into knocking one of the stacks over. She scrambled to catch the aged books before they fell to the floor.

Darien plopped down into his leather chair and read over the story. "Oh, oh no," he exclaimed when he got to what the fay had done to turn human. Shutting the book, he shook his head. "No, no, no." Standing up, he slipped the book back on the shelf.

"What?" Vicky asked. Her curiosity was killing her.

Darien started picking up the books and returning them to their original places. "I didn't do that."

"Didn't do what?" Vicky pushed as she handed books to him.

"Well, he ate the hearts of several young girls." Darien paused in his movement and shuddered. "But it was how he got them out that..." His words trailed off.

Vicky considered pushing for the rest of the story but decided not to. "I don't even want to know." She shook her head and let it go. If it was gruesome enough to make a vampire falter, it must have been bad. Vicky already had enough of her own nightmares to last a lifetime; she didn't need any more.

Vicky rolled over and stretched out the sleep from her muscles. She rubbed her eyes and looked around the empty room. Since Darien had been so sick yesterday, she had taken the liberty of clearing his Friday schedule so he would have time to recover. She had expected him to sleep in a little, but he was already gone. Zak had taken up sleeping with Sue since the wolf's arrival. In fact, he had barely left the wolf's side. Vicky pushed back the covers and pulled on the man's robe Darien had given her. She loved the feel of the woolen dressing gown.

Slipping into her bedroom, she checked on her guest. Sue and Zak were curled up on the bed.

Zak turned his beady, little eyes towards Vicky and gurgled quietly.

Vicky reached out and ruffled his tentacles before turning to leave. Sue was snoring lightly in her sleep, and Vicky did not want to wake her. They were going to have to do something about her soon.

The house was unusually quiet as Vicky made her way through it, looking for her love. She checked the office Darien kept filled with unusual things but didn't find him. Walking through the living room, she pushed back the wall to the family room. He wasn't there, either. Leaving the wall open, she went to the other side and passed through the dining room to the kitchen. There were two plates of untouched food waiting in the breakfast nook, but no sign of Darien. Concern filled Vicky, and she searched for her link with him. She could feel his contentment, but there was something else—a rage she couldn't quite explain. It didn't match the rest of his feelings. Vicky followed the feeling up the steps to the rooftop terrace.

Drawing the long robe tightly around her, Vicky stepped into the cold, December morning. Her breath fogged the air as she exhaled. It only took her eyes a moment to find the man she was looking for, sitting on the stone walkway with his face turned up towards the sky. He was only wearing a T-shirt and pajama pants from last night.

Vicky rushed over to him. "What are you doing?" The patch of sunlight he occupied didn't do much to break the chill carried in the air.

"It doesn't hurt." Darien's voice was filled with wonder.

Vicky knelt down in front of him so she could look at him better. His lips were a light purple, and he shivered from the cold. Her shadow blocked the sunlight from his face, and he opened his eyes to look at her.

"I didn't realize how good it could feel." His eyes flipped back and forth between hers, imploring her to understand him. "I don't remember a time when the touch of sunlight didn't hurt."

Vicky's eyes softened as she caught on. "Yes." She smiled at him and reached for his hand. He gave it to her. His long fingers were ice cold, and Vicky rubbed them with hers to warm them up. "It is very nice, but you need to come inside now. You've already been sick once this week."

"Oh, *Vicky!*"

Vicky squeaked as Darien surged forward and caught her up in his arms.

Pulling her to him, he crushed her in a hug. "I had forgotten what it's like to be truly alive." He let her lean back enough to look at him. "I want to do everything."

Vicky looked at him, shocked by his enthusiasm. "Okay," she agreed as she gathered up her scattered thoughts.

Darien pushed her from his lap and stood up.

"Like what?" Vicky asked as she let Darien help her to her feet.

Darien grinned at her. "Like eat!"

An amused smile turned the corner of Vicky's mouth. "You eat all the time."

"Yes, but I'm always careful about it." He grabbed her up, and she giggled as he spun her around, listing all the food he wanted to eat in excess. She was breathless when he put her back down.

Grinning at him, she said, "You've been sick, so maybe we should start off slowly." His excitement was infectious.

Tugging her to him, he kissed her softly. "I also want you," he said softly against her lips.

Vicky tightened her arms around him and pulled back with a warm smile on her lips. "You've already had me," she teased.

Darien drew her against him again and rubbed his cheek on the side of her head, feeling her. "I want you like *this*." His voice was soft and low. "I want you without the call for blood at the back of my mind."

Vicky stiffened a little as he nuzzled the soft curls of her hair.

"Just your soft skin against mine, with no push, no drive, overshadowing it. It's something I've never known."

She relaxed into him, enjoying the soft caress of his hands.

He tilted his face to the nape of her neck and drew in a deep breath. "And I want it now," Darien breathed out across her skin.

Vicky's breath caught at the desire in his voice. Before she could react, Darien stooped down, caught his shoulder in her stomach, and lifted her up in one swift movement. She laughed as Darien's stride took him to the stairs, unwilling to wait for the elevator. It took almost no time to get back to his penthouse. The stairwell door opened after a quick knock, and Darien had Vicky in his bedroom before she could see who had opened the door. Setting her on her feet, he kissed her again, harder.

"All right," Vicky agreed when he finished with her lips. She rubbed her hands up and down his chest. "Since you're feeling so much better…"

Darien made a contented noise at her.

"But, then it's breakfast time. And you're going to need to shave." She reached up and rubbed the day-old scruff on his cheek.

Surprise lit Darien's face, and he reached up to feel the prickly skin. "Should I do that now?" he asked in concern.

Vicky shook her head and circled her arms around his neck. "Not now." She gave him a light kiss. "I kind of like it."

Darien growled in desire and reclaimed her lips more passionately—a prelude of things to come.

6

THERE WAS NO DIFFERENCE BETWEEN THE TWO SWATCHES OF FABRIC VANESSA had insisted Vicky compare. She held up the antique white square next to the champaign one. "Which do you think is better, Sue?" Vicky held them up where the wolf could see.

Sue looked from one to the other and laid her head back on the rug next to Vicky's leg without comment.

Vicky looked at the two pinkish squares. "I can't tell the difference, either." A chuckle rolled out from the end of the couch where Darien was sitting.

"I don't think her eyes see enough of the color to tell a difference," he elaborated.

Sue snorted out a breath in response.

Darien smiled at the wolf and reached for the swatches. "But, I can't, either," he added after Vicky handed them to him.

Vicky shook her head and took the material back. She folded them neatly into the tablecloth file and stuck it back in the box Vanessa had left. There were color samples for everything from ribbons for the bridesmaid's hair to containers for the party favors. One whole box was filled with arrangements of pressed flower petals. The file that surprised Vicky most was the one filled with plans for her bachelorette party. Not only did it have addresses and prices of local male strip clubs, but it also had photos and cards for the dancers in case they wanted to have a more private session. And the party favors listed in this file would make sailors blush.

Vicky put the lid back on the file box. "I never would have thought about half these things."

Darien turned the page in the newspaper he was reading. "And that's why people hire wedding planners."

Vicky made a scoffing noise and opened her mouth with a retort, but she was interrupted by the sound of the phone in the kitchen ringing. Surprised, she popped up from the floor and went to answer the mostly unused phone. "Hello?" she asked timidly.

"Good afternoon, Miss Westernly."

Vicky recognized the voice of Ethan, the building's concierge.

"I'm sorry to disturb you, but there is a gentleman here by the name of Karl McDowell asking to see you."

"Oh, yes!" Vicky smiled as she recognized the name. Rupert had said that he would send Karl to talk to Sue. "We've been expecting him."

"Very well. Would you like me to send him up?" Ethan asked politely.

Vicky thought about that for a moment. It would give her time to let Darien and Sue know he was on his way. "Yes, please."

Ethan confirmed her request, and Vicky hung up the phone.

Darien looked up at her when she came back into the room. "And?"

"Karl's on his way up."

Sue growled a little from where she lay on the rug but didn't move.

Zak wiggled against her side protectively. Vicky was starting to feel a little neglected by the small fay. He had been Sue's constant companion since she had arrived.

Vicky lifted up the box containing the stuff for her wedding, deposited it in the dining room, and slid the wall back in place. She would just have to look over it later. The sound of the elevator door pulled Vicky from her thoughts, and she went to meet Karl.

"Hey." He greeted Vicky with a halfhearted smile. "Is she here?"

Vicky smiled back and ran her eyes over him. He looked like he'd been under a lot of stress lately. There were dark circles under his eyes, and his wavy, brown hair was sticking up where he kept running his fingers through it. "She's in the living room." Vicky held out her hand so that Karl could lead the way into the room.

He stopped just past the end of the fireplace and looked at Sue, still lying on the rug with Zak.

Zak gurgled a warning at him.

Ignoring the small fay, Karl came around the seating area so that he could see Sue's face.

Sue lay there, snubbing him; but once he was in her line of sight, her eyes tracked him.

Darien folded his newspaper and got up from the couch. "I'll be in the other room if you need me." He slipped from the room so he wouldn't be in the way.

Vicky turned to follow him. These two obviously had something to work out.

"Please stay," Karl called from where he was crouching next to the loveseat.

Vicky turned back to look at the pair of wolves standing off. There was a palatable tension hanging between them.

Karl looked up at Vicky for a moment. "She may not want to talk to me."

Smiling reassuringly at him, Vicky moved to sit on the arm of the closest couch. "She isn't talking to anyone right now," she said, folding her arms across her chest.

Zak gurgled at her.

"Except maybe Zak."

The little fay wiggled his ends over Sue's fur in a reassuring way.

"Please," Karl begged.

Vicky could see that the man was at a loss, so she slid over the arm of the couch and onto the cushion to watch.

Karl turned his attention back to the wolf lying on the rug and a dropped to his hands and knees. He crawled towards her very slowly. Sue's ears swiveled back as Karl pushed the glass table across the rug, giving them more room.

Vicky had never studied wolves, but she could tell that this was some sort of dominance display.

Never taking his eyes from Sue, Karl lay down and rolled to his back. Slowly, he closed his eyes and stretched his neck out, exposing his throat to Sue.

Sue stared at the offering for several long minutes, but Karl never moved. Finally, she got up and moved to him. She stood over Karl's prone form for another long moment before lowering her head and tightening her jaws around Karl's neck.

Vicky held her breath as Sue's white teeth pressed into the medic's throat, stretching the skin.

Karl swallowed, waiting for Sue's decision.

After another unending minute, Sue released her hold on his uninjured skin. She licked his face a few times before nosing him up from the floor and sitting down beside him.

Karl wrapped his arms around Sue's neck. "I'm sorry." He buried his face in her fur. "For everything." Their embrace lasted a long time before he pulled away and looked into her golden eyes. "Can you shift back now so we can talk?"

Sue let out a loud whimper and lay down against him.

"Come on, Sue." Karl sunk his fingers into her thick fur, rubbing her on the back of the neck. "Rupert is beside himself with this whole attack thing."

A rumble of anger rose from the tawny wolf.

"I know you wouldn't have done it without reason, but we need to know why."

Sue whined again and wiggled closer to him.

Karl let out a frustrated growl.

Vicky considered the problem, and an idea popped into her

head. "I've got it!"

Karl, Sue, and Zak all turned as Vicky jumped up from the couch and practically ran from the room.

She was back in a few minutes with a small, velvet bag. "The problem is Sue can't talk in wolf form, and she won't shift back," Vicky stated matter-of-factly.

Karl nodded. "That's part of it."

Vicky waved the rest of the issues away. "Come here." She went over to the open floor behind the loveseat. Karl and Sue slowly followed, their curiosities piqued. Vicky turned to look at them with a grin splitting her face. She opened the bag and dumped the contents over the bare floor.

Karl's eyes widened as he recognized the square, wood tiles from a scrabble board. "This is prefect." He knelt to the floor and started flipping the squares over so the letters were up.

Vicky helped, and they soon had most of them spread out where Sue could touch them.

Karl looked over at Sue studying the letters. "Can you tell me what's wrong, now?"

Sue shifted so she could paw at a letter.

Karl picked it up and read it. "P."

Sue pawed another letter.

"R." He moved this one over with the first.

She picked out another.

"E."

Vicky's eyes found the next letter as Sue touched it.

"G."

Vicky grabbed Karl's arm. "Oh my God! She's pregnant!" She squeezed his arm in emphasis.

Sue chirped at her.

Karl looked at Vicky in shock and turned back to Sue. "Is this true?"

Sue sat down and solemnly nodded her head.

"Is it mine?"

Sue snarled, making Karl fall backwards, away from her.

"Okay, okay," he said defensively. "It's just that we haven't been seeing much of each other recently."

Snorting at him, Sue relaxed.

Karl sat back up and reached out to caress her fur. "I'm sorry for that, too."

She leaned in against him, forgiving him of his errors.

Vicky smiled at the two werewolves. They looked so content with each other. A soft touch on her arm drew her attention to the little fay.

Zak wiggled into her lap and nuzzled his face into her stomach.

"You knew, didn't you?" Vicky petted his top tentacles back. They curled around her fingers as she worked them around. "That's why you've been so protective of her."

Zak purred and wiggled around until he could look at the wolves. They had turned their eyes to the hellhound. Zak gurgled again and waved his ends.

Karl closed his eyes and nodded his head at the fay. "Thank you." Zak purred louder as the wolf looked back up. "I'm going to be a father."

Vicky saw several emotions race across Karl's face, but elation was the last one she saw before he buried his face into Sue's neck. "Well, if you need anything else..." Pulling Zak's tentacles away from the wooden tiles he was playing with, Vicky stood up with the fay in her arms.

Sue gave her a grateful look before closing her eyes and leaning back into Karl.

Vicky took away the last of the tiles Zak was trying to eat and slipped out of the room quietly. Now that part of the mystery was solved, things could start to get better.

Pushing the door to the kitchen open, Vicky dropped Zak to the floor.

The hellhound scampered over to Darien standing at the stove and bowled into the back of his legs, trying to get at the hamburger the vampire was frying up.

"Monster," Darien growled at him, but he scooped out a spoonful of the crumbled meat and dropped it to the floor in front of the fay.

Vicky smiled at them as Zak greedily lapped the chunks up and licked the floor clean.

Darien turned his attention to Vicky. "So?"

She came over and leaned against his back lovingly. "Sue's pregnant."

Darien stilled at her words. He turned his head so he could see her from the corner of his eye for a moment, and then went back to cooking his hamburger. "You know," his words were thoughtful, "that actually makes sense."

Vicky rubbed her cheek into his back, enjoying the feel of his voice rumbling through her.

"That explains why she couldn't change." He stirred the meat around thoughtfully. "How did you figure this out?"

Vicky let out a contented breath and pushed away from Darien's back so she could talk to him. She leaned her backside against the counter and crossed her arms. "I broke out the Scrabble tiles."

Darien snickered. "So, did you find out how she got hurt?"

"Not yet," Vicky said, letting out a long sigh. "They needed some time alone." She thought about the couple wrapped up together in the other room. They were going to be parents. A flash of melancholy skimmed through her, making her heart hurt. With Darien as a lover, she would never have children. She pushed the pain away and forced herself to be happy. Sue was going to be a mother.

Darien leaned over and gave her a quick hug, banishing the rest of her unhappiness. "So, I take it Karl will be staying for dinner?" He released her and reached for the can of sloppy joe mix.

Vicky chuckled. "Most definitely." So far, this had not been a boring week.

The sound of Darien's voice drew Vicky out of the trashy romance novel she had been attempting to read. Her eyes had skimmed across the same passage six times, but she was just not absorbing the words tonight. So much had happened in the last few days that her mind just couldn't latch onto the story tonight. She looked up from where she was sprawled across the bed as Darien came into the room.

"I see," he mumbled into the phone as he went about gathering up clothing.

Vicky closed her book and scratched Zak where he was curled up next to her. Her eyes followed Darien as he continued to listen to the phone. She was used to him choosing his work clothing in the evening, but tomorrow was Saturday, and none of the articles he had pulled out were suitable for work.

"Have it ready by then." Darien paused to listen again. "Thank you." Hanging up the phone, he set it next to his stack of clothing and came over to sit on the edge of the bed.

Vicky rolled over and looked up at the pensive vampire. "What's up?"

"I just got a call from Clara." His voice was slow as he thought about his conversation with the head of the local Vampire Council. "The Council is still having issues with random attacks in the city. There's going to be a meeting at the end of the week to discuss this rogue. She wants me to help."

Vicky considered him for a moment before answering. "Did you tell her about your issues?"

Darien got real still for a moment before glancing over to the new mirror over his dresser. The glazier had done an excellent job replacing the glass Darien had shattered in a fit of rage. "No."

He breathed the word so softly Vicky almost didn't hear it. Confusion crossed her face as she pushed up to a sitting position. "Why not?" she asked. "Isn't losing your vampire powers something she needs to know?"

Zak rubbed up against Darien's hip.

Dairen weaved his fingers deep into the little horror's feelers. "This isn't something I can let them know about." He paused, choosing his words carefully. "The council here may respect me enough to let this weakness slide, but there are other things out there that would see my failings as an opportunity not to be missed."

The seriousness of his voice caused Vicky to sit up a little straighter. She touch Darien's arm reassuringly. "This isn't your fault."

He turned and gave her a thin smile. "Maybe not, but it still leaves me vulnerable."

Zak gurgled and wiggled into Darien's lap.

He let out a chuckle and rubbed the small fay. "There's not much you can do to protect me."

Growling, Zak rubbed his face into Darien's stomach.

"So, what do we do?"

Darien turned to look at her and sighed softly. He loved that she was willing to help him without his needing to ask. "Well," shifting Zak to the bed, he stood up, "I know of someone that might be able to help, but I have to go to them." He turned and gave Vicky a cryptic grin. "How would you like to go drop in on them tomorrow?"

"Sure," she agreed. "Will it be okay to drop in unannounced?"

Mischief bloomed in his eyes as his smile widened. "Oh, it's expected."

This confused Vicky, but she let it go. When Darien got into a mischievous mood, it was best just to roll with it. It didn't matter how many times or ways she questioned him, he would not give her a straight answer. "All right." She smiled. "So, where are we going?"

Darien's grin got bigger as he tapped his long index finger on the side of his nose.

Vicky just laughed at him.

"Find a set of comfortable clothing." He turned back to the clothes he had pulled out. "It'll be warmer than here, but you will still probably need a jacket."

Vicky let out a long sigh and went to get some clothes. She was definitely not getting anything out of him tonight.

Zak led the way out of Darien's bedroom. Vicky had been sleeping in there for a while now, but all of her stuff was still in the dappled green room she had originally moved into when an ifrit had set fire to her apartment.

Tapping lightly on the door to let the werewolves inside know she was there, she pushed it open when Karl's voice called in answer. "Sorry," Vicky said as she slipped into the room and grinned apologetically to her friends stretched out on the soft rug. The Scrabble letters were scattered across the floor so Sue could communicate. "I just need some clothing." Zak wobbled over to the pair as she moved to the dresser and pulled out two sets of clothing. Peeking over, she found Sue watching her. "Darien wants to go out tomorrow, and we might be gone all night." Vicky gathered the stack of clothes to her chest and turned to her friends. "Will you guys be okay here?"

Sue chirped, and Karl patted her lovingly.

"Of course." He smiled. "We really appreciate Darien letting us stay." Darien had invited Karl to remain with Sue for as long as he liked. With her still unable to shift back to human form, it was not safe for her to return to Rupert and the local pack.

"It's no problem at all," Vicky reassured them. She reached down to scratch Sue behind the ear and stopped just short of the soft fur. Somehow, Vicky has started to think of Sue as more dog than a human.

Karl caught her internal conflict and grinned. "It's okay." He reached up and scratched Sue behind the other ear.

Sue rocked her head so his fingers dug in a little deeper.

Vicky let her fingers fall to the fur and scrubbed them in the same way she knew Zak liked. "It just seems so rude to pet your friends like that."

Sue let her tongue loll out of her mouth in pleasure.

Karl chuckled at her. "Wolves are very social animals," he explained. "Most of us are very comfortable with ourselves and enjoy being touched."

Vicky nodded her head, slowly taking in his words. "I seem to remember that." She raised an eyebrow as she thought about a very interesting poker game she has walked into in this very room.

Karl laughed at the look on her face.

"Oh," she pulled her hand back and readjusted her pile of clothing, "I don't mind you using this room, but my stuff is stowed in here. If you don't want me coming in at odd times to get something, you may want to move to either the yellow room at the end of the hall or the room downstairs. But, I don't want you to think I'm running you out of here." Vicky added the last bit quickly so they wouldn't misunderstand.

Sue snickered—a very disturbing sound coming from a large wolf.

"We understand." Karl reached out and touched Vicky's leg where he could reach it. "It would probably be a wise idea to move to the room downstairs, anyway." He turned loving eyes on his wolf lady. "Once Sue starts showing, it would be best if she avoided stairs."

Sue snorted at his overprotectiveness, but she tolerated it.

"Well, let us know if there's anything else we can do for you." Vicky stood up and looked at the hellhound that had come in with her. "Zak!" She called to him. "Drop those, and spit out what's in your mouth."

Zak had been playing with Sue's Scrabble tiles. He rapped a few on the floor before dropping them and spitting out a well-chewed, wet glob that had once been a game piece.

Vicky rolled her eyes in exasperation as the little fay came over to cuddle against her leg. "Sorry about that." She smiled at her guests. "I'll get something to clean it up."

Karl reached over to the basketball-sized mass of tentacles

and ruffled a few of the smaller bits. "Don't worry about it."

Zak turned to nuzzle Karl's hand.

"I'll get it."

The fay wrapped some of his grasping ends around Karl's fingers and was in the process of licking their tips when Vicky nudged him lightly with her foot. "Then, I think I had better get him out of here before he decides he wants to chew on something tastier."

Karl's eyes widened, and he carefully pulled his hand away from the fay's mouth.

Vicky nudged the hellhound towards the door. "Come on, you little horror."

The fay gurgled happily and rolled out of the room.

"Have a good night," Vicky called as she followed Zak out to the sounds of Karl's mirth. It was going to be interesting having other people in the house.

Vicky made her way back into Darien's bedroom and added her things to the pile the vampire was sorting into a bag.

Darien looked over her choice of jeans and a dark, woolen sweater. "You might need something else." He considered his options for a second before turning to his walk-in closet. "I think I have just the thing." When he came back out, he held a black, hooded sweatshirt and a white, long-sleeved T-shirt. Darien folded them and replaced Vicky's sweater. "Now, you just need some comfortable shoes." Going back to the closet, he found Vicky's running shoes. She only wore them to run on the treadmill in the exercise room. "There." Darien looked over the new outfit, pleased. "That should work for our meeting tomorrow."

Vicky raised an eyebrow at the new outfit. "I thought we were going to a meeting." Lifting the zipped hoodie, she looked at it closer. The golden word 'Saints' was split in half by the zipper. This was definitely inappropriate for the types of meetings they usually had.

"Well," Darien shrugged as he dropped the filled bag on the

floor, "these people aren't the type of people I usually meet with." He gave Vicky an odd look. "They're people from my past."

"Oh." Vicky nodded slowly and folded the shirt back onto the pile. "This is going to be interesting."

Darien chuckled as he turned to pull her into his arms. "It's nothing you should be concerned about." He kissed her lightly on the forehead. "Now, go get ready for bed. We have to head out early tomorrow."

Vicky leaned her head onto his shoulder and breathed out a resigned sigh. At times, Darien's mysterious side infuriated her, but she had learned that pushing wouldn't get her the information she wanted. All she had to do was practice a little patience and all would be revealed tomorrow.

7

Somehow, Vicky wasn't really surprised when Darien got them up before dawn and drove out to the little airfield on the outskirts of Brenton. She had been there before—she picked him up from Hawking's Field during the first week she had worked for him. Just the memory of how he had recoiled from the sun brought a smile of amusement to her face. At the time, she hadn't known about vampires and had thought he was reacting due to a hangover. Oh, how wrong she had been.

"So, are you going to tell me where we are going?" Vicky asked as she opened the door to let Zak out.

The small fay shifted into his Shih Tzu form, jumped out of the car, and scurried around, sniffing things.

Shutting the door, she pulled her coat a little tighter around her before slipping her satchel over her shoulder. The weather had turned colder last night, and the air bit as they got out of the car.

Darien smiled at her and grabbed up the backpack he had stuffed their things into. "You'll see." He wrapped his arm around her shoulder and guided her into the hangar. "Come on, Zak."

Zak peeked up from where he was digging in the grass and sprinted his way over to the waiting plane. He paused when one of the ground crew whistled and reached down. Zak's tail wagged happily as the little horror rubbed into the man's outstretched hand. After a few good scratches, the fay shook off the man's attention and scampered up the steps into the plane.

"Good morning, Mr. Ritter." A well-dressed man greeted him as Darien got closer to the small jet waiting for him. "She's all ready to go." He held out his hand, and Darien handed over the bag to be stowed.

"Good. Thank you, Michael," Darien said as he led the way to the plane.

The man nodded. "Watch your step, Miss." Michael stepped up and held his hand out so Vicky could follow Darien into the aircraft.

Vicky looked at the offering for a moment before using it to climb up the steps of the private jet.

The man followed her up and turned to help the ground crew secure the door.

Vicky paused to look around the aircraft. She had never been inside a private jet before, but she had seen them in movies. Darien's jet looked exactly like she would have expected. The interior of the plane was done up in varying shades of beige.

On one side of the room were two comfy-looking armchairs attached to the floor. There was a wooden folding table attached to the wall between them. At the moment, it was stowed away for liftoff. Zak had jumped up on the long couch that ran the length of the other side of the cabin. The dark brown cushions accented the rest of the space, making the beige less overwhelming. The doors at either end of the cabin were done up in mahogany. Overall, it was a rather simple, but elegant, design.

Vicky pulled her bag off and headed for one of the chairs. She slipped off her overcoat and looked around for someplace to hang it. To her surprise, Michael stood ready to take it from her. "Thank you." She handed the coat over.

Michael folded it over his arm before taking Darien's jacket as well. "The captain is running through the last of the preflight checks now," he explained, taking the bag and jackets to a small closet in one of the bulkheads. "There's a cold front over Mississippi, so we could run into some turbulence there, but otherwise, it will be calm air clear to New Orleans."

Vicky's eyes widened when she heard their destination. She had always wanted to go to New Orleans but never had the chance to go.

Darien sunk into the chair farthest from the door. "Very good."

Michael nodded and disappeared through the door to the cockpit.

"New Orleans?" Vicky asked as she settled into the other chair.

Zak jumped off the couch and came over to climb onto Vicky's lap.

Darien gave her a lazy shrug. "I have a contact there who owes me a favor or two." Leaning back into the seat, he crossed his legs at the ankles and folded his hands over his stomach. "They deal with a different type of magic than the fay. I'm hoping the different perspective will shed some light on the situation." He closed his eyes and relaxed back into the chair.

"So what type of magic do they deal with?" Vicky tried to draw Darien into a conversation, but all she got was a rumbling noise from deep in his chest. Smiling, she turned her attention to the windows. With all the stress from the last few days, Darien hadn't been sleeping well. It was probably best to let him rest a little. After all, he was still recovering from his bout of stomach flu. She wiggled her fingers deeper into Zak's fur, setting him to purring.

When the plane started to move, Vicky looked around in surprise. She had been on a few planes before and was expecting the whole safety demonstration thing from a flight attendant. As far as Vicky could tell, there wasn't a flight attendant. While the plane hurdled down the runway, she considered waking Darien to ask, but he looked so peaceful stretched out in his chair. Vicky decided to wait for the plane to level out and ask Michael. When the plane finally stabilized, she picked up Zak and went to tap on the pilot's door.

"Can I help you, Miss?" Michael asked when he opened the door.

Vicky took a quick look around the small room before answering. She had never seen the cockpit of a real airplane before. Shaking her head to realign her thoughts, she turned back to her question. "Is there some kind of security or safety stuff we have to do?" She held Zak tightly against her. He was trying to get down to investigate the little room.

Michael chuckled and opened the door, inviting her into the small cabin. He went back to the copilot's seat. "That's only for aircraft over 12,500 pounds," he explained. "We miss that mark by about 2,000 pounds."

"So, what about the whole flight attendant thing?" Vicky asked, curious.

An attentive look crossed Michael's face, and he sat up taller. "Did you need something?"

"No." Vicky held out her hand to keep the man from jumping up to help. "I've just never flown by private plane before."

Zak made an attempt at escape, but Vicky caught him before he could leap from her arms.

"Then, welcome aboard." The pilot smiled over his shoulder at her. "I'm Terry."

Vicky looked over the well-spoken man. His skin was so dark it was nearly purple, and he would probably be tall when he stood up. Right now, he was folded neatly behind the controls of the plane. "If you need anything, Michael here can help you find it."

Michael nodded his head in agreement.

"I'm Vicky." She smiled warmly at him. "And this is Zak." She bounced the fay in her arms. He was still trying to get down to look around the room.

"You can let him down." Terry reassured her as he watched the little dog struggle to get free. "He can't hurt much."

Vicky snorted in mirth but let Zak down. "You don't know him very well." She smiled.

Finally free, the fay sniffed around one of the panels. He turned his attention to Michael holding down his hand. Zak sniffed it before rubbing his face into the man's palm.

Michael lifted him to his lap and ruffled his fur. "Oh, he seems nice enough to me."

"That's what he would like you to believe." She chucked at Zak sniffing the instrument panel. "Come on, Zak." She patted her leg. "Let's leave these nice men to do their jobs."

Zak shook his head in a great sneeze and jumped from Michael's lap.

"Sorry for bothering you," Vicky backed out of the small room.

"You're no bother at all." Michael stood up to see her out. "If you or Mr. Ritter needs anything, please let me know."

Vicky thanked him again and went back to her seat. The air temperature in the plane was comfortable now that the cold December air had been shut out. She unzipped the Saints hoodie and relaxed back into the chair, giving her lap back to Zak.

Closing her eyes, she tried to remember everything she had ever learned about New Orleans. Unfortunately, it wasn't much. She knew the city was most famous for Mardi Gras and drinking. There had been a few extensive articles on the city's rich history after Katrina had devastated the region, but she had mostly read the parts about the pumping and levee systems. There had also been a recent kids' movie about the darker side of the city.

Vicky pulled at her memory trying to get it to work. She had stopped to watch part of that show when she had gone shopping. There was a man with a strangely painted face and little shrunken heads singing a catchy song, but she just couldn't recall what he was. Vicky shook the thought away and let her mind drift. She would find out the answers soon enough.

The morning sunlight twinkled off the water as the plane circled, preparing for landing. The little airport was on the edge of the biggest lake Vicky had ever seen. Darien pointed out the thin line that crossed the waters of Lake Pontchartrain and explained that it was the longest bridge in the world at a whopping twenty-four uninterrupted miles. Zak perched on the back of the couch, looking out the window as the plane touched down. By the time they taxied into a waiting hangar, he had jumped down and was romping around the cabin, ready to get out and explore the new area.

"Should we warn New Orleans that he's coming?" Vicky laughed as she gathered her bag.

Darien smiled at her. "No," He chuckled as he went to get their coats and bag. "This city's seen worse."

Michael stepped out of the cabin and almost ran into Darien. "Sorry, Sir," he apologized and slipped passed the vampire to crack open the hatch.

Zak bounced over and rubbed against his leg.

"Come on, Zak," Vicky called the little horror away so the man could work.

"He's all right." Michael leaned over and scratched Zak's ear before lowering the door to the waiting ground crew.

As soon as the steps were completely down, Zak bounced out to investigate the new smells.

Darien laughed as Michael tried to catch him before he slipped away. "Just let him go," he reassured the man trying to scramble after the dog. "He'll be fine."

Michael looked out the door before nodding and climbing out of the cabin at a more dignified pace.

Vicky glanced around to make sure she hadn't left anything before following Darien out of the plane.

He held his hand out to help her down the steps.

Vicky looked around, slightly disappointed. "So, this is New Orleans." Even though the air temperature was warmer than Brenton, it didn't seem much different than home.

Darien snickered and wrapped his arm around her, pulling her to his side. "This is the New Orleans Lakefront Airport." He steered her towards a black sedan. "You don't get a good feel for the city until you get to the Quarter." A dark-skinned man, dressed in a suit, stood by the car with keys.

"Welcome to the Crescent City, Mr. Ritter." He held out the keys for Darien to take. "She's all gassed up and ready to go."

Darien thanked him and tossed his bag and coat in the back seat. His long-sleeved T-shirt was enough to cut what little chill there was in the air.

Vicky added her coat and bag to the back seat as well.

"Zak!" Darien called to the fay. "We're leaving."

Vicky had to suppress a smile when she heard the surprised squeal of some unseen groundskeeper. Zak must have startled him when he bolted out of whatever mischief he was getting into. Vicky opened her door, and Zak launched himself into her seat.

"Little monster." Darien grinned as he got in.

Vicky had to shift the excited fay around so she could get in. "Do you like it here?" she asked as Zak bounced from looking out the front window to looking out the passenger window.

The fay tried to get into Darien's lap so he could see out his side, but the vampire grabbed him up and handed him back to Vicky. Zak gurgled excitedly and went back to pressing his nose all over the passenger window.

Vicky ruffled his fur excitedly. His enthusiasm was catching.

"Oh, he should love it here," Darien answered as he drove out of the airport. "This area has a long history of magic use. Several large lay lines cross under the city." He glanced at Vicky from the corner of his eye. "Why else would they build a city right at sea level?"

Vicky thought on this for a moment. "I thought New Orleans

was a port city founded by the French."

"It was," Darien said with a nod, "but there were several better places to put a city than in the middle of a swamp. And, you're going to get laughed at if you continue to call it 'New *Or Leans*'." Darien stressed the way Vicky had been pronouncing the city's name. "It's 'New *Orlens*'," he said, stressing the Southern pronunciation. "Or, if you really want to fit in, '*Naw'Lens*'."

Vicky giggled and repeated them. "I think I'll stick with 'New *Orlens*'. I feel weird saying '*Naw'Lens*'." She looked out the windows at the little houses lining the road. It was surprising how many still had boards over their windows. "Why are all these houses abandoned?" She could still see signs of the flood that had devastated the city.

"We're driving through some of the areas hardest hit by Katrina," Darien said solemnly. "Some of these homes had over ten feet of water in them. Most of the families in this area were evacuated to other places, and a fair number of those people decided to stay in their new locations versus coming back." He looked over the deserted scene. "Most of the people that lived around here were renters. With the renters gone, the landlords are either not in any hurry to rebuild, or they don't have the funds to do it."

"But, didn't their insurance cover it?" Vicky asked, concerned.

"Some did." Darien shrugged again. "Others either didn't have enough insurance, or they didn't carry the right type. A lot of these houses held storm insurance, but not flood insurance."

Vicky gave him a bewildered look.

"That means the insurance would only pay for the damages done by the wind and rain, but not the damage done by flooding."

"But, wasn't this," Vicky waved her hand at the passing houses, "done by the storm?"

"Yes and no. Yes, the storm battered the area, but it was the failure of the levees that caused the flooding," Darien explained. "So, most of the damage was not a direct result of the storm."

Vicky worked this over for a moment, trying to see it from

the insurance companies' point of view. "So, since the damage was caused by a failure in the levee verses wind and rain damage, the insurance companies see it as flood damage, not storm damage," she reiterated.

"Exactly." Darien nodded.

Vicky scrubbed her fingers into Zak's fur, annoyed. "That's stupid." To her, all of this damage was caused by that one storm and should be covered under storm insurance.

"Yes, but it saved the insurance companies a lot of money."

"What about the people?" Vicky's voice was filled with indignation. *How could a company hang so many people out to dry like that?*

"That's how it works." Darien shrugged again. "I never said it was right."

Vicky grumbled and watched as the neighborhoods slipped past. They were starting to look more populated.

Soon, Darien was zigzagging his way through the city. Most of the main roads held large, grassy medians between the lanes. Sometimes they would follow one of the many canals that cut through the city. Several times, Darien had to pass his turn and loop around to the other side of the street before he could get to the road he wanted.

"What's wrong with the road systems in this town?" Vicky asked as they made another U-turn. "Can't you turn left?"

Darien laughed at this. "There are a few places in the area where you can turn left, but most of the time it's restricted."

"Why?' This concept seemed stupid to her. Even in Brenton, where most of the roads were one way, you could make a left without much issue.

"Maybe the planners were thinking of all the people that come down here to get drunk." Darien grinned as he made the next right-hand turn. "You know, UPS drivers aren't allowed to make left-hand turns in most cities."

Vicky looked at him in disbelief.

"It's true. There was a study done that showed the drivers would use less time and gas making all right turns."

Vicky raised an eyebrow as she took this information in. "Really?"

"Yes." Darien nodded. "They didn't have to sit at the light, waiting for cross traffic. And there were also fewer accidents. Trying to turn through traffic in such a large vehicle is hard. If they only make right-hand turns, they avoid that whole find-a-hole-and-hurry issue. If they go around the block, they can just go straight through at the light. Much safer."

"True." Vicky had not thought about that. She turned her attention back out the window to the passing world.

Darien made a right-hand turn and pointed towards his window. "That's Vieux Carré. Also known as the French Quarter."

Vicky craned her neck trying to see the famous area. It didn't look very exciting from here.

"How would you like some breakfast?"

"Sure." They had skipped out on breakfast when they left this morning.

Darien drove them down the divided road to another major road. "This is Canal Street," he explained as he stopped at the light.

Vicky looked up and down the street. She could see a trolley running along the tracks between the lanes. This road was starting to look like what she expected New Orleans to look like. There were several large neon signs that would be brilliant in the evening. "Why is it called Canal Street?" Vicky didn't see any canal splitting the median.

"It was named for the canal that was going to be built here, but never was."

Why would they name a street after something that they never built? Vicky thought. Of course, these *were* the same people who deemed that left-hand turns were useless.

Darien passed Canal Street and drove into a more city-like area. The little buildings and trees were replaced with the taller architecture of a city. Turning at the first road, he circled the block to get back onto Canal Street.

Both Vicky and Zak twisted from one side to the other as they looked over the flashy signs that lined the street. There were a few people out, but not many. This place would be amazing after dark. Vicky could see strands of beads stuck on some of the signs. They swayed slightly in the morning breeze. "Are the beads left over from Mardi Gras?" Her eyes caught more hanging from other, out-of-reach places.

"Yes." Darien watched traffic as he came to the end of Canal Street and followed the road as it turned left alongside some railroad tracks. Pulling into a parking lot at the end of the road, he found a parking space.

Vicky looked around but didn't see any place to eat. "So, where are we going?" she asked as Darien got out of the car. Vicky stepped out and debated whether she needed her coat. The long-sleeved shirt and sweatshirt she wore felt pretty warm with the sun shining on it, so she grabbed up her bag and slipped it over her shoulder.

"There's no parking in the Quarter," Darien explained. "We'll have to walk a bit." He held out his hand.

Vicky took it. For some reason, he seemed older to her.

Darien folded her hand around his arm and led her out to the street.

Zak started to bounce along in front of them.

Pausing, Darien looked at the fay. "Come here, Zak." Kneeling down, he picked the little horror up so they were eye level. "I'm sorry about this, but we need to put you on a leash."

The fay growled at him.

"I know, but it's the law."

Zak sneezed his displeasure and whined at Darien.

"We'll get you something special," Darien said, offering the fay a bribe.

Zak finally gave him a sulking look and nodded his head.

"Good." Darien ruffled the hellhound as he set him down. Turning, he pointed to Vicky's bag. "I need in that."

Vicky shifted it around so Darien could search in it without standing back up.

After a few moments of digging, Darien pulled out a black collar with a dark green leash. He fastened it around Zak's neck. "Here." Handing the end to Vicky, Darien stood up. "I think it would be better if you held him."

Vicky looked down at the disgruntled fay. He had already gotten the leash in his mouth. "Zak." She pulled him over so she could pet him. "I don't like this any more than you do." Wiggling her fingers into the fay's thick fur, she scratched the sweet spot behind his ear. "But it's only while we're in the city." She continued to rub him until he purred. "Once we're back to the car, we can take it off."

Zak rubbed his head into Vicky's leg and pranced around at the end of the lead. The tips of his hair wiggled unnaturally in his excitement.

"Now," Darien reclaimed Vicky's free hand, "where were we?" He wrapped her hand back around his arm and led her to the street. "You know, I didn't come out here very often in the daytime." They headed away from Canal Street, past more parking areas. Most of them were fairly empty at this time of day. After a few blocks, the road they were on joined with another.

"This is Decatur," Darien explained. "The Quarter runs from Decatur up to North Rampart Street, and from Canal Street clear over to Esplanade Ave."

As they walked, Vicky could just see the green of a park up on the left-hand side. "So, you know this area well?"

"Oh, yes," Darien answered. "I've spent a great deal of time here." His accent slipped a little, picking up a hint of the French that the area was so well known for.

Vicky raised an eyebrow as they walked on.

"I came to New Orleans in 1810." Darien got that faraway

look that he often had when remembering things from his past. "That was a different time. The area was being flooded with immigrants from the Haitian Revolution just a few years before. With the active ports and the influx of people, this was the perfect place for vampires." His demeanor took on that edge of danger that Vicky had learned stemmed from his darker nature. "No one questioned if someone went missing every now and then." This was the side of Darien that scared Vicky. She had only seen it a few times, but it unnerved her to know that such darkness lurked in his soul.

"At that time, there were several masters in this city." He looked around as if seeing the area in a different light. "Most of them are dead now, too eager in their lust for blood to not draw attention. I was always careful. Life is too precious to be taken so recklessly." He caressed Vicky's hand where it touched his arm. "But, like draws like, so I spent more than my fair share of time in their company. Fortunately, by that time, I was old enough to not be pressured into moving with the crowd."

"You mean, other vampires could pressure you into things you didn't want to do?" Vicky asked. It was hard to believe that anyone could force Darien into doing something he didn't want to by peer pressure alone.

Darien smiled at her. "It was hard to go against what others of my kind were doing. A lesser vampire would have been looked down on as weak or afraid for taking the route I chose," he explained. "Murder and death are part of what we are."

Vicky shivered. "No," she said, shaking her head and resting her other hand on top of his arm. "You're not like that."

Darien covered her hands with his again. "Yes. I am," he answered. "I have been every bit the dark villain, and it will always be part of me."

"Did you enjoy it?"

Darien paused to consider his answer. "At times."

"And do you still?" Vicky pushed.

"Not so much anymore," he answered truthfully.

They walked on in silence. The bit of green ahead of them opened up on both sides of the street. Vicky tore her mind from their conversation and looked around her. On the left side of the street was a line of carriages. Beyond them was a black, iron fence, separating the sidewalk from the famous Jackson Square. Wrapping around the edges of the square were the redbrick buildings with the amazing balconies that the area was known for. "Wow," Vicky breathed in awe. They were as beautiful as she had imagined.

Darien pulled his arm from hers and wrapped her up against his side. "Is beautiful, no?" He looked out over the square. "I've been through here hundreds of times, but one never appreciates a place when they live there." Pulling her along, he urged her farther down the road. "Where we're going is just over there."

Vicky looked back down Decatur Street. She felt a tug on the leash and looked to see Zak straining against the lead. He'd smelled something he wanted. Just past the trees on the right was a building with a green roof. She could just make out the many tables and familiar, green logo on the side of the building.

"Really?" Vicky bounced as she realized where Darien was taking her for breakfast. She sped up and spun around to face Darien without stopping. Darien smiled as she took up his hands and continued their walk backwards. "We're going there?" She swung his hands excitedly.

"But, of course." His thick, French accent made Vicky giggle. Twirling her back around to his side, Darien pulled her into the line of his body and kissed the curls at the side of her head lovingly.

Vicky let out a soft hum of contentment. "I really do love it when you speak with an accent." Snuggling closer into him, she felt him stiffen slightly as they walked on. Peeking up, she saw surprise on his face. "You didn't realize you were speaking with a French accent, did you?"

Darien chuckled a little and relaxed. "No, ma chérie." He shook his head but didn't lose the foreign inflection in his voice.

Vicky giggled again and leaned into his side.

Café Du Monde was much larger than Vicky had thought. She'd expected a place that served mainly donuts and coffee to be rather small, no matter how famous they were. The recognizable green-and-white striped awning only covered a small portion of the seating patio. Just outside the fenced-in area, a man sat, playing soft jazz on a saxophone, the white of his suit shone brightly against his dark skin.

Pulling out a bill from his pocket, Darien dropped it in the man's case as they passed. He led Vicky through the archway and into the end of a long building that housed the restaurant. There was already quite a crowd. "Come; let us find a table before le petit horreur eats the place."

Vicky looked down to find Zak trying to get to a chunk of beignet someone had dropped. She loosened his lead a little so he could reach it.

Darien escorted her under the awning to an empty table near one of the fences. "I'll be right back," he reassured her and headed into the main part of the building.

Vicky settled into the padded chair and studied the café. The open floor plan and high ceiling gave the building an airy quality, while the wooden ceiling warmed it. Fans hung overhead, ready to move around the air when the temperature climbed in the summer. The gentle murmur of the crowd soothed her as the delicate voice of the saxophone wafted in from the street. Even though it was busy, there was no hustle or bustle like the coffee shops back home. No one was rushed or hurried here. She was starting to understand why they called this place 'The Big Easy'.

The speed in which Darien returned with a tray full of food surprised Vicky. She was sure he hadn't been gone long enough to get the delicious-looking treats. Time didn't seem to run the same way in this place, or it felt that way. She sat back so Darien could place a cup of coffee on a saucer in front of her. Someone had filled it so full that the coffee sloshed over the sides of the cup even though he tried to be careful with it.

After unloading several plates of beignets heaping with powdered sugar and a bottle of milk, Darien claimed his own overflowing cup and dropped the tray on the empty table nearby. Settling into the chair next to Vicky, he shifted the food around, dividing it out.

"Thank you," Vicky said as she turned the very full cup around on the saucer. She leaned forwards and sipped some of the hot liquid. The chickaree coffee laced with milk was both very hot and slightly bitter. Picking up her spoon, she looked around for the sugar. Finding their container was empty, she scooped up some of the powdered sugar from the edge of her plate and added it to the coffee until it was sweet enough.

A whine from Zak drew Darien's attention away from the food he was sorting. "I didn't forget about you."

Zak pawed at the vampire's leg, trying to get into his lap and at the food.

"Keep your fur on." Darien pulled one of the plates over and set it on the ground for Zak.

The little hellhound circled it before shoving his face into it greedily. Powdered sugar puffed out from where he snorted into the plate.

Darien laughed and took the saucer from under his coffee. He cracked open the bottle of milk and filled the plate before setting it down for Zak to lap up.

Vicky smiled at the two. "He's so spoiled."

"He'll take what he wants, anyway," Darien shrugged, "so why not give it to him?"

Vicky conceded his point before turning to her warm, sugar-covered bread. With all that powder covering the beignets, how was she supposed to eat them without getting making a mess? She watched Darien pick one up, tap it on his plate, and bend in to take a bite. Amazingly, he didn't come away covered in the sugar. Vicky mimicked him. "Mmmm," she moaned in pleasure. "These are so much better when they are hot."

Darien nodded his head but didn't answer around the

beignet stuffed in his own mouth.

Vicky snickered at the eagerness in which Darien was consuming the pastry.

Catching her mirth, Darien looked up at her. "What?" he asked around his mouthful.

Vicky snickered even more as Darien finished chewing and swallowed.

"It's the first time I've had these and not had to worry about it."

The French accent was gone, and he sounded so much like a scorned child that Vicky had to laugh harder.

He gave her a hurt look.

Vicky wiped her eyes. "Sorry." She reached out to touch his hand and soothe his bruised feelings. "It's just, there are times you go from mysterious and foreboding to such a child, that it surprises me." Reaching up, she brushed some powdered sugar from the corner of his mouth. "You know I love you and would never laugh at your situation." Her voice had lost most of its joy, turning serious due Darien's strange predicament.

Darien caught her hand and pressed it to his cheek, enjoying her touch. "I know." Pulling it around, he kissed the back before releasing it. "Finish your food," he said, pointing to the barely touched plate in front of her. "We still have a long walk and not much time to get there."

Vicky looked around for a clock but didn't see one. They had left so early in the morning that it couldn't be later than ten AM. "Where are we going?" she asked as she picked up her beignet.

"To visit an old friend of mine." Dairen picked up his final beignet and dug in with the same enjoyment he showed earlier.

8

VICKY DUSTED AWAY THE LAST TRACES OF POWDERED SUGAR FROM HER HANDS and stood up. For just bread and sugar, the beignets were mighty filling.

Zak nosed around on the ground under the tables, hunting for scraps that had been overlooked. He had even begged a few bites from some of the nearby patrons.

"So, where are we going?" Vicky asked as she drained the last of her coffee. Several of the tables around them had filled up in the short time they were there, and Darien had been reluctant to talk about his plans for the day. It had also been hard to get words out of him around the pillowy doughnuts he kept stuffing in his mouth. She had never seen him this eager about food before.

"It's on the other side of the Quarter," he said as he stacked the dishes together on the table. "They close early on Saturday, so we need to get going."

Vicky reclaimed Zak's leash and stood up.

Darien reached out for Vicky's satchel. "Let me take that."

Surprised she had it, Vicky slipped off the bag and handed it over to Darien. She really shouldn't have been surprised; this wasn't the first time she had picked the bag up without thinking. After all, Darien had bespelled the satchel to ensure it would not be lost or stolen.

Once the bag was settled on his shoulder, Darien led the way back out to Decatur Street. When they were free of the confines of the café, he took Vicky's hand and led her through traffic to the other side of the street.

Fascinated by the sights, Vicky turned her head back and forth, trying to take it all in. The fence around Jackson Square was covered with artwork being hawked by starving artists. As Darien led her along, she glanced at each of the pictures. A little farther down, there was a woman with a table draped in cloth. A crystal ball sat on the corner of the table, while the woman folded large cards to the cloth-covered surface. From the way the woman was dressed, the word 'gypsy' popped into Vicky's head. But it was obvious from the woman's pale skin and blonde hair that she did not belong to this iconic group of people. Following Darien's pull, Vicky rounded the corner to find a whole row of people selling things.

"Is there a bazaar today?" Vicky asked as she looked at a man completely painted silver standing on a box. He held perfectly still as people took his picture.

"No." Darien looked around at the scene. "This is a normal Saturday. It's actually pretty light, considering the weather."

Vicky looked up at the brilliant blue, winter sky. The air was actually comfortable.

Darien's eyes caught something, and he adjusted their course to intercept the hawker.

Seeing Darien's intention, a man holding a basket of roses stopped and waited for him. "A flower for a lovely lady?" He held out a single, red rose.

"Please." Darien took it. "I will also need six more wrapped together, if you please." After paying the man, Darien turned and presented the single rose to Vicky. "For you, my love."

Vicky blushed with pleasure as she accepted the flower. She kissed Darien's cheek.

The man presented the six roses wrapped in a piece of green tissue paper. "Your roses."

Darien thanked him and tucked the small bouquet into the crook of his arm. "Shall we?" He held his arm out for Vicky to take.

She nodded and slipped back to his side.

"Come on, Zak," Darien called the little fay away from where the rose seller was petting him.

Zak barked and shook his Shih Tzu-like body before falling in to walk with Vicky.

Darien led them across the open area in front of the church at one end of the square.

Vicky looked up to the three towering spires. "I've seen pictures of this church so many times, but I have no idea what it's called."

"Cathedral-Basilica of Saint Louis, King of France," Darien said, looking up at the impressive, white building. "Or, St. Louis Cathedral. It holds the prestige of being the oldest continually operated cathedral in the United States."

Vicky gawked at the building as they passed.

"I remember when they put the clock tower on it." He was quiet for a moment. "But, that was before they made it bigger." Darien led her down the side of the church to a small alleyway.

Vicky suddenly felt so meek compared to him. "You must remember a lot about this city." She clutched the rose to her chest as she thought about it.

Darien let out a soft chuckle as he looked around. "So much has changed since I lived here." They passed under some trees and stepped onto a brick street. Turning left, they walked down the middle of the road. Black metal markers had been raised at the intersections to keep cars from turning down it.

"How so?" Vicky asked as she studied the tightly packed buildings they passed. These stores were filled with knickknacks and artwork.

"Oh, the layout and buildings are all the same, but the flavor isn't." Darien turned right at the next corner. "At one point in time, this place was a bustling port. You could see and get all manner of things here. There were so many different people flowing through here. And each brought something with them.

"When the Haitians introduced Vodou, they stirred the pool of power that had been collecting. At that time, the magic in this area was tangible. It wasn't uncommon to see loa possession in the middle of the street. Nowadays, most of the city's energy comes in through the tourists." Darien paused to let out a sigh of regret. "The land still draws in a large quantity of energy from the people, but drunken debauchery doesn't provide a very stable pool to draw from."

As Darien talked, Vicky thought about the energy pooling around her. Now that he had drawn her attention to it, it tingled across her skin from everything. It was like waking up to a fuzzy blanket wrapped around you—you could feel it, but you didn't know how it got there. Vicky returned her attention to Darien's musings.

"There is still a great deal of power here, but it's not as alive as it once was." He turned left down the next street. "Well. This is Bourbon Street."

Pausing on the corner, Vicky glanced up and down the road. It looked to be just another long street. There were people milling about, and she could hear some music coming from a building down the block.

Darien turned right onto the street, and they continued on their way.

Zak sniffed at piles of garbage and spills along the sidewalk. It was surprisingly dirty.

"Hey man!" One man cried out as they got close to him. He might have been twenty, with skin the color of dark chocolate. "For five bucks, I'll tell ya' where you got your shoes."

Vicky's eyebrows raised in wonderment. She dropped her gaze to the sneakers Darien was wearing. How could this man tell where they had come from?

Darien smiled. "They're on my feet," he said and continued without pausing.

Surprise and disappointment flashed across the man's face. He hadn't expected Darien to know the answer to the question.

Zak yipped at him as they passed.

"What was that?" Vicky glanced back at the man returning to the wall he had been leaning on.

"Panhandlers," Darien explained. "It's a form of begging." He watched as another young man approached another target. It looked like his ruse was going to work. "They pretend to provide a service while getting as much money out of people as possible." Shaking his head, Darien escorted Vicky down the street. "At one point in time, you could at least get a good shoe polish out of someone like that."

"Darien!" Vicky scolded, shocked he would say something like that. "Isn't that kind of racist?"

Darien chuckled a little. "It might have been if I were referring to his skin tone." After two blocks, Darien took another turn and left Bourbon Street behind. "Begging and offering meager services to passing people is a profession practiced by all races."

Vicky looked around at the street. "You still might want to be careful how you say things." They had left most of the crowds back on Bourbon Street. "Some people are really touchy about things like that. You *do* have an image to uphold."

Darien let out a laugh. "Like these people would know who I am. Anyway, if they want a fight, I'm sure my lawyers can give them one."

Vicky could hear the smugness in his voice. She just shook her head and thought back over the exchange. "How did you know the answer?"

Darien gave her a confused look.

"To the shoe thing."

"Oh." Enlightenment lit his face. "It's a bit of slang and the way they talk down here," he explained. "Sometimes 'got' can mean 'to have', but don't worry about it. You only really run into that type of thing on Bourbon Street."

Vicky nodded and turned her attention back to the street. "I honestly expected this place to be more crowded." There were a few cars parked alongside the road, but there wasn't a lot of activity going on.

"This place doesn't pick up until after noon." Darien peeked at his watch. "It's only just after ten in the morning."

"Really?" Vicky glanced up at him. "I expected it to be much later than that."

"We did get an early start on the day." The street they were walking on came to a divided road that looked vaguely familiar. Darien stopped and waited for traffic to clear before hurrying them across to the median.

"Where are we going?" Vicky asked as she looked back across the road. She was sure this was the road that marked the northern edge of the Quarter.

"It's just over there." Darien nodded in the direction they were going. "About another block." He hurried them across traffic again.

Vicky looked around for anything that might be their destination, but all she saw was a gas station and what looked to be a police station.

Darien ignored these and went to the next road. This time, he waited for the crosswalk light before leading her across.

A light-colored, stone wall stretched down the block to the left. Darien took them to a split in the wall, but the iron gate was shut and chained. Making a confused noise, he looked at the heavy padlock. "I know they close this place early on Saturday, but it should have been at one." He pulled out his phone and consulted it. "We should still have a few more hours until they lock it up." Rattling the chain, he looked around for an answer. The wall was too high to get over without someone noticing. "Let's go around to the side." Darien took Vicky's hand again and headed off to the side entrance. This gate was also chained and locked.

"Rats," Darien growled. "I didn't come all the way down here to be stopped by a chain." He pulled on it but lacked the strength to break it. An angry growl rumbled from his chest as he glowered at the lock.

Vicky pulled on his arm. "Maybe we can call the keepers." From what she could see, they were standing outside a cemetery. Suddenly, the roses tucked in Darien's arm seemed much more appropriate. A gurgle from Zak drew Vicky's attention.

The little fay rubbed up against the gates, testing them. Before she could stop him, Zak dropped his Shih Tzu disguise and reached tentacles up to the chain.

"Zak!" Vicky hissed and looked around for anyone who might have seen his transformation. "You can't do that here." She shoved her rose into Darien's free hand and grabbed up the little horror, trying to hide him.

Zak held tight to the gate, forcing Vicky to step into the wall more. Thankfully, no cars passed them on the road, but several had passed at the corner.

"Stop that," Vicky scolded him, trying to get him away from the gate.

Several of his grasping ends wrapped around the chain and pulled the links into his mouth.

"No," she hissed as his teeth sank into the metal severing it. "Zak!" she said, exasperated with the fay.

The little horror spit chunks of metal out on the ground. In a blink, he shifted back into the loving Shih Tzu he liked to pretend to be.

Vicky stepped back from the gate now that Zak was no longer holding to it.

"Well," Darien pulled on the damaged chain and the gate squeaked open, "that's one way to do it. Good boy." He reached over and scratched Zak's head before stepping through the opening into the cemetery.

"Darien!" Vicky hissed, her exasperation with Zak flowing over to his actions. How could he just walk into a place that was *supposed* to be locked? She glanced up and down the street, then slipped in behind him. Darien had stopped a few steps inside the gate to get his bearings. "We can't just break in here."

Vicky struggled to hold on to Zak. Wanting down, the little fay wiggled until she finally gave up and dropped him to the ground. He scampered off, dragging his leash behind him. With a frustrated huff at the little fay's behavior, she let him go. He could take care of himself.

Darien turned to the right and headed towards the front of the graveyard. "Why not?"

Vicky hurried to catch up to him. "We're going to get arrested," she growled at him. Her eyes scanned over the graves as they walked. They were nothing like any graves she had ever seen. There were hundreds of small, stone buildings lined up across the space.

"No, we won't," he reassured her as he turned from the main path and proceeded between the tombs. "We won't be here that long." Darien weaved his way through the stones, looking for something.

Vicky dogged his footsteps, still worried they would be caught. "Where are we, anyway?" she asked looking at the unusual graveyard.

"Welcome to Saint Louis Cemetery Number One. It the oldest 'City of the Dead' in New Orleans."

"City of the Dead?" Vicky thought this was an unusual name for a cemetery, but looked more closely at the small buildings. They did look like little houses. Some even had iron fences around them. She almost ran into Darien's back when he stopped suddenly.

"I know it's here somewhere." He looked back and forth at the tombs. "It can't be that hard to find."

While they were stopped, Vicky reached out to touch one of the crumbling buildings. "They're tombs." She rubbed the sun-bleached stone.

"Family tombs," Darien clarified as he gained his bearings again and headed off in another direction. "In the early years of the city, the high water table made burying the dead in the ground difficult. One good rain and the airtight coffins popped right out. And when packing them under rocks and drilling holes in them didn't work, the people turned to the French and Spanish traditions of family vaults above ground."

Vicky listened, fascinated by the history around her. "So each of these is for a family?" She looked at one stone vault. It was about six feet tall and just large enough to lay a man in. "How did they get an entire family in there?" All the buildings varied in size, but none were large enough to hold more than two or three bodies.

"When someone died, the tomb was opened up, and the body was placed in the compartment on the top. The dead were given a year and a day, undisturbed, for their souls to rest. During this time, the heat and the sun would decompose the body," Darien explained. "When the next family member died, the remains of the first were pushed to the back, where they fell down into the bottom of the vault. Then, the next body was put in. Nowadays, they give the bodies two years to decompose, and the remains are wrapped in a special burial bag when their time is up. The remains are then deposited into the bottom of the tomb."

"What happens if someone else dies before the end of the year or two years?" Vicky asked.

"The cemetery has special holding vaults in the walls." Darien pointed towards the wall two rows over. Vicky could see little doors lining it. "The second body is placed in one of those until the first has had its time in the tomb. Then, the family clears the first body and moves the second into its final resting place. Then that person's time starts." Darien stopped when his eyes caught something. "There it is." He cut between two tombs.

Vicky followed, curious to see what had Darien wandering around such an old graveyard.

The tomb Darien had been looking for was hard to miss. There were candles and beads strewn about it, and the sides were covered in hundreds of little Xs. Darien stood in front of the tomb quietly for a moment. Other than the many offerings and markings, the only thing that distinguished this tomb from any of the others was a small, bronze plaque on the lower left-hand side.

Vicky bent to read the name and inscription. "Marie Laveau?" Standing up, she looked at Darien. "It this really her grave?" Even Vicky had heard of the Voodoo Queen of New Orleans.

"No," Darien answered as he placed the roses at the foot of the grave. "Her remains were removed from here a long time ago."

"Then, why are we here?" Now she was really confused.

"Because this was her original resting place and where she is now is lost to time." Darien held Vicky's rose out for her.

She took it, not sure what to do with it now. Should she put it on the grave with the others?

Darien dug around in the bag and pulled out a handful of gaudy bead necklaces. "Here." He held them out to Vicky before digging in the bag again. This time, he pulled out a small bottle of rum and a pack of cigars.

"Okay." Vicky finally voiced her thoughts as Darien placed the bottle and smokes against the grave. "Now I'm really confused."

Darien snickered and stood up. "Why don't you arrange those beads around the bottle, and I'll explain."

Vicky handed him back her rose and artfully draped the beads over the bottle and box. "Okay." Pushing up from the ground, she dusted off her hands. "Explain." She looked back to find him holding out a stick of red chalk. Not sure what was going on, she took it and waited for him to explain.

Placing his hands on her shoulders, he spun her around three times and pointed towards the tomb. "Knock three times," he instructed her.

She looked over her shoulder at him in confusion but rapped her knuckles on the stone three times.

"Now draw three Xs." He pointed to an open spot on the white stone.

Holding up the chalk, she paused, not wanting to deface the tomb, but Darien urged her on. She drew three tiny marks on the tomb.

Darien wrapped his arms around her and raised her hand up to press it over the marks. "Now make a wish," he whispered into her ear. "And make it a good one."

Shocked by this, it took Vicky a moment to think of things she might wish for. The obvious wish would be for them to not get caught, but she nixed this idea for a better one. She closed her eyes and wished for an answer to Darien's problem. After a moment, she drew her hand back and opened her eyes. "Now explain," she demanded.

Darien kissed the side of her head. "It's an old tradition to wish on Marie Laveau's tomb." He released her and stepped back.

Vicky turned to face him. "Does it really work?" she asked curiously.

Darien shrugged and reached out to take her hand. Turning, he started back for the gate. "Tradition says it does, but I've never tested it," he confessed.

Vicky looked at him, shocked. "You mean that I just marked up some tomb in hopes that it would grant my wish?"

Darien nodded.

"And this is okay?"

"Not really. It makes the Glapion family furious." He shrugged again. "They have been after the police for years to stop the vandalism."

Vicky's mouth dropped open as she stopped to stare at him. It was outrageous that he knew this and still had her do it.

Darien stopped and looked back at her, unashamed.

She thought of several things she wanted say to him but decided not to. Yelling at him was not going to get him to behave. Vicky let out another exasperated sigh. Shaking her head, she stepped into him for a hug. "I love you." She put all her frustration, indignation, and irritation into those three words as she squeezed him. "But, it's times like these that I wonder why."

He chuckled and squeezed her back, getting the meaning she implied. Kissing her softly, Darien pulled her around to his side and held the single rose out to her.

She took it, and they continued walking.

"So..." Vicky thought over their little ritual back at the tomb. "I understand the roses," she twirled the one in her fingers as she thought, "but what's with the bottle, cigars, and beads?" She could almost come up for a reason for the Mardi Gras strands.

"It wouldn't be right to bring a gift for Marie and not bring something for the loa," Darien explained as if Vicky knew what he was talking about.

Vicky let out her amusement in a soft snort. By now, she should be used to him using terms she didn't know. "What are the loa?" she prompted, unsure if she really wanted to know.

"They are Haitian spirits."

She waited for Darien to explain more, but he didn't. "*And...*" Vicky pushed for more.

Darien chuckled. "They are the connection between the human world and God."

Vicky rolled her hand in front of him, wanting Darien to give her more.

"In the practice of Vodou, the loa are called on to take mortal requests to the Creator," Darien began. "There are lots of different loa, but the two main ones are Papa Legba and Baron Samedi."

Vicky could almost feel the air thicken as Darien said those two names, like speaking them out loud drew something's attention. She looked around but didn't see anyone watching.

Darien went on. "Papa Legba is the intermediate between the loa and humanity. He's the one you go to if you want to speak with any of the other loa; therefore, he is known as the gatekeeper."

"So who's the key master?" Vicky beamed up at him.

A grin turned the corner of his mouth, and he ignored

the sarcastic movie reference. "Papa Legba definitely deserves respect, but the loa you really need to watch out for is Baron Samedi." Darien's voice grew a little more serious, and the air thickened a touch more.

A spot between Vicky's shoulder blades itched as if eyes were on her back. She looked around again, but the cemetery was still deserted.

Darien continued. "He's the master of the dead." This time Darien looked around as if expecting the loa to step out from between the tombs. He drew Vicky a little closer to his side. "The rum and cigars were an offering to him." His steps quickened just a little.

Vicky could tell he was anxious to get out of the cemetery. Could he be having that same itching feeling of being watched? "If he frightens you that much, why did you leave him an offering?" Shivering, she pressed closer to Darien.

Darien laughed out loud but didn't slow. "He doesn't frighten me, but I do respect him and the power he wields." His eyes locked on the gate just a few feet ahead of him. "I've been loa-ridden before, and it really wasn't pretty. I would like to avoid a repeat performance."

The itchiness on Vicky's back grew warm, making it harder to breath. She felt a soft touch on her ankle and looked down to see Zak wobbling along in his fay form. He had reached a feeler up under the edge of her pants leg to wrap around her skin. The warmth on her back cooled, but she could still feel eyes on her.

Darien ushered her out of the gate and turned around to string the broken chain back through it so it looked secure.

Vicky took several deep breaths and looked around. Her eyes caught on a flash of red at the far corner of the cemetery. She focused on it to see that is was an old black man in a red coat and a straw hat leaning heavily on a cane.

He pulled the stump of a pipe out of his mouth and nodded his head slowly at Vicky.

"Darien!" Vicky hissed and grabbed at his arm.

He turned to meet her eyes. "What?"

She looked back at the corner, but the old man was gone.

Darien followed her gaze to the corner.

Zak stared down the road and chirped before wiggling back into his Shih Tzu disguise.

"I think it's best we get out of here now." Darien pulled the still-shocked Vicky into his side and led her back to the main street.

The walk back to the car was nowhere near as enjoyable as the trip to the cemetery had been. The air was still thick with the presence of something Darien had unintentionally attracted. Vicky huddled close to Darien's side as he picked out the most direct route back to the car. She could feel Zak bouncing against her leg every step of the way. The tingling sensation subsided as they put more distance between themselves and the cemetery, but feeling of eyes on her didn't ease until Darien loaded her and Zak in the car and pointed it away from the Quarter.

Darien finally drew a cleansing breath as he slipped the car on to I-10 and pointed the black sedan west. "That was close." He clicked on the cruise control. Reaching out, he scratched his fingers into Zak's neck. "Thanks."

The little fay nuzzled him before burying his face into Vicky's stomach. His fur curled around her fingers where she held him. When Vicky unzipped her "Saints" hoodie and opened it, Zak dropped the dog act and slipped inside, wrapping his appendages around her.

"I guess we dodged a bullet back there with those loa things." Vicky zipped her hoodie back up with Zak cuddled inside. His warmth and the soft rumbles from his purring were very soothing. "Are we safe now?" The slightly manic laugh Darien let out surprised Vicky.

"Oh, we definitely dodged a bullet back there. Mostly thanks to this one." Darien patted the lumpy shape under Vicky's sweatshirt.

Zak pushed back playfully.

"But, are we safe?" Darien gripped the wheel hard and stared down the road for a moment before answering. "No one is truly safe from the loa. They go where they wish, when they wish. There is very little magic that can protect you from the Baron if he wants you as a host. I wasn't expecting such a small offering to draw that much attention."

Vicky sat quietly as she processes this information. "A host?" She didn't like the sound of that. "Like possession?"

"Exactly." Darien nodded. "But, they call it 'being ridden'. See, the loa are spirits and can't manifest physical forms, so they chose a horse—a servant—to ride."

"Oh, that doesn't sound pleasant."

"It all depends on the loa who's riding." Darien shrugged a little. "I mean, once you get past the flailing and convulsions, the actual possession doesn't usually last very long."

Vicky's eyes widened in disbelief. *How could he be so calm about being possessed?*

"The real trouble comes in from the loa themselves. Some of them can be rather harsh on their horses."

Vicky could see remembered displeasure cross Darien's face.

"And then there are others that are rather loud or randy." The hint of a grin curled Darien's lip. "A good Vodou ritual can make for a very interesting night." He glanced over at Vicky for a moment.

She did not like the look in his eyes as he considered the possibilities.

"No." He turned back to watch the road. "I don't think so. Too many things already have an interest in you. I would rather the loa not be added to that list."

Zak gurgled his agreement from inside her shirt.

Turning her attention to the window, Vicky watched the town slip past as she thought. She had no idea why she warranted so much attention. The only thing unusual about her was her connection with Darien. She peeked over at the vampire-turned-human. There was a good possibility that they were only interested in her because of her connection with him.

From what she could gather from her friends among the vampires and wolves, Darien was different from most other vampires. Sure, his age and power made him stand out, but it was something more than that. He was well respected and accepted by every supernatural group. It had taken a while, but she finally understood that this was highly unusual. She had also learned that the peace in Brenton was mostly due to Darien's presence.

In most places, werewolves and vampires were bitter rivals, always thirsty for one another's blood. The presence of the fay seemed to be a mystery to everyone. Since the addition of Christian's people, Vicky had discovered that the fay were much more active around Darien. Even the oldest of Christian's humans had only heard of the fay in passing. None of them had ever seen one before Darien's Halloween ball.

Her mind turned to the sensitive spot on her back where she still bore a faint outline of wings. She and Darien had worked hard to remove the delicate appendages the lesser fay had graced her with, but they had only succeeded in getting them to fade into her back. Vicky had asked if they should go ask the Lady Aine for help, but Darien didn't want to take her back to see the Fairy Queen until they had exhausted all other possibilities. With Darien's new responsibilities, there had been little time to worry about that problem.

"Darien." She turned from the window to look at him. "How long do you think you have been losing your powers?"

Darien looked at her, surprised. "I'm not sure." He focused his attention back to the road. "It couldn't have been long. I would have noticed."

Vicky smiled. "I have a strange feeling this all started sometime before Halloween."

Darien's head snapped over to meet her eyes again. Concern

filled his face.

Vicky pointed at the road with her chin reminding Darien to watch where they were going. "It would explain some of the things that happened then, Mr. Vampires-don't-get-drunk."

One corner of Darien's mouth turned up in amusement at the dig. "That and the episode at work." He recalled his bout of low blood sugar.

"How about falling asleep at the Council?"

Darien actually laughed at that one. "And here we thought that was your influence."

"Me!" Vicky gasped. "How did I make you fall asleep?"

"Well," his grin turned mischievous, "if you weren't keeping me up all night…"

Vicky huffed and crossed her arms over her chest.

Darien laughed softly. "Seriously, Clara was sure it was because I was sleeping with you." The look Vicky shot him held daggers. "That's not what I meant." He reached over and pulled her arm over so he could catch her hand. Lacing their fingers together, he raised it up to kiss the back of her hand. "We've only spent a few nights apart since the thing with the ifrit."

Vicky shuddered at the memories of blood and dark demons. She still had nightmares about nearly being killed.

Darien rubbed her knuckles as Zak squeezed her reassuringly.

She pushed the memories away and turned her mind back to the subject at hand. "So, if you were having issues clear back there, that might explain why we haven't been able to break the fay's spell," Vicky pointed out.

Darien nodded his head thoughtfully.

"That might also explain the power fluctuations Jakob mentioned."

Darien shot her another confused look. "What power fluctuations?" His voice held a note of concern. Even though Darien hadn't made them, he truly cared about the people he had taken in.

"Well," Vicky started slowly, not sure how to pass on what

she had learned from Jakob, "when I ran into Jakob in the club, we talked about the differences between our marks. I think he was a little jealous that my connection was much stronger than his."

"I remember him testing it," Darien said, a little displeased with the memory.

She blushed in embarrassment. It felt odd to talk about this. It seemed so intimate. "He also mentioned that the kiss was worried at first. They didn't think you were strong enough to support them all."

Darien let out a snort of disbelief. "That's absurd. There are only seven of them." He shook his head in disgust. "It's insulting that they would even question my strength. At one point, I held nearly two dozen in my keeping. And I wasn't even five hundred at the time."

Vicky was surprised by this. It didn't seem like something the man she knew would do. "You made nearly twenty-four fledglings at one time?" she asked skeptically.

"Of course not." Darien sounded indignant. "I would never do something so reckless. The more fledgling you have in one place, the more likely someone is to notice." His voice softened, and he rubbed Vicky's hand where he still held it. "I saved them when their sire was killed."

Vicky grinned at him. "Sounds like you do that a lot." She thought of Elliot and the fact that Darien had saved him that way.

Darien chuckled at her. "I've adopted more than my fair share." The smile slipped from his face. "Most aren't around anymore."

"I'm sorry." Vicky squeezed her reassurance into his hand.

Darien squeezed back, letting her know he appreciated the support. "The world is not a safe place for those who don't respect it." He let out a soft sigh. "You would think that as one grew older, one would gain wisdom and respect for life." Shaking his head, Darien took another deep breath. "It amazes me to see how many vampires get themselves killed by getting cocky and careless." He rubbed Vicky's knuckles absentmindedly as he thought about those he had seen pass. After a moment, he shook the memories away. "So, what did Jakob say about his mark?"

"Oh, yes." Vicky shook herself and returned her mind to the conversation they were having. "Well, umm… He compared the bond he has now to the one he held with Lillian. Apparently, she held them very close to her."

"Lillian always loved a strong bond with her people." Darien nodded his head. "I didn't feel right holding them the way she did."

"Why not?" Vicky asked, puzzled. Wouldn't he want to keep them close to make sure they were okay?

Darien gave her a quick glance before answering. He continued to caress her knuckles as they talked. "The stronger the bond is, the deeper the connection," he explained. "We have a strong bond. Your presence and feelings are always at the edge of my mind." Darien stretched for his connection with Vicky, but couldn't reach it. He could just barely feel it there, but it was like grasping at illusions. "Or, we had."

Vicky could hear the worry in his voice. Reaching for their bond, she felt it secure in her mind. She could feel Darien's frustration hinted with an edge of rage. Studying his profile, she didn't understand the anger she felt in him. It didn't show anywhere on his face. She pushed love and warmth at him.

"I can feel that." He smiled and squeezed her hand. "The bond is there; I just can't reach it," he explained.

Vicky patted their joined hands with her free hand. "We will figure it out."

Darien nodded his head and went back to the topic they had been discussing. "While I like Lillian's people, I'm not sure I want that level of intimacy with them," he continued. "The connection I have with them now will allow me to feel if something's wrong, but they won't be slipping into my thoughts constantly like you do."

"I'm sorry." Vicky stiffened at his words. Even though it had taken her some time to get used to his presence in her mind, she hadn't realized how much of a distraction she would be for him.

"Don't be." He lifted her hand up to kiss its back again. "I enjoy our closeness."

Zak gurgled his agreement from within her sweatshirt.

Vicky rubbed the little fay lovingly and relaxed again.

Darien dropped their hands to rest on her leg. "But, you said something about power fluctuations."

"Oh, right!" Vicky paused as she recalled exactly what Jakob had said. "Apparently, when you first marked the Kiss, there were days when they had trouble keeping their link with you. Jakob also said he knew when you marked me because the power stabilized into something quite amazing."

Darien sat for a moment quietly processing this information. "I didn't know," he said softly. His thumb worried her knuckles as he turned this over in his mind. It wasn't surprising that the vampires had felt him mark Vicky. He was just a node in the center of a wide web. Every mark he made bound another mind to that web, and each person was connected to the rest through him. Vicky's addition shouldn't have made more than a tiny ripple along the strands connected to the rest, even if her mark brought Zak into his power base. It definitely gave him something else to ask about when they reached their destination.

9

The ride south from I-10 had taken nearly an hour as Darien weaved them deeper into the wetlands of Louisiana. Finally reaching their destination, he shut the car off at the end of a gravel drive and relaxed for a moment.

Vicky looked over the house tucked into the cypress trees. It was mildly surprising there was even a building there, considering they were in the middle of a swamp.

The house itself was nothing much to speak of. It was a very simple design with yellow clapboard siding done up in white trim. Overall, the place looked well cared for. The remarkable thing about the home was the three-foot stilts it sat on. A line of wide steps came down from the ample front porch. Vicky could see the glitter of sunlight reflecting off the water not far from the back of the house. Strands of Spanish moss clung to the trees, giving the area a very mystical feel. This was exactly what she had imagined the bayou to look like.

Darien stepped out of the car and stretched out his fatigue. Since he'd always made this trip at night, it had taken him longer to find in the light of day.

Vicky opened up her door and let Zak hop out. The creak of a screen door drew their attention as a woman stepped out. She was slightly older than Vicky, with warm brown skin. Her dark hair was short with golden highlights woven through it. Vicky's eyes caught on the woman's bright pink T-shirt, which read 'Kiss Me, I'm Creole'. The woman took up a loose defensive stance on the porch at the top of the steps.

Darien laughed wryly as he looked up at her. "I didn't expect this." He came around the car as Vicky shut her door. "This should only take a few minutes. Please, wait here."

Vicky could see the seriousness in Darien's eyes. She raised an eyebrow at him but leaned her backside against the car and crossed her arms, willing to wait.

Darien nodded his appreciation and turned to face the woman. With squared shoulders, he strode forwards with determination.

"How *dare* you come by day, demon of the night?"

The woman's words forced Vicky to stand up straight. Her Cajun accent was thick, but she was well spoken. Vicky hadn't expected such a welcome.

Darien paused for a moment a few feet from the bottom of the steps. "I have come for what is mine." His voice was strong and sure, but it didn't carry the power it usually did.

The woman's eyebrow rose at the lack. "Take it if you can, foul one." The woman raised her well-manicured hands. Several long strands of beads hung loosely in her right hand. She grabbed up the loose end in her left hand and stretched them out in front of her to the sounds of a word Vicky recognized vaguely as French. The air crackled with the power of the spell the woman invoked.

Darien laughed at her and took a few measured steps forward.

Vicky could feel him fight his way through the spell the woman cast. The stray magic hit Vicky hard, and her head swam. She leaned back against the car, trying to let the power wash over her. A slight pressure on her ankle drew her attention, and Vicky's head cleared. Looking down, she found that Zak had pressed himself to her leg. His eyes watched the woman challenging Darien, but he did not move to help the vampire-turned-mortal.

Slowly, Darien moved to the bottom of the steps. His eyes never left the woman chanting softly on the porch. She did not move as Darien pressed his way up the stairs. With each step he took, she snapped the beads.

Vicky could feel waves of energy pulsating from the woman as she fought with Darien.

When he reached the landing at the top, the woman stepped back, giving him space. She snapped the bead strands one more time before Darien reached out and pulled them from her hand.

A look of defeat crossed the woman's face as she hung her head. "I have failed." She tilted her head to the side, exposing her pulse to him. "Take what is yours."

To Vicky's stunned amazement, Darien pulled the woman into his arms and placed the barest of kisses on the side of her neck.

Surprise flashed across the woman's face as he released her and stepped back with her beads in his hand. "No blood?" she asked as if she expected him to feed from her.

Darien chuckled at her. "Not today." He looked over the stands of rose quartz beads before giving them back to her.

The woman looked over the beads, confused. "I was sure these were going to work today, L'aimè." She looked up at him. "They should have done something. I soaked them in holy water right before you got here."

Darien laughed out loud. "Under normal circumstances, that might have worked." He leaned in a little closer to her. "But, I know of your little trick now, chère." A mischievous grin spread across his face before he turned and headed back down the steps. "It's alright now," he called to Vicky. The sound of the screen door squeaking drew his attention, and he turned just as a small child flung herself from the porch at him.

"Uncle L'aimè!" the girl squealed as Darien caught her and spun around so her momentum wouldn't topple them.

"Marie!" the woman on the porch scolded. "How many times

have I told you *not* to do that?"

Darien laughed as he repositioned the small child in his arms. She couldn't have been more than five or six.

Vicky was even more shocked when the little girl completely ignored her mother and tilted her head over, giving Darien access to her throat.

He placed a light kiss over her pulse point. "You must listen to your mother," Darien reprimanded her lightly.

The little girl nodded seriously. "I promise, Uncle L'aimè." She looked at him and then up at the sky. "What 'chu doing in da sun?"

Darien chuckled again. "That's a long story." He carried the little girl back up the steps to the shade of the porch.

Vicky's stunned feet had moved her to the bottom of the steps.

"Delia, I would like you to meet Victoria Westernly, my fiancée."

This time shocked surprise crossed Delia's face.

"Victoria, this is Delia Toutant."

"It's an honor, My Lady." The woman dropped a curtsy to Vicky. It looked odd from a woman in a hot pink shirt and jeans.

"Please, it's Vicky." Vicky had no idea how to respond to this woman. The warm welcome didn't fit with Delia's previous attempts to banish Darien. It made Vicky's mind reel.

Seeing her confusion, Darien explained, "Delia and her family are in my service."

Delia grinned widely. "Until one of us can break your control."

The warmth and humor in the woman's voice still confused Vicky.

Darien laughed again. "If you want out of our contract, all you have to do is ask."

The arms the little girl had wrapped around Darien's neck tightened as she waited for her mother's response. It was obvious that she like him.

"Of course not." Delia smiled at her daughter. "Marie would

never forgive me if I sent you away, L'aimè."

The little beads on the end of the child's many braids clicked as she nodded her head vigorously.

"So how did you know we were coming?" Darien looked down at the crystal strands.

"That's a question for Marie."

Darien turned his attention to the little girl in his arms. "Marie?"

She grinned, showing off two rows of very white teeth. "Papa told me."

"Papa?" Darien looked over at Delia. "Loa?"

Delia nodded.

The little girl pulled something from the pocket of her light jacket and held it out. It took her a moment to work it over Darien's head. "Papa said 'chu need dis."

Darien looked down at the thing. It was a red piece of cloth tied up with a length of yarn. "Thank you." Recognizing it for the good gris-gris it was, he touched the pouch to feel what was inside. Several small objects clicked together, but the one that surprised him the most was long and hard. He looked up to the little girl's mother.

She shrugged unknowingly.

"It's very well made," Darien complimented her.

The little girl wiggled in his arms, trying to get down. As soon as Darien sat set her on the porch, she went to the top of the steps and looked down at Vicky. She held out another handmade pouch.

Vicky looked from the expectant little girl to Darien and back. Slowly, she climbed up the steps and lowered her head.

"Papa said Uncle heard 'chu knock'n." Marie spoke as she put the second gris-gris over Vicky's head. "He tinks 'chu need dis."

Surprise stole across Vicky's face, and she looked up at Darien again.

"Uncle?" he asked Delia.

"Baron," she explained.

Vicky looked at the small child and stood up. "Thank you." She placed her hand over the bag where it rested in the center of her chest. It didn't tingle with magic, but there was definitely a weight to it that its small size couldn't account for.

Maria nodded solemnly and turned to her mother. "Can I's play wif da puppy?"

All eyes turned towards Zak, sitting quietly by the foot of the steps. Delia looked over to Darien for permission.

The vampire looked down at the fay.

Zak tensed in anticipation and gurgled.

"Sure," Darien answered.

Zak barked his agreement and bounced up the steps to the little girl. He licked at her hands until she giggled, and the two scampered down the steps to the yard.

"You be nice to him," Delia yelled after her daughter.

Darien snickered. "I doubt she could do him any harm," he reassured the worried mother. "And she'll be safe in Zak's care."

Delia watched for a moment before the two playmates disappeared around the side of the house. "Well, come on in," she said as she opened the door for her guests. "Mama's waiting for you."

Darien held out his hand for Vicky to come to him.

She fingered the little pouch as she moved to his side, still a little lost. "What just happened?" Vicky asked.

Delia laughed as Darien leaned over to kiss the hair at her temple.

"I'll explain inside." He ran his hand down her back and propelled her through the door.

The inside of the house was cozy and clean. It held all the comforts a good, country home should, including afghans on the back of a soft couch and handmade rugs breaking up the wooden floor. An older Creole woman stood just inside the doorway on the other side of the room. The tiny woman was almost lost inside the shapeless housedress she wore. Some type of brightly colored cloth was wrapped tightly around her graying hair. She studied Vicky and Darien as they came into the room.

"Hi, Mama." Darien went to give the lady a hug.

Glancing over him, she pulled him down to her. "What have you done to yourself, L'aimè?" she asked.

Vicky had to listen hard to hear the English words through the woman's thick, Cajun accent.

Darien nearly picked her up as he embraced her. "That's what we're here to find out, ma chèrie." He made sure the woman was on her feet properly before he let her go.

"Delia. Bring tea for everyone, tout de suite," the woman ordered.

Delia raised an eyebrow and looked at Darien.

"Everyone," Mama confirmed before making her way to a large armchair.

Delia shrugged in resignation and went to get refreshments.

Mama turned her attention to her guests. "Come sit." She waved at the couch.

Darien went to Vicky and guided her around to sit on the couch with him.

"So," the old woman looked pointedly at Darien. "Spin your tale, L'aimè, and we shall see what can be done."

Darien smiled at her. "Impatient as always," he reprimanded her lightly.

"Ahh, but you came to me this time," she said, smiling at him wickedly, "and with such a lovely cherè." Her smile warmed towards Vicky.

"Victoria, I would like you to meet Marie Benoit." Darien held out his hand to make the needed introductions. "Marie, this is my fiancée, Victoria Westernly."

The old woman looked at him in surprise and lowered her head in greeting to Vicky. "Welcome to my home, amie. Call me Mama." The woman grinned at her. "And congratulations. L'aimè is a hard one to catch." Her eyes shifted over to Darien, and her smile held a touch of unrequited love. "Lord knows we have all tried."

Darien chuckled at her. "And I would have driven you all crazy." He took up Vicky's hand reassuringly and turned to talk to her. "I've known their family since shortly after I came to New Orleans. I ran across the most extraordinary young woman one day while getting my hair styled." Mischief shone in his eyes as he explained things to Vicky. "She had a power I had never encountered before, so I followed her. Of course, she recognized me for what I was right away, so she was wary at first. But, eventually we came to an agreement. She would teach me about Vodou, and I would teach her how to tap into the natural energies of the earth."

"And that is how Marie Laveau became the Voodoo Queen of New Orleans," Mama added with a knowing smile.

Vicky eyes widened. She looked at the woman, then back to Darien.

They both grinned widely.

"So, you're related to Marie Laveau?" Vicky asked, confirming her thoughts.

"On my mother's side." The woman nodded. "We have served Master L'aimè since her pact with him all those years ago."

"And in return, I teach each new generation the secrets of Vodou and magic." Darien turned his attention back to Mama. "Speaking of new generations, should I start making time for Marie?"

"The child does have a strong connection with the loa, but she is still young." Mama turned to look at the window. She could just see her granddaughter romping on the grass with Zak. "Let her be a child for a while longer. There will be plenty of time for magic later." Smiling, she turned her attention back to Darien. "That is, if we can manage to straighten you out. You still haven't told me what you have done."

Darien sighed, trying to think of where to start. "It's a long story."

"Well then, we best get started. But first," Mama turned her attention to the doorway into the house, "Delia, where is you?"

"Coming, Mama." The answering call wafted in from the other room. In a few moments, the missing woman came in with a tray full of glasses and a pitcher of iced tea. "Sorry," she apologized, setting the tray down and passing out the cups. "I had to pick up the mess Marie made putting together your gris-gris. That child dumped the trashcan over to get at last night's chicken bones." Picking up her cup, she took a seat in the other armchair.

"Chicken bones?" Vicky asked as she reached up and grabbed the charm around her neck. It was warm and almost comforting to the touch.

"Gris-gris can be made for all types of things," Darien explained. He looked back at Delia and touched the bag on his chest. "Do you know what these are for?"

Delia shook her head. "I caught Maria this morning digging through my scraps bag for the cloth. She just said that Uncle L'aimè was coming, and that Papa told her you needed gris-gris. When I asked her what for, she said it was to keep the boogie man away."

Darien raised an eyebrow at her. "The boogie man?"

"She's five." Delia shook her head. "Sometimes I wonder if she even knows what she is saying. The other day, she told me Lucifer was chasing her around the playground at school."

"I'm sure Morningstar has much better things to do than harass children at school." Darien smiled.

"Don't be so sure about that," Mama warned. "The Devil always be looking for a way in." Both women crossed themselves.

Vicky shot a questioning look at Darien. She was not sure what to say about this whole conversation. Were they really talking about the Devil as if he were a real person? And if that was the case, was God real, too?

"So tell us, L'aimè, why have you come, and what have you done?" Mama pointed their conversation back to where it needed to go.

Darien picked up his glass of sweet tea and took a sip to

wet his mouth. He was a little embarrassed to come to them seeking help like this. "I haven't done anything." Carefully, he set his glass back to the coaster and fidgeted with it a little. "I woke up the other day unable to take blood. I spent the day sick in bed."

"The stomach flu," Vicky elaborated.

Darien nodded. "When I was well again, I could not reach my powers, sunlight no longer hurt, and my body..." Darien actually bushed a little as he thought of the changes that had occurred to him. "Well, my body has started doing things, on its own that it hasn't done in a very long time." The two women looked on in shock as Darien laid out his issues.

"And this started a few days ago?" Mama asked.

"Yes," Darien confirmed.

"Well..." Vicky interjected, and the women turned to look at her. "Everything Darien said started a few days ago, but I think it started earlier than that."

Darien let out a heavy breath; he hadn't wanted to admit that this issue could have started much earlier without his noticing.

"When?" Mama asked.

Darien shut his eyes, blocking out the room. He knew the information could be important, but he didn't wanting to admit his faults or the fact that he had nearly killed Vicky in his stupidity.

Seeing that he wasn't going to tell them, Vicky answered for him. "Sometime before Halloween." She told them of his confusion at work, his slow healing after the accident, and his inebriation at the party.

Darien braced himself for condemnation of his fouled-up mark, but she skipped over it. She did tell them of his increased appetite over the last few weeks.

Mama and Delia listened closely as the details piled up.

"And you didn't see any of this as possible problems?" Delia asked in wonderment.

"Of course I did." Darien tried not to snap. Having Vicky lay everything out made it very clear that there had been something wrong for months. "The last few months have been very... busy."

Vicky nodded her agreement.

"Besides, I called on a fay friend of mine for help, but he could find nothing wrong before a few nights ago."

"The fay are creatures of magic and can overlook the simplest things because it seems right to them." Mama pushed herself up from her chair. "Come here and let me look at you."

Darien stood up in front of the old woman.

Laying her fingers on Darien's chest like Lord Dakine always did, Mama closed her eyes, searching him. "L'aimè, I am not sure what has happened, but something has hooked out your essence. Bare traces of it still cling to you, but those, too, will soon be gone." She looked at Darien, worried. "If you lose those, you may not be able to regain what you have already lost."

Real fear crossed Darien's face for a moment before he pushed it back. "Is there some way to stop it?" he asked.

Vicky could feel the anxiety bubbling inside of him. She reached up and took his hand, offering what little comfort she could.

Mama gasped and snapped her head to look at Vicky. She looked back at Darien, then to Vicky again. "Let him go," the old woman commanded sharply.

Startled, Vicky dropped his hand.

Mama looked at Darien again before pushing him out of the way.

He moved, but watched carefully as Mama went to Vicky.

"Stand, child."

Vicky looked up for Darien's approval before rising from the couch.

Mama placed her hand on Vicky's chest. "This can't be," she gasped, looking up at Vicky's blue eyes. "Are you human?"

"Yes," Vicky answered, unsure where this was going.

"We've had a few run-ins with the fay," Darien admitted.

A smile slowly crept across Mama's face before she broke out in laughter. "This is rich!" she chuckled as she went back to her chair.

Slightly stunned, Vicky reclaimed her seat on the couch.

"What?" Darien settled next to her.

Mama worked to calm her mirth but couldn't get the smile off her face. "She has your powers."

Darien looked at Vicky in shock.

Vicky was stunned by this announcement.

"But, how?" Darien touched Vicky, probing her with what little power he could still call. "She's not a vampire."

Mama chuckled again. "No, but she can call on them." Picking up a letter opener from the table next to her chair, Mama threw it at Darien. The knife-like object sunk into his leg before he could even register the attack.

"Darien!" Vicky gasped as he clutched at the fresh wound, hissing in pain. Without thinking about it, Vicky grabbed up some napkins from the iced-tea tray and yanked out the opener. She pressed the tissue to the gushing wound. "What the hell is wrong with you?" she cursed as she applied pressure, trying to get the cut to stop bleeding. The blade had gone deep, and the blood quickly soaked through the paper.

Amusement lit Mama's face as she watched them.

Vicky scowled at her and grasped for another handful of tissues.

The front door banged open, and Zak came bubbling through, spoiling for a fight. He had dropped his dog act and waved tentacles menacingly at the old woman as he came to check on Darien.

The little girl came in right behind him.

"It's all right," Darien soothed the little fay.

Pulling the blood-soaked tissue away, Vicky went to press the new wad to the wound. What she found showing through the hole in his jeans stopped her. She looked at up at Darien before slipping her finger into the slit. The skin below was smooth and unbroken. The wound had completely healed, leaving no signs of a mark.

Amusement crossed Darien's face as he released his hand from around his leg.

Zak ran his feelers over Darien, checking him for any other injuries before turning and growling at Mama.

"I didn't know you had a guardian." Mama looked over the upset hellhound.

Darien leaned forwards and pulled the grumpy fay into his lap. He patted Zak softly, settling him. "He claimed Vicky." Darien shifted the mess of tentacles over to Vicky's lap.

Zak gurgled at him and buried his face into Vicky's middle. One lone tentacle reached out and wrapped itself around the belt loop of Darien's jeans.

Mama studied the trio on the couch. "I see." She turned her attention to the wide eyes of the little girl watching them. "Come here, Marie."

"Yes, Gama." The child came over and crawled up in her grandmother's lap. Her eyes never left the fay she had been playing with.

"Are you afraid?" Mama kissed her granddaughter on the top of the head.

The little girl shook her head and stared at Zak in amazement.

Zak wiggled around so he could look at his playmate.

"Can I keep 'em?" she asked softly.

Mama laughed lightly. "No, sweetheart." She kissed the child's hair again. "He has to stay with L'aimè. He may very well need a protector in the next few weeks."

Zak gurgled and wrapped a few more ends around Darien's arm.

Darien glanced down at the unexpected contact but stroked the grasping ends. "But, if you like, you can go back outside and play," he offered.

Delia looked ready to object, but Maria hopped back up from her grandmother's lap excitedly.

"Really?" She looked over at her mother.

Delia let out a long sigh and nodded her head.

Zak gurgled excitedly and wobbled out of Vicky's lap. He led the way to the door and opened it to let the child out.

Delia watched as her daughter disappeared with the small fay. "Will she be okay?"

Vicky watched the pair leave. "Zak wouldn't let anything happen to her." An agreeing gurgle brush her mind pulling a smile to her lips. Turning her attention back to the old woman that had stabbed Darien, she opened her mouth to tell the woman off, but Darien's hand fell to her leg, stopping the reprimand.

"You've made your point." Darien glared at her. "I would suggest you not do it again."

Mama's grin widened. "Of course, L'aimè." She leaned forward in her chair. "But, it was a good demonstration."

Darien snickered at her.

She leaned back in her chair again. "And I seem to recall a few similar demonstrations, only in reverse."

"True." Darien nodded his head. "So, Victoria has my powers?" He turned the subject back to the topic at hand.

"Not exactly." Mama shook her head. "They do not reside inside of her, but the mark that binds you allows her access to them. Why she can wield them, I cannot say."

Darien caught Vicky's eye before looking back to Mama. "Vicky has a piece of my soul," he admitted.

Mama's face lit with surprise.

"It's a long story," he said, cutting her off before she could ask.

"That could explain why she can use them, but that doesn't explain why they are missing, or where they have gone," Mama pointed out.

Darien nodded. "Is there a way to find out?" he posed the question that had been plaguing his mind.

"Perhaps." The old woman leaned forwards and took the bloodied letter opener from where Vicky had dropped it on the table. She held it up to look at the wet redness glistening on the end. With her free hand, she reached down and popped open the door on the end table next to her. Rummaging around, she pulled out a small sack.

Vicky listened closely as the woman started a low chant. Delia picked up the words, adding to the repeating rhythm. After a few passes, Darien also picked up the chant, growing its power. Vicky listened carefully, not sure if she was supposed to add her voice to group.

Before Vicky could dissect the unfamiliar words, Mama's voice peaked, and she threw a pinch of dust from her pouch onto Darien's blood. Their chanting fell silent, and all held their breath, waiting for the spell to take effect.

Vicky drew in a startled breath when a line of gold dust shimmered out of the tip of the opener.

"There you are." Mama's voice held a note of deviant glee. The faint line of gold twisted its way through the air and brushed against Darien's lips.

He held very still as the gossamer thread continued on to touch the side of Vicky's head where Darien often kissed her hair.

She felt a warm weight wrap around her as the spell encircled her. The warmth pierced her chest right over her heart. It didn't hurt, but the spell pulled power from her mark. A line of gleaming gold shot out of her and followed the line of dust back to the knife-like tip. Once there, it ricocheted back in a northerly direction.

"That's why your fay couldn't find your spell. This magic wasn't set on you." Mama moved the blade around, bending the line back and forth examining it. "It looks like fay magic." She followed the gold strand to Darien's mouth. "Maybe something sealed with a kiss?"

Darien turned his mind back over the last few months. A lot had happened, but only twice had they dealt with the fay where they worked magic on Vicky. The most recent was the Halloween ball; but if what Vicky suspected were true, the magic had to have been done on that first encounter. His mind recalled an image of Vicky laid out in a white, spider-silk dress on a bed of flowers. He could still hear the lesser fay calling for him to wake her with a kiss. Darien let out a deep sigh and dropped his face to his hands.

"We have to go see the fay." Darien rubbed the spell from his face. The gold line disintegrated. He had wondered why the little ones had been so adamant about getting him to kiss Vicky. It also explains why he had not been able to find a way to break the enchantment on Vicky's dress. When he broke their sleeping spell without kissing her, they must have used the sweet gum balls to force her into his arms in hopes that Darien couldn't withstand the magic she'd been wrapped in.

Thinking back over the events of the weeks that followed, Darien tried to recall the first time he kissed her. It was to the side of her head when they were folded together on the Twister board. No wonder it had taken the magic so long to affect him. The potency of the spell must have been weakened by the banality of the real world and the location in which he had kissed her.

"Then you must do it soon," Mama warned him. "Your powers are very nearly gone as it is. There is no telling what will happen if you delay and they disappear entirely. You may never regain them, even if you break this enchantment."

Darien swallowed hard and nodded his understanding. "How long do you think I have?" he asked, trying to figure out how long it would take to get an invitation to see Lady Aine.

Mama took Darien's hand and felt him. She sighed at how little of his power was left. "A day." She dropped her hand away from him. "Maybe less."

He could hear the worry in her voice. Darien drew in a cleansing breath and set his resolve. If he had so little time, there would not be time to send a request for an audience. He would just have to go to Fairy and speak with Lady Aine, hoping that his standing with her would be enough to get him back out. A vibration from his pocket drew him out of his thoughts before the music of his cell phone split the air. "Pardon me." He stood up and slipped the phone out of his pocket. No one would call him on this number unless it was important. "Hello?"

"Darien." Elliot's voice echoed down the line.

Darien shifted around the room to see if he could get better reception. "Elliot?" he asked. It was much too early in the day for Elliot to be up and about.

"Where are you?"

The line crackled with so much static that Darien could not hear his friend's response. "Elliot?" He covered his other ear, hoping to pick up the other man's words. "The reception here sucks. What's up?" Static hissed across the line.

"Rupert… wol… wn… Sue."

Elliot's words were fragmented, but Darien caught the need in them. Suddenly, he could feel Elliot's mind pressing on his, calling him home as fast as he could get there. Darien snapped the phone shut and turned to look at Vicky. He could see that she was getting the same feeling.

Mama sat waiting for him to explain.

"Thank you for everything." Darien came over to hug her. "Something has happened at home, and we need to leave. Now."

Mama stood, hearing the urgency in his voice. "Go." She pushed him towards the door. Turning, she ushered Vicky along at the same time.

Vicky got up and followed him.

"*Zak!*" Darien called out as soon as he hit the door. It took the hellhound a moment to scamper around the corner of the house with the little girl in tow. "Sue's in trouble." Darien nearly ran down the steps and yanked open the passenger's side door of the car.

Vicky followed, calculating the hours it would take to get back. If things were as bad as Elliot's panic led her to believe, they would be much too late to help.

Darien yanked out the messenger bag from the front seat and slammed the door before Vicky could get it. He tossed the keys to Delia. "Someone will be by later to get this."

Delia nodded.

Settling the bag over Vicky's head, Darien turned to Zak. "Take us home." He grabbed Vicky's hand and looked at Zak expectantly.

The little fay stared at him for a moment and wiggled his end reluctantly.

"I know you can feel Elliot through Vicky," Darien pleaded with the fay. "We need to get back *now*."

Zak writhed on the ground, still unwilling to open the way for them.

Darien looked at Vicky, then to Zak. "She bears your mark and my protection; nothing will harm her in-between."

Whining louder, the hellhound flailed around more.

"Darien?" Vicky pulled on his hand to get his attention. From the one-sided conversation, she figured that Zak could get them home faster, but had to do something that might endanger her. "Is this dangerous?"

"Only if you go unescorted and unprotected," Darien reassured her.

Turning this over for a moment, Vicky tried to figure out the problem Zak was having. "Zak's mark protects me," she confirmed.

Darien nodded. He was starting to get upset with the fay's delay. Every second could count in the world of the supernatural. He pleaded with the fay again, but only got a reluctant whine.

"What about you?"

"What?" Darien looked at Vicky, not understanding the question.

"What protects you?" she asked again.

"I'm a vampire, I don't need..." His voice trailed off as he realized the problem. Drawing in a deep breath, he let it out, trying to think of a solution. "It's a risk I'm going to have to take." Weaving their fingers together, he squeezed her hand. "Just don't let go." He prayed that with her touch and Zak as escort, they would get through unscathed.

Vicky turned her attention to Zak and knelt down. "Zak." She reached her free hand out to the fay and ruffled his feelers. "Can you get us there?" Zak whimpered at her, but she heard the positive note in his tone. "*Please*," she begged him. The urgency beating at her from Elliot drove her to take chances she normally would not.

Zak studied her for a moment. His tentacles stilled as he considered her request.

"For Sue."

Snorting his acceptance, the hellhound wobbled around on the ground unhappily.

"Thank you." Vicky rubbed him and stood back up.

Zak rolled over and nuzzled her leg where she bore his mark, testing the link to make sure it was solid.

She pushed back against him mentally, showing it was firm.

Zak wiggled between Darien and Vicky, touching both of them.

"Ouch!" Darien jerked his leg away from the fay, who had just sunk his teeth into the back of Darien's calf. "Damn it, Zak!" Releasing Vicky's hand, he limped away from the fay. "I know this doesn't make you happy, and you can eat my pants later if you want, but leave the flesh, little horror." He paused a few steps away and lifted up the leg of his jeans to look at the wound.

"Zak!" Vicky snapped as she dropped down by Darien's leg. She wiped away the blood with her sleeve to find two neat rows of teeth marks marring the skin. "Oh, Zak." She reached up and touched one of the cuts.

"Ow, ow, ow, ow." Pulling away from her probing finger, Darien limped around as he tried to ignore the pain ripping up the back of his calf. "I think the little monster is poisonous or something." He flexed his leg. "It burns."

Zak whined in response and rolled around.

"It's okay, Uncle L'aimè." Marie came over and tugged on Darien's sleeve. "Da puppy only wanted to help."

Darien clenched his teeth together hard, trying not to speak his mind in front of such an impressionable child. "Yes, help." Sitting down hard, he squeezed the knee of the leg Zak had bitten. "Can I get some water, please?" he asked before closing his eyes on the tears forming, rocking to try to block out the burning in his calf. It was the worst pain he had ever felt. "Why don't you just eat me and get it over with?" Darien growled at the fay behind him.

Zak gurgled and wiggled over to where Darien clutched at his leg. Sweat had broken out on the vampire's forehead as tremors ran through his body.

Vicky moved to his back and touched him gently, not sure how to soothe his pain. "Stop this, Zak," she reprimanded the hellhound.

Zak whined and touched Darien with several tips.

Delia approached him with a glass of water, but Darien's attention was on the burn spreading up his leg. He could feel his heart pushing the pain from his leg into his body. The heat marked exactly where his veins ran under his skin.

Vicky took the glass of cool water and held it to him. She could feel his temperature rising as she rubbed his back, trying to comfort him.

Snatching the glass of water, Darien drained half of it before pouring the rest over his head. The cold water did nothing to calm the fire running through him. He dropped the glass to the ground, forgetting it in his plight. The heat climbed to his chest, making it hard to breathe. Gasping, he tried to drag air into his aching lungs.

Vicky grabbed his hand as he started to tear at the collar of his shit. "*Zak!*" she begged the hellhound as she pulled Darien into her lap. His skin was flushed, and he moaned from the agony consuming him.

Tears streamed from Darien's eyes as he gripped onto Vicky for dear life. His breath came in short, ragged pants.

"*Please!*" she begged Zak again. Holding Darien, she tried her best to help him. She could feel the warm brush of feathers on the inside of her skin, only this time, the feathers flowed out of her and into Darien. Opening herself as wide as she could, she let the power work as it willed. At the back of her mind, she could feel someone's confusion. It came from the area she associated with Darien, but it wasn't him. His thoughts were filled only with the pain threatening to break him. Vicky leaned forwards and soothed his hair back from his face as the magic worked to heal him. Slowly, he relaxed as the pain eased.

Now that she had opened herself up fully, Vicky could feel the edge of Elliot's panic rubbing on her mind. When Darien's pain had begun, Elliot had stepped in and blocked the master's connection with the rest of the kiss. Vicky agreed that this was not something Darien needed to share with the people he was taking care of. She sent a wave of gratitude and reassurance to Elliot. A responding wash of relief and curiosity rolled back to her. Unable to express anything in words, she thought of patience, and Elliot backed off her mind.

Vicky looked down to where Darien was curled on his side with his face almost buried in her stomach. His breathing was better, and his color was returning to normal. "What did you do to him, Zak?" Vicky turned narrowed eyes to the fay.

Zak flattened himself out and whined. Only the tips of his tentacles wiggled where they touched Darien.

Vicky could feel his confusion and regret pushing at the edge of her mind. She touched that point and gasped at the overwhelming mix that was Zak's mind. His consciousness pulled back, leaving her with a very clear picture of what he had intended.

Marking Darien had been the only way Zak felt he could ensure the man's safety through the between place. The hellhound had chosen to do so through a bite because it was the fastest way to set a secure mark. The type of fay mark Vicky carried would have taken days to settle on Darien and would not have given the protection needed to move through the between places immediately. Zak also didn't think Darien would have agreed to the claiming.

"Well, you didn't give him a choice," Vicky huffed at the fay, rubbing Darien's back. The man was completely relaxed now. His consciousness had fled when the fire burning his insides had ceased.

Zak wiggled and whined at her again.

Letting out a deep breath, Vicky held her hand out to the fay. Now that she understood why he had bitten Darien, she really couldn't stay mad at the little horror. The mark was for the man's own good. "Next time, ask."

Zak wiggled over and rubbed up against her side. His tentacles tangled through Darien's hair, petting him.

"Is Uncle L'aimè dead?"

The little voice startled Vicky back to her surroundings. In her attempts to help Darien, she had totally forgotten about the people around her. Vicky smiled up at the child watching them. Shifting her gaze, she took in Delia and Mama waiting anxiously behind her. "No," Vicky reassured the child. "He'll be alright. He's just tired."

Marie nodded as the two older women let out relieved sighs.

"It's not da puppy's fault," the girl pointed out adamantly. "Hims was try'n to help."

Vicky smiled soothingly at the girl. "I know." And she did, because Zak had shown her.

Zak was truly confused by Darien's reaction. He had expected the magic of his mark to spread throughout the man's body, carried by his blood, but it shouldn't have hurt the way it had. The only time Zak had ever seen a reaction this bad was when another fay had tried to claim something of light that had fallen to earth. The creature had writhed in agony for days before dying a most horrendous death. Afterwards, Lady Aine had forbidden the marking of such things. Their magics didn't mix, and the consequences were much too high.

Vicky looked down at Darien asleep in her arms. His pain was gone and the bite mark was healed, but the magic had used most of his energy. He needed to rest, but Elliot's call still pressed on her mind. Darien's recovery would have to wait—they needed to leave soon. Rubbing the wet hair back from his face, Vicky leaned over to kiss his cheek. "Darien," she breathed his name.

His brow furrowed as he rubbed his face harder into her middle.

Vicky patted him on the back. "You have to get up now."

He groaned in response.

"Come on." She shifted him into a less comfortable position on her lap.

Darien groaned again but opened his eyes. Rolling to his back, exhausted by the experience, he studied the swath of blue shimmering between boards of green. It had been a long time since he had lain back and stared at a sky the same shade as Vicky's eyes. Taking a deep breath, he concentrated on his body. The pain was gone, but the memory of it lingered just under his skin. The feather light whisper of power rubbed against the inside of his skin. He knew this feeling, had used it to heal many times, but this was the first time he had no control over it. It was... odd.

"Thank you," he breathed softly to Vicky. "You can stop now." Reaching over, he touched her on the leg.

She cocked her head in confusion before realizing his meaning.

Darien felt her pull the power back and close up. The sensation left him slightly empty, but it made room for something else he had not felt. Worry pressed against the edge of his awareness. He touched it and let out a manic laugh when he felt Zak's mind.

"All that for a mark." Darien pushed up from the ground and rolled to look at the hellhound. Holding the fay's unwavering gaze, he let out a deep sigh. How could he reprimand the fay for doing what needed to be done? He would have done the same thing if their roles had been reversed, but that didn't mean that he was going to be happy about it. Darien sat up and pulled his pant leg up to look at the form Zak's mark took. "At least it's not flowers." He shifted to show his new mark to Vicky.

Vicky studied the back of Darien's calf. She had expected to see two rows of teeth marks but was surprised to find what looked to be a tattoo filling the space between the lines. A mass of black and green was swirled over his skin. A few flecks of silver floated along the twisting lines. It was very abstract but amazingly beautiful. Vicky blinked a few times and reached out to touch the image. It was solid and still, but it felt as if it were swirling too slowly for her eyes to catch. "Amazing," Vicky breathed.

Darien snorted and pulled his damaged jeans back down. He looked up to the ladies watching him. "Just remember, the help of the fay always comes with a price." He caught Zak's shining eyes. "Sometimes that price is more then we bargained for."

Zak wobbled over and rubbed up against Darien.

Darien stood up. "I'm fine now," he reassured everyone. Exhaustion clung heavy on him and he would rather have laid back down for more rest; but something was wrong at home and he needed to get back as soon as possible. "Let's get this over with." Darien held his hand down to help Vicky up. He made sure she had the messenger bag before turning to Delia and Mama. "I will see you again soon."

"Travel safely." Mama waved to them.

"Bye, Uncle L'aimè." Marie waved to them from where she stood by her mother.

Darien bid her farewell and turned to where Zak was now waiting for them. "Let's go." He took Vicky's hand and laced their fingers together. "Whatever happens, don't let go." Patting her hand, he turned to Zak.

The fay looked over them for a moment before reaching out and grabbing each by an ankle. Grabbing at reality, he split the air in front of them.

Vicky didn't have time for her mind to respond to the impossibility of this before Darien and Zak took off at a run pulling her along. Memories of danger and pain burst forth as the darkness of the between places closed around her. Terror bubbled up, paralyzing her as her mind shut down. Darien caught her as she stumbled, unable to move.

"Victoria." He pulled her against him.

She clung to him, terrified. The feel of Zak urging them on pressed at her, but she just couldn't get past the fear of the darkness. Even though the ifrit had healed the damage to her mind, the near-death experience still showed from time to time.

"I've got you." Darien pressed her face into his shoulder and swept her legs from under her. He settled her in his arms and took off after Zak as quickly as he could.

Vicky could feel how his pace has slowed, but she could not face the blackness clutching at them. Even now, with her eyes shut, clinging to Darien, the dark was cold against her skin. "I'm sorry," she sobbed into Darien's shoulder.

He shushed her as he ran. "It's okay." Carefully, he squeezed her, offering what comfort he could. "We all have our moments."

A reassuring gurgle sounded from Zak somewhere below and in front of them.

This brought a smile to her face and a tear to her eye. Even when time is of the essence, her boys cared enough to comfort her. Vicky rubbed the tear that slipped from her closed eyes on Darien's shirt and kissed him where her head rested. "Put me down." She shifted in his arms as he ran. His breath had started coming in more labored pants as he fought against his fatigue. His pace slowed as she wiggled to get loose.

"Are you sure?" he asked as he released her legs, swinging her down.

"Yes." Vicky found her feet without opening her eyes. If she didn't think about the darkness, she could do this. "Just don't let me go." She gripped at Darien's hand for dear life.

"Never." He spared a moment to kiss the side of her head before following the pull of Zak's tentacles.

With her feet on the ground, Vicky matched Darien's pace as they pounded through the unfathomable distance.

10

VICKY'S CHEST AND SIDES WERE BURNING BY THE TIME ZAK TORE ANOTHER HOLE in reality and they spilled out onto the streets of Brenton.

Darien placed his hand against the wall of the alley and huffed, trying to catch his breath. Turning around, he leaned on the wall, about ready to pass out.

"Keep moving," Vicky warned and dragged him up from where he was sliding down the bricks. "If you stop now, you will cramp up." She pulled him to her side and forced him to walk slowly into the gathering twilight.

Darien nodded his head and followed her lead, huffing.

Zak whined as he slipped into his Shih Tzu form and circled them.

"I forgot what it's like to have to worry about things like muscle fatigue." Darien stretched his legs as they moved. "Whee!" he said giddily as the endorphins running through his system hit him hard, making him stagger.

Giggling, Vicky clutched at him to keep him from falling over. "Welcome to oxygen deprivation and a runner's high." She led him down the alley to the cross street. It took her a moment to recognize where they were and turn in the direction of home.

Darien tilted his head back and stared up at the sky, enjoying the head rush. "This is fantastic."

"Give it a minute." Vicky laughed. "You'll change your mind."

It was only a few minutes before she could feel Darien come down from his high.

He leaned on her heavily as his legs turned to jelly. "And people do this willingly?" Darien moaned as fatigue hit him.

"People train extensively for what we just did," Vicky explained. She didn't know how far they had gone, but it had to have been quite a ways without a pause.

Darien eyed her suspiciously. "How come you're not feeling that run?" Vicky had already recovered mostly.

"Because I run several times a week," she pointed out, "while you sit around and don't exercise."

Darien scoffed at her. "I've never needed to work out," he huffed. As a vampire, he didn't require the same type of body conditioning humans did.

"Well, maybe you should think about it until we get this thing straightened out." Vicky sighed. "Speaking of straightening out." She opened herself to Darien's power and let it pour into her again. Pushing the healing force into Darien, she cleared the lactic acid from his system and soothed the stressed muscles.

"That is so weird." Darien held his hand out in front of him as if he could see the energy coursing through him. His stance and walk had both become stronger. "But you better stop before you overtax your system."

Vicky nodded and let the power go. As it receded, she could feel a touch of confusion coming from the point where she pulled. Reaching out, she recoiled as soon as her mind touched it. She had expected to feel Darien, but the mind she touched was hard and cold, filled with bitter rage and confusion. Vicky shuddered, trying to remove the lingering chill from the contact. "Someone else has your powers." She leaned into Darien for comfort.

He looked down at her, shocked. "What?" Slipping his arm around her, Darien pulled her tighter to his side.

"I can feel them... no, him. It's definitely a 'him'." Vicky swallowed as she reached for that point again, not quite making contact. "There's a presence where you normally are, but it's not you." Looking up into Darien's eyes, she tried to make him understand. "It's cold and dark and filled with so much anger it hurts." She buried her face into him as they walked.

"Can you still feel me?" Darien pushed on their connection as hard as he could, sending her love and comfort.

A smile bent the corner of her distressed mouth. "Yes," Vicky sighed, relieved by his touch. "It's faint, but it's there."

He rubbed her shoulder, giving as much comfort as he could. "We'll go see the fay as soon as possible." Darien kissed the side of her head before turning the corner onto their street. "Let's deal with this, first." A large crowd filled the sidewalk in front of the Touraine building. Darien let his arm drop from Vicky's shoulder and stood up straighter. Even without his vampire powers backing him, he still held a commanding presence from years of walking in the human world.

Zak wiggled up between them, letting his aura of power mask what Darien was not putting out.

"Can I help you?" Darien let his voice boom out over the crowd.

Vicky recognized several of the Rupert's pack as they moved back to let them through. They stepped into the white stone lobby to find Rupert standing to one side and two wolves Vicky didn't know squaring off with Ethan. The poor concierge stood between them and the elevators, determined not to let the intruders pass.

"Is there a problem here?" Darien's voice rang through the crystals of the overhead chandelier. He could see relief flood Ethan's eyes. Rupert looked amused, while the remaining two wolves almost quivered with frustration.

"Mr. Ritter." Ethan nodded his head in greeting. "These men came in demanding to see you. I told them you were out, but they insisted that I let them up. They tried to slip past me when I went to call security about their gang outside."

"Thank you, Ethan." Darien looked at the four men, amused.

"I'll take it from here."

"Would you like me to call the cops for you?" Ethan started to move over to his counter and the phone he had dropped when he went to stop the men from passing.

"That won't be necessary," Darien reassured him. "I will take care of this."

"And who the hell are you?" the older of the two men growled at him.

Darien cocked an eyebrow at him while Zak growled from his place at the vampire's feet.

"Can't you tell? He's Master Darien Ritter."

Relief swept through Darien at the sound of Elliot's voice from the doorway.

A smirk stole across Rupert's face as the color drained from the other two wolves.

The older one snapped around to glare at Rupert. "You didn't tell me she was staying with him." He jabbed his thumb at Darien.

"I *did* tell you that she had taken the protection of a..." Rupert glanced over to the human watching them and changed what he was going to say. "...of someone important."

"Maybe we should take this upstairs," Darien offered. He could see Ethan's hand hovering over the phone, ready to call for help as soon as they were out of sight.

Elliot nodded. "That's a good idea." He turned his attention to Rupert. "Send your people home. There's no need for them to be caught up in this." Elliot tipped his head towards the concierge poised for action.

"Of course." Rupert went to the door to disperse his pack.

Darien looked over to where his friend had taken up a place by his side. Their eyes met for a moment, and he felt Elliot understand the gratitude he couldn't show. Darien turned his attention back to the waiting werewolves. "Gentlemen, if you will please come with me." He held his hand out towards the waiting elevators. "I'm sure we can discuss this in a civilized fashion." Reaching over, he touched Elliot's shoulder, drawing the man's attention to him. "Do you mind?" He nodded to the counter where Ethan was watching them.

"Not at all, My Lord." Elliot raised his fist to his chest and bowed before turning to alter the poor man's memories.

Darien hooked his arm around Vicky and led her past the waiting wolves.

She looked back to where Elliot held Ethan enthralled. "Will he be alright?" Vicky remembered how Elliot had changed Vanessa's memories.

"The things that man has seen and does not remember could fill books." Darien smiled at her. "But, Elliot will make sure he doesn't notice them."

Vicky glanced back. She worried for the man's mental health, but she knew they had to mess with his memories. He couldn't be allowed to inform the world of the things he had seen.

Darien punched the call button for the elevator. Rupert and Elliot rejoined them just as the door slid open. Darien waved his guests inside. "Shall we?"

Picking up Zak, Vicky stepped inside the door as Darien punched in the code that would take them to his penthouse.

Zak turned his dark, beady eyes to the two new wolves and stared at them hungrily. They shifted, uncomfortable in the little fay's gaze. The tension in the elevator was tangible by the time the doors opened to let them out.

"So, what may I do for you gentlemen?" Darien asked as he crossed his foyer. He causally leaned his elbow on the railing of the stairs, effectively trapping them in this first room. Vicky and Elliot took up places on either side of him, showing their support. The two wolves looked around the spacious entryway. Rupert eased his way to one side, abandoning the two wolves to Darien's questioning.

The older of the two wolves drew himself into a dignified stance and glared at Darien. "We have come for the rogue wolf," he announced.

Darien cocked an eyebrow at him, curious at his lack of manners. He studied the man for a moment before answering. The man was heavyset and squat, with gray touching the edges of his brown hair. His eyes were root-beer brown and held the light of authority in them.

"Well, Mr...." Darien cocked his head, waiting for the wolf to supply his name.

"Eckert," The older wolf offered, realizing his faux pas. "Corban Eckert. And this is Ross Umlad," he said, introducing himself and his companion.

"Under other circumstances I am sure it would be a pleasure to meet you, Mr. Eckert." Darien inclined his head in greeting but did not move to offer the man his hand. "But at the moment, we have business to settle. As for the 'rogue wolf', Miss Marshal is under my care at the moment." Darien offered them a smile that didn't reach his eyes.

Corban cleared his throat and cocked his head, uncomfortable with the situation. "Then, we have a problem," he said very politely. "She must answer for what she has done."

Darien's eyebrow raised again in curiosity. "And what, pray tell, had she done?" He shifted his eyes from the wolves to Rupert, standing silently away from them, and back.

"She tried to kill my lieutenant." Corban held out his head to his companion. The second man stood up to his full height.

Darien looked over him. The second wolf was taller than his commander was and darker in complexion. He held an edge of violence to him that Darien did not like. "He looks perfectly fine to me." Darien shot him another warm smile.

Ross glared at him. "She tried to rip my throat out," he growled, knowing the vampire was egging him on. An answering growl from the doorway drew all their attentions.

Sue stepped into the room and bared her fangs at the man.

"See?" He pointed towards the angry wolf. "Even now she threatens me."

Darien looked over Sue's raised hackles. "I'm sure she had

just cause," he said calmly.

Zak wiggled in Vicky's arms so she had to put him down. He scampered over to Sue and rubbed up against her legs reassuringly.

Ross bristled in anger.

"Then make her shift and defend herself," Corban demanded.

Darien moved to stand next to Sue to soothe her. "That would be troublesome at the moment." He pushed his fingers into the bristling hair at the back of her neck. "Such a feat would endanger her unborn children." He spoke softly, but his words seemed to echo across the silence this revelation brought.

Rupert stared at him in shock as the other two wolves stiffened. "Is this true?" he snapped at Sue.

She lowered her head and licked the side of her muzzle, unable to properly answer him.

"It's true," Karl replied as he stepped in from the living room. "She's only about three weeks along, but she is most definitely pregnant."

"You lie!" Ross growled.

Corban grabbed him by the arm, warning him back. Werewolf pregnancies were rare, but when they happened, the expecting mothers were treasured by their packs.

Sue raised her eyes to the offending wolf and growled menacingly.

Zak added his voice to hers and shook out of his disguise. The wolves took a step back as the fay waved warning tentacles at them.

"Zak seems to think she is." Darien nodded to the fay, placing himself between Sue and the new wolves. "And I doubt he would be wrong."

Zak chirped at him without taking his eyes from the wolves.

"Very well." Corban pulled on Ross's arm, steering him back towards the elevator. "We will drop this matter for now."

Ross growled his discontent with the conclusion.

"But once the bitch has birthed her pups, she will answer for her actions."

Darien curled his fingers into Sue's fur, holding her back as she tensed, ready to attack the offending wolves.

Zak wobbled a step forward and growled menacingly at them.

"Once the children are safe, we will discuss the incident," Darien corrected. "And the guilty party will be dealt with properly." He caught Rupert's eyes, reading the wolf's satisfaction with this decision. The two visiting wolves didn't look happy at all. "Is there anything else?" Darien's voice held the finality of his choice.

"No." Corban bowed his head to the vampire, not wanting to offend him. If he were as strong as the stories told, fighting with him in his home would only end in their deaths. "We will take our leave of you for now."

"Then I will bid you good night." Darien stepped past them and pushed the button to open the elevator doors.

Corban corralled Ross back into the elevator.

Rupert placed his hand on Darien's upper arm as he passed. "We'll talk later." He slipped into the elevator and punched the button for the lobby.

Darien nodded to the local alpha and stepped back. He let out a cleansing breath as the door closed on the three wolves.

"Well, that was fun." Elliot chuckled from his position leaning against the banister.

"How *dare* he call her a bitch?" Vicky said indignantly as she went over to rub Sue on the ears.

"Technically, she is," Karl answered from where he stood patting Sue on the back hip.

Sue snickered and rubbed her head against Vicky's thigh.

"Well, he didn't have to use that tone," Vicky huffed.

Darien came over and wrapped his arms around her. He kissed the side of her head soothingly. "Thank you for not making a scene of it." Releasing her, he turned his attention to Sue and Karl. "You both have my protection until this is over."

"She didn't do it," Karl growled at Darien, still upset over the wolves' visit.

Darien cocked an eyebrow at him.

"Okay, well, yes. She did try to rip the guy's throat out," Karl clarified, "but it was in self-defense. He tried to kill her first."

Darien laid a calming hand on the agitated wolf's shoulder. "Once the children are born and she can speak for herself again, I'll make sure justice is served." He released Karl with another pat. "You're safe here."

Sue licked the side of her muzzle again and turned to head into the living room.

Karl followed behind her.

Turning his mind away from the wolves, Darien went to Elliot. "Thank you for calling us back." He touched his friend on the arm.

"Cassie called to let me know that the visiting wolves were calling for blood on Sue." Elliot shrugged. "I figured you would want to know when a pack of angry wolves were about to rain havoc on your place." He looked over Darien and Vicky, noting the blood on Vicky's dark sweatshirt and Darien's rumpled and torn pants. "What have you two been up to?"

Darien chuckled at his friend and turned up the stairs. "We went to New Orleans."

Elliot followed.

Zak scampered past them, almost knocking them over.

"I'm going to go check on Sue," Vicky called up after them.

Darien raised his hand in acknowledgement and continued on his way.

"Did someone get upset with you." Elliot made the comment a statement as he studied the hole in the back of Darien's jean leg.

Darien looked back at the flap of material that was barely hanging in place. "I asked Zak to bring us in between." He sighed as he led the way into his room. "Due to my... predicament, he wanted a firmer connection to ensure my safety."

Elliot chuckled. "You've been fay marked!"

"And it hurt like hell," Darien growled.

Zak gurgled as he wobbled into the room in front of the vampires.

Elliot stopped and looked at the cross hanging just inside the doorway. "Did you do something to this?" He reached his hand out towards the holy item. Usually the cross would drain his strength, but today it didn't.

Darien stopped and looked back at him, then to the wooden carving. "No." He turned to examine the object again. "It's the same as always." Reaching out, he laid his hand on it fully. "It's so odd to touch it and not have it bite."

Elliot had never been able to touch the consecrated item. Reaching his hand out, he brushed against the wood. The angry sizzle he was used to ran over his skin, and he pulled his hand back, confused. "Yes." Elliot rubbed his palm trying to figure it out. "It is."

Darien turned back to his room.

Elliot shook himself free of his thoughts and followed Darien. The cross seemed to be tied to Darien somehow, so maybe its power reflected that of its owner. Since Darien had weakened, maybe it had, too. "So, what did you learn from the priestess?" Elliot turned back to the subject at hand.

"Not as much as I'd have liked," Darien answered as he went over and pulled the gris-gris over his head. He dropped it on the top of his dresser before pulling the dirt-covered shirt off. "My loss of power has nothing to do with anything I did." He tossed the shirt in the hamper and pulled out a clean one. "Apparently, when I first took Vicky to Fairy, the lesser fay found a kink in her protection and set a spell on her to drain my powers." Drawing the clean shirt over his head, he settled it in place before pulling off his pants. He looked at the bite taken out of the pant leg and chucked the damaged jeans in the waste can.

Elliot looked at the black and green swirl on the back of Darien's calf. "He got you good, didn't he?"

Darien looked down at his fay mark again. "At least it's not flowers."

Zak gurgled from where he had jumped up and spread himself out on the bed.

Elliot laughed and leaned his hip against the doorframe and watched his friend change. "To what ends?" he asked, pushing the subject back to the original topic.

"I don't know," Darien said as he slipped on another pair of jeans, "but I intend to find out." Darien's stomach rumbled loudly, surprising both of them.

Elliot smiled at him. "Maybe you should eat first." The worn look around Darien's eyes told Elliot that he was exhausted.

"Point." Darien laughed. "Have you eaten?"

Elliot considered him. "Not yet," he said softly.

Darien raised an eyebrow at this. "'You've helped me so much in the last few days." A cockeyed grin split his face as he held out his wrist. "It's only right to offer."

Elliot tensed up against the wall. "No," he clinched his jaw against the temptation, "and you should not offer your blood to anyone else, either."

Darien's lighthearted manner dropped as he took in his friend's discomfort. "What's wrong?" he asked. Something struck a chord in Darien's memory, but it was a fleeting thought.

Elliot swallowed hard, trying to control himself. "Your blood tastes different than anyone else's." He so wanted to taste Darien again.

Darien's brow furrowed in thought as he worked his mind around why this would strike his memory so. Unable to make any connection, he shook the feeling away. "It's probably the fay magic at work." He dismissed Elliot's concern. "Or, maybe my age."

Elliot stepped back so Darien could lead them out of the room.

Zak jumped from the bed and wobbled out after the vampires.

"Well, it's unlike anything I've ever had," Elliot cautioned him. "Even now, I can feel its call."

Darien looked back over his shoulder, concerned. "Then I will be careful," he promised before turning his attention to where he was going.

Elliot let out a relieved sigh. He didn't know how to describe the way his friend's blood had affected him. The warmth that had filled him from just a few pulls, the bloodlust that had risen in him, or the fact that he had not hungered since he found someone to quench his thirst that first night. Even after two days, he could still feel the powerful blood moving through his system. "So, what do you plan to do now?" Elliot asked. "There's going to be a special meeting of the Council at the end of the week to see what can be done about the rogue vampire."

"I know." Darien nodded as they went down the steps. "I'm going to have to get this solved before then." He paused as he considered his course of action. "I'm going to see Lady Aine tonight."

Elliot looked at him with concern. "Does she know you are coming?"

"No." Darien shook his head and pushed through the door leading to the kitchen. He held it so Zak could pass before following the fay in.

"So, you're going to drop in on the queen of Fairy unannounced," Elliot clarified.

Darien nodded.

"While you're mortal?"

Darien let out a sigh. "Not the brightest decision I've ever made, but it's something I've got to do." He opened the fridge and looked to see what was in there. He hadn't eaten since the beignets in the Quarter. "I don't know how to break the spell, and Maria said that it may already be too late to regain my powers." He grabbed up a handful of cherry tomatoes and shut the door, not seeing anything he really wanted. "And that means I'm going to be stuck as a human, unless you want to turn me again." He dropped some tomatoes down to Zak wiggling next to him.

The little fay batted them around on the floor before pouncing on them.

Elliot chuckled at him. "I don't know if I could stand you as a fledgling."

"I don't know if I could stand being a fledgling again." Darien popped one of the fruits into his mouth while he continued his quest for food. Everything he saw would take too much time and energy to cook. He wanted food now. "To be held by the power of the sun. Oh, God, how would I run my business?"

Elliot laughed at him again. "We'll get it worked out," he soothed the older man. "Let's just get you something to eat." Seeing Darien wasn't really focusing on the task, he pushed his way through the swinging door and out of the kitchen. The panel between the dining room and living room was open, and he found Vicky, Karl, and Sue sitting on the floor behind the love seat.

"How do you all feel about pizza?" Elliot asked as he pulled out his phone. A murmur of agreements and a quick round of 'what toppings' got dinner ordered and on the way.

"Thank you." Darien patted his friend on the arm and went to sit down in the breakfast nook. He rested his head on the table, weary from the long day.

"Why don't you put off the trip to Fairy until tomorrow?" Elliot suggested as he joined his old friend and master at the table.

Darien rolled his head to take in his friend. "I don't have the time to waste," he complained. "I need to get an answer as soon as I can."

"You can't go as you are right now. You're much too tired. If you wait until tomorrow, you'll be well rested and ready to face the fay," Elliot pointed out. "Without your powers, you are going to need all your wits about you."

Darien let out a deep breath as he considered his friend's

words.

"I could go with you if you want," Elliot offered.

"Thank you, but no." Pushing up from the table, Darien leaned his head back to stare at the ceiling. "You don't have the same standing with the courts that I do." He rubbed his knuckles into his tired eyes. Darien let out an oomph as Zak jumped up into his lap. Dropping his hands back down, he rubbed them into the little fay. "You're right." He looked over at his friend. "It has been a very long day."

"Well, once you get food, I would suggest that you get some sleep." Elliot laced his fingers together over his stomach and leaned back in his chair, studying Darien and the hellhound. "I'll stay to ensure you and yours are safe."

Darien let his head rock over and blinked his tired eyes. "I can't ask you to do that." He protested weakly. "I'm sure you have other things to do. Zak and I can take care of things here."

Zak gurgled softly at Darien.

"I'm sure you can." Elliot reached out to play with one of Zak's feelers that had reached over to wrap around the vampire's knee. "But, it would ease my mind to know that you were safe."

Zak squeezed, drawing Elliot's eye to his. The little fay shot him a look of gratitude.

Elliot patted him reassuringly. When no answer came for Darien, Elliot looked up to find his friend had nodded off in his chair. Snickering, he stood up and patted the sleeping man on the upper arm to wake him. "Darien."

Darien's eyes popped open, and he looked around, startled from his sleep.

"Let's head out to the living room to wait for food," Elliot suggested.

Zak slipped from Darien's lap and Elliot pulled him up.

Darien nodded his agreement, not quite awake. He followed as Elliot guided him out to the soft couches in the living room where he could rest more comfortably until food got there.

11

Vicky looked out into the leafless trees of Sharon Woods. Since her first visit to the fay, she would never be able to look at this forest the same again. Just knowing that it held something magical changed it.

Zak wiggled up into her lap and licked her with his little, pink tongue, breaking her out of her thoughts.

"Silly mutt." Ruffling him, she opened the door of Darien's SUV. The Range Rover was almost too big for the tiny parking lot closest to the entrance to Fairy. She touched the silver medallion Darien had insisted she wear. It was the same medallion that had failed to protect her properly the first time they had entered the realm of the fay. This time, Darien had assured her that it would work. Zak had even helped when he invoked the spell. She looked over to where Darien was locking up the car.

"Did you think about protection for yourself?" she asked.

Darien shook his head. "If I can't convince Lady Aine to help us, nothing I can do will save me." His voice held a note of despair.

Zak scampered over to him in his dog form and rubbed up against his leg reassuringly.

A smile worked to gain ground on Darien's face as he reached down to pick up the little fay. He let Zak lick him a few time before joining Vicky at the entranceway to the path. "At least we have someone on our side."

Zak barked his agreement and jumped down from Darien's arms.

"Maybe we shouldn't do this." Vicky swallowed her anxiety as Zak started up the trail. She took Darien's hand and let him pull her along.

"We've got to do this." Darien sighed. "I have to find out what the fay have done and how I can stop it." He set a determined look on his face. "Just remember what we talked about."

"Don't turn you loose. Don't accept anything from anyone. Don't eat anything." Vicky ran over the list of warnings he had given her before they left.

"And whatever happens, do not react to anything Lady Aine does or says," Darien warned.

Zak barked his agreement.

"Just the slightest insult, intentional or not, could cause major problems."

"I do know how to behave," Vicky huffed, insulted that he would warn her about her manners.

Darien lifted her hand to his lips and kissed the back of it lovingly. "I have no doubt that you can," he soothed her. "But the fay love to play games. They will push us both as hard as they dare. If we don't follow their rules, we lose. We can't afford that."

"What are the rules?" Vicky asked. The more information she had, the better prepared she would be to face the games the fay would play.

"That's the problem." Darien said. "The rules change at the whim of the Queen."

"Then how are we supposed to follow them?" Vicky asked crossly.

Darien let out an exasperated chuckle. "It's something we have to figure out as we go." He paused, remembering the conversation from last night. "Elliot was right to make me wait until morning to do this. We would have been eaten alive if I had tried this last night."

Vicky looked at him with shock-filled eyes. "Seriously?"

"Oh, I am sure they wouldn't have *eaten* us," Darien reassured her, but the gurgled warning from Zak said differently. "Well, not much," Darien added.

"I don't think I will ever be ready to face the fay." Vicky sighed as they made their way down the increasingly wild trail.

Darien moved her hand to the crook of his arm and patted it. "Don't worry," he comforted her. "We have Zak to help us through today."

Zak gurgled his agreement and came back to rub against her leg before leading them onward.

Vicky let her mind drift, preparing it for the fantastical things she expected to find in Fairy.

The clearing that led to Fairy opened up in front of them. Zak shook out of his dog form and wobbled around the edge of the trees, looking for the entrance. He warbled out to Darien and Vicky, calling them to him.

"Are you ready?" Darien asked as he repositioned Vicky's hand in his and laced their fingers together. He led her across the small, open area to the waiting fay.

Zak writhed, growing in size as he waited for them.

Vicky's eyes widened as the small fay tripled in size. "I guess," she answered, not seeing any way out of this trip. Since the enchantment had been set on her, she was needed. Plus, she was not about to let Darien walk into Fairy alone without his powers. Even with Zak as his guide, she had a feeling that he would never come back out without her.

Darien took a deep breath, calming his nerves. "Then lead on." He called to Zak.

The fay slipped his bulk between them and wrapped tentacles up around their joined hands. Binding them tightly together, he pulled them across the stone marking the entrance to the fay's realm.

Vicky closed her eyes as the familiar feel of cobwebs whispered across her skin. Once free of the barrier, she opened her eyes to the long, dark tunnel. They walked on in silence as the light from the outside world faded.

"It's so weird not to be able to see in here." Darien's voice split the darkness.

Vicky could just make out his outline, a darker silhouette in the blackness of the long hall.

He lifted his hand up to wave it, unseen, in front of his face. "I guess I took for granted how much being a vampire changed me."

"It's not that dark in here." Vicky reached over with her free hand and grasped the hand Darien had raised to his face.

He gasped at the contact and clutched at her fingers. "I couldn't see that at all," Darien admitted as he turned his face, looking for her in the dark.

Vicky looked at him wide-eyed for a moment before releasing his hand. "You're all darkness and shadows," she admitted.

Laughing, he turned his attention back to the front.

"So, our tables are reversed this time." He squeezed the hand he still held.

Vicky turned this over in her mind as they made their way down the rest of the hall. Soon, the light from the Fairy realm seeped in to push back the darkness.

Zak led them from the narrow hall into the large, open area beyond.

Vicky remembered this room from the first time she had visited. The long banquet tables were empty except for a few fay clearing away spent dishes.

"Looks like we missed the meal." Darien glanced around the room.

Vicky took in the scene, too. "Where are the lesser fay?" The small, winged creatures had flocked around them the first time they had come. Their absence was suspicious.

Darien let out a joyless laugh. "They know we're here." The smile that split his face held the promise of pain for someone.

Zak rumbled a warning, and giggles could be heard from

the edges of the room. Tightening his hold on their hands, the hellhound led them across the long hall and through the second set of trees leading to Lady Aine's main hall.

This time, Vicky's eyes picked up every creature hidden in the dark recesses of the hall. She stood straighter and bolstered her courage. With Zak's touch and Darien by her side, she could face the monstrous things waiting here.

The fay watched as Zak pulled those he protected between the tall columns of stone to the hearth where Lady Aine and Lord Dakine waited for them. They stopped just short of the woman sitting on her low, carved stool. Today, her dress was a deep plum with bronze accents around the neckline and sleeves. Lord Dakine's flowing robes were of a deep maroon. The pair looked regal together in front of the crackling fire. A hint of surprise shone in Lady Aine's eyes as Darien dropped her a respectful bow. Vicky followed his lead and curtsied.

"Kian; Cailín," Lady Aine greeted her guests. Her voice rang out through the room, carrying a note of curiosity. "And what brings you to my warren so unexpectedly?"

Darien stood up, bring Vicky with him. "Please forgive our intrusion." He nodded his apology to her. "We are in need of your wisdom."

Surprise filled Lady Aine's face. She looked up to Lord Dakine, who nodded, confirming her suspicions. Turning delighted eyes back to the pair in front of her, she laughed.

Vicky did not like the joy the woman took in Darien's plight.

"This is rich!" The Queen stood up and closed the space between her and Darien. "Oh, the times I have dreamed of you mortal, Kian Dubhlainn." She reached out and touched his chest over his heart.

Darien squeezed Vicky's hand in warning but held still as the Queen petted him.

"Years I have studied ways to steal your powers from you—to have you at my mercy—and here you are." She placed her other hand on his chest and stepped in against him. "Too bad you are bound to another and protected by something older than I." Stepping back, she ruffled a few of Zak's feelers. She circled the trio, studying them. "So tell me Dubhlainn, what have you done to yourself?" The queen trailed her fingers across his back as she passed. Her fingers ran down his arm and up Vicky's. "I see you still haven't released cailín from my grasp."

Vicky shuddered as the Queen touched the sensitive spot on her back where the outline of the wings remained.

Lady Aine stepped up and wrapped her arms around Vicky, pressing herself into Vicky's back. "Or do you just need my help to unravel this spell?"

"I believe we'll be able to handle that on our own," Darien said, politely refusing her assistance with that matter.

Lady Aine sighed and released Vicky. She came back around to look at them from the front. "As you wish." Moving back to her chair, she sat down. "But you must tell me, how did you make yourself mortal?"

"That's why I've come to you." He tilted his head at her. "I believe this is the work of your little ones."

"Of course it's the little ones." Lady Aine grumbled. "It's always the little ones." She looked up at Lord Dakine. "I assume you know about this?"

The elf lord nodded. "I knew of Kian's issue, but I don't see how the lesser fay could have stolen his powers away." Dakine came over and touched Darien on the chest. "They would have left some enchantment on him, but I feel none." He dropped his hand away and studied Darien. "And how would they get pass the protection you have already been given?"

"The spell isn't set on me." Darien raised an eyebrow at his friend. "I believe they set this enchantment on Victoria."

Dakine's eyes darted to Darien's companion. "Cailín?" He moved around Zak to look at the woman. Reaching out, he touched her gently on the chest. "I feel her enchantments, but it's hard to tell what they are."

Vicky felt warmth radiate out from where the elf touched

her.

"It's there," Darien assured him. "I had a Vodou priestess identify it for me."

Lady Aine clicked her tongue at him, annoyed. "Are you still dealing with those ghosts?"

Darien shrugged. "Only on occasion." He slipped his hand into his pocket to touch the gris-gris hidden within. It was another of the precautions that he had asked Vicky to carry into this meeting. Maria wouldn't have made them if there weren't a need for them.

"I'll have to take a closer look at you." Dakine reached for Vicky's hand to pull her closer to him.

Zak gurgled a warning as Darien's squeezed her hand in his.

Dakine raised an eyebrow at them. "I promise she will come to no harm in my hands."

"Thank you," Darien nodded his head to him, "but Zak's mark and Victoria's touch are the only things keeping me safe."

Vicky swore she heard a giggle off to one side of the room as if something were waiting for Darien to be vulnerable.

"Poor Kain Dubhlainn… master no more." The queen's voice was sickeningly sweet with joy and mockery.

Darien's jaw tensed at her words, and he stood up as tall and imposing as he could. "Lady Aine," Darien began, throwing his voice so it carried to every corner of the room. "Oh, most powerful queen of the fay. I beg of you, grant Victoria and I safe passage; to guard us and guide us until our time in your home is done." He used the most formal request that he could.

Lady Aine leaned back to stare at him, intrigued with the way he made his request. "And why should I do this, mortal?"

"For years I have come when you called," Darien reminded her. He focused all of his attention on her as his voice dropped in pitch. "I have done your bidding, fought your wars, run with your hunts, and I have asked little in return. I have been confidant and advisor, friend, and yes, even lover."

Vicky looked at him, wide-eyed, as he went on.

"I come to you now in my time of dire need. I implore you: find it in your heart, in all that we have shared, in all the future possibilities that may be, grant me this one request and help me." The urgency and need etched in his voice rang throughout the room.

The queen sat up in her chair. She had not expected such seriousness from him. He had always been such a lighthearted soul. "Well." Wiping her palms on her skirt, she looked from the normally indomitable man begging, to the shocked woman holding his hand, then down to the hellhound joining the two. "How can I say no to such a passionate plea?" The queen waved her hand at them. "You are safe, for your stay, to come and go in the normal time of mortals."

Darien relaxed a little and dropped her a deep bow. "Thank you, my most benevolent Queen." His voice showed his relief and gratitude.

Darien's actions pulled Vicky from her surprised stupor, and she dropped another curtsy to the queen.

"Don't thank me so quickly, Kian," Lady Aine warned. "I have promised my protection, but my help is never free."

"I am fully aware of that." Darien nodded his head. "Once we know the source of the problem, I am prepared to negotiate terms for your assistance."

The queen cocked her head at a curious angle. "Then by all means." She waved her hand to Lord Dakine, who was waiting. "My Lord, if you would, please."

"But of course," Dakine answered.

Darien released Vicky's hand so the fay could examine her further.

Vicky looked to Darien for reassurance. When he nodded, she stepped into the circle of the elf's arms.

Dakine's hands slipped inside her jacket and pushed it off her shoulders. He let it drop to the floor, forgotten. His fingers found the knot on Darien's medallion and pulled it off.

Zak caught it in one of his grasping ends as the elf lord

dropped it.

Dakine fitted Vicky against him as if she were a lover.

She stiffened at the close contact.

"Relax." He breathed the word into her ear as he shut his eyes and pressed the side of his face into her hair. His warmth enveloped her, making her muscles slowly lose their tension, until they were molded together.

After a few more moments, Vicky closed her eyes and wrapped her arms up around Dakine's back, burying her face into the crook of his neck.

He made a pleased noise and held her just a little tighter. The world seemed to back away, leaving the two of them tangled together for all time.

Darien watched the fay lord wrap Vicky up in his arms. His heart jumped at the sight of his love in the arms of another man. In his mind, he knew Dakine was searching Vicky for the enchantment, but it killed him that the fay had to get that close to her to do it.

"Jealous?" Lady Aine whispered into his ear.

Darien jerked back from where his mind had been at the queen's unexpected presence at his back. Lost in his thoughts, he hadn't noticed her move from her chair. He didn't want to admit to being jealous, but he couldn't lie to her; it wasn't part of the game she played. And he could tell that she was still playing from the way she leaned into and caressed him.

"He may hold her close, but he will never touch her heart." Darien spoke the words softly, more to remind himself than for the queen's benefit.

She laughed and wrapped her arms around him, pressing her ample chest into his back. "I could always take your mind off them..." Lady Aine nuzzled the nape of his neck as she ran her hands over his chest and down the smooth planes of the coat covering his stomach.

Darien moved to take her arms and hands before they could drop below his belt. "Thank you, but I must decline." He turned his head to look at her out of the corner of his eye.

Lady Aine studied his profile for a moment before letting out a tinkle of laughter. She raised her arms to a more appropriate level and rested her chin on his shoulder to watch the elf lord work. "Zak's mark must be so infuriating." She smiled as she spoke.

Darien chuckled. "It drives me nuts."

Zak gurgled from the floor next to Darien. The hellhound had not taken his eyes off Vicky.

"I really could help you with her," the queen offered.

Darien cocked an eyebrow at her. "At what cost?" Freely given help was never to be passed up.

"Nothing that you haven't already done." She smiled up at him, a wicked gleam in her eye. "Although, it might be a little outside your lady's comfort."

Darien chuckled and patted her arms. "I'll have to pass for now." He turned his attention back to Vicky. "I'm sure I can deal with her issues once my power has been restored."

The queen shrugged and looked back to her lord. "As you wish."

Darien knew he was a fool for passing up the queen's offer of help a second time, but it wasn't something he felt Vicky would freely accept. Given enough time, he was sure that he could unravel whatever spell the lesser fay had placed on her. Plus, this one was not hurting anyone, or at least not as far as he could tell. Lord Dakine would be able to tell them better once he had worked out what enchantments had been placed on her and when.

After what seemed like forever, Lord Dakine let out a long breath and eased himself away from Vicky. He placed a soft kiss in the center of her forehead and supported her by the upper arms as he stepped back.

Lady Aine released Darien as he came to take Vicky from the elf lord. The men's eyes met for a moment of silent understanding before Darien parted his trench coat and pulled her into the warmth of his body.

Vicky's mind was hazy as she wrapped her arms up Darien's back under his coat. She rested, her face pressed into the side of his neck, as the magic Dakine had searched her with drained from her system.

Lady Aine stepped around the pair to her lord. "And?"

"There are many layers of magic on cailín." Dakine pulled Lady Aine in against him as he spoke. He turned her so her back was against him and wrapped his arms around her chest. They studied Darien and Vicky as Dakine went on. "The strongest and hardest to see past were the spells placed on Halloween, but they were all in good fun."

Vicky snorted her amusement at the fay's idea of fun into Darien's neck. Her head was feeling better, but she stayed in Darien's arms for support.

Darien patted her on the back, showing his own amusement.

"The most intriguing is the mess Kian made trying to mark her. How she survived that one, I will never know."

Darien tightened his hold on her as he was reminded of his near-fatal error.

Zak rubbed against their legs reassuringly.

"Oh, you *have* been a bad boy," the queen scolded him mischievously.

Darien chose to ignore the comment.

"There were a few broken enchantments scattered here and there, making the path hard to follow, but I think I found the bit of mischief causing the issue."

Darien looked up, hopeful for an answer.

"A spell, laid by the lesser fay during your first visit, drains your power."

"Just as we thought." Darien swallowed back his frustration with the situation. "Can it be undone?"

Dakine took a deep breath and let it out. "The spell is interwoven with cailín's life force. It draws out your power and transfers it to another," he explained. "I dare not try to break it without first knowing how the little ones spun it."

"Then I think we should find out." Lady Aine pulled herself free from Dakine's arms and returned to her seat by the fire. She drew a deep breath and started into a song.

Vicky closed her eyes and let the haunting sound drift over her. She didn't understand the ancient words, but she could feel the call in them. After a few bars, the soft rustle of wings drew Vicky's attention, and she turned in Darien's arms to watch as the lesser fay fluttered into the room.

"Our lady calls."

Vicky picked out the English words in the white noise of the fay's chatter.

"Dubhlainn is mortal!" another excited voice cried as the flock of lesser fay swarmed them. "Let us play! *Let us play!*" The demand echoed through the group.

"Please," Lady Aine held up her hands to suppress the excitement, "my children, calm yourselves." The deafening roar tapered away to excited babbles as the lesser fay tried to contain themselves.

"Who is responsible for Kian's mortality?" she asked the group in general.

Whispers ran the gaggle for a moment, but no answer was given.

"Come forth or all will be punished."

Finally the flock drew back, leaving three small fay grouped together with their heads hung low.

Lady Aine looked over the three guilty fay. "I should have known."

The three winged people trembled as they waited for her judgment.

Holding up her hands, Lady Aine drew them closer to her. "And why would you do this to one such as he? You know my guests are not to be messed with for trivial matters." The little creatures fluttered their wings as they worked up the courage to answer.

"We *had* to," the smallest of the three blurted out. "He wouldn't release us unless we granted his wish." The rest of the lesser fay picked up and echoed the first's plea.

"Quiet!" Lady Aine cried, and the fay fell silent. "Who would do this?" There was anger in the queen's voice.

"The mortal that caught us on All Hallows' Eve." The smallest fay's voice was almost too soft to hear. "He trapped us with iron." The fay's voice grew with anger.

"He threatened our wings." The second fluttered her wings madly, rising a few inches.

"He forced us to promise him magic." The third dropped a few inches as his wings stilled in rage.

"And what were you doing out in the mortal realm on All Hollows' Eve?" Lady Aine asked, eyeing them angrily.

The three fay sunk into silence, knowing they had done wrong.

Seeing no answer was coming, Lady Aine let out a long sigh. "And what did this mortal want?"

"The power of Darien Ritter," the smallest fay answered again.

"The keys to his life and empire," the female answered.

"But Kain was beyond your reach," Lady Aine pointed out. "How did you plan to grant this wish?"

"We only promised to do what we could," the third answered. "We never expected a possibility."

"...And in steps cailín." Lady Aine said softly.

"So vulnerable," cooed the first.

"So mortal," sighed the second.

"So tempting," giggled the female. The laughter ran throughout the room.

Vicky's breath caught in her throat as she listened. Why had the fay used her to get to Darien? They hadn't been more than coworkers at the time, had they? She looked up at him, but his eyes were pinned to the three fay who had stolen his powers.

"So, you set your spell on cailín." The fay nodded their heads as Lady Aine spoke.

Vicky turned her attention back to the inquisition taking place.

"How did you plan for the spell to reach Kian?"

The entire flock of fay answered, but each individual yelled slightly out of unison, so the word 'kisses' was hard to make out.

Lady Aine raised her hand to calm them again. "But Kian didn't play your games."

"He resisted," one of the three grumbled unhappily.

"Did you send Zak to help with this?" Darien's voice was hard as he asked the question.

Zak growled and thrashed his tentacles at the accusation in the question.

"No," the smallest one admitted. "He nearly ruined our plans."

Zak growled at them.

Lady Aine smacked his grasping ends away from the three fay. He has slowly wiggled them out while the fay had answered. "I will deal with these little ones." Pulling one of the tentacles up, she rubbed it lovingly. She looked back to the three fay that had raised up away from the floor now flowing with feelers. "You are lucky I don't let the hellhound have his way with you."

Zak gurgled his anger at them.

"I assume if Kian had kissed her, your spell would have been immediate."

The fay nodded their heads in agreement.

"Then we could have kept him," the smallest admitted.

Darien rested his head on top of Vicky's. He was starting to see the entire scope of the fay's intentions.

"And you let him escape?" Lady Aine sounded disappointed in the little ones.

"Cailín's protections were too great for the sleeping spell," the female in the group admitted.

"And that was why you enchanted her dress," Darien added as he put things together. The giggles sounded again, and a few fay zoomed around in excitement.

"Still, Dubhlainn was strong," the girl sighed.

"So how did you do it?" the Queen finally asked.

"The spell was weak," the smallest giggled.

"It did no harm to any," said the second fay.

"It ties them all together," the female added.

"Can you undo it?" the queen asked. All three of the fay shook their heads.

"We gave our word," the smallest explained.

"And you can't break your word." Lady Aine sighed and nodded her head. "Very well, I'll deal with you later." She waved the three away. They fay zoomed up to the rest of the waiting lesser fay. They quickly scattered, leaving the air in the great chamber empty. Lady Aine turned her attention back to where Vicky and Darien were standing together. "Does that answer your questions?"

"Some of them," Darien admitted, "but how do we unravel the enchantment?"

"Don't you like being mortal?" Lady Aine smiled.

Vicky shivered from the look in her eyes. The queen was definitely enjoying his plight.

Darien drew in a deep breath and let it out heavily. "It's not the matter of enjoyment," he explained. "I have responsibilities to others that require my strength. Plus, there is a man out there using my powers to hurt others. He has to be stopped."

"Always the noble one." The queen shook her head. "So, Lord Dakine, what do you think?" They all turned eyes to the waiting elf lord.

"The only way I can see to break it is to destroy one of the anchors."

Vicky tensed up and shifted, uncomfortable in Darien's arms. "What do you mean by 'destroy one of the anchors'?" she asked, not liking the thoughts that popped into her head.

"Since the anchor is in the life force," Dakine explained, "you would need to end the subject's life."

"Like, kill them?" she said, shocked that he would even

suggest something like that.

"Yes," Dakine clarified, "like, kill them."

"But, how do we find them?" Darien asked the question that he really wanted the answer to.

"You have one of them right here," Lady Aine pointed out with a wicked smile. "But, with so little of your power left in you, if you cut this end of the spell, you may lose the rest to your foe."

"Out of the question." Darien shot down this idea before Vicky could process the suggestion. "How do we find the other anchor?"

"A tracking spell is what you need." Lady Aine stood up from her chair to bargain with them. "I could help you with that, for a price."

Vicky turned to look at the queen.

Darien held her tightly to his chest as he considered the offer.

Seeing how hard he was thinking about the possibilities, Lady Aine added, "I am sure your simple magics could get the job done, but how will you identify the culprit? I have the three responsible and everything they used to set the spell."

Seeing her logic, he tipped his head forward in surrender. "And what is your price?" Darien asked.

"In a few months' time, you will both come to me and submit to one request without question or pause." Lady Aine held up her hand to stem the flow of Darien's immediate refusal. "I give you my word that my request will cause no harm to you or yours, and it will not compromise cailín's ideas of decency."

Darien bit his lip, considering the demand. To give this woman carte blanche on one request was just asking for trouble. He looked down at Vicky. "What do you think?" This was not a decision he was about to make on his own.

Vicky looked up into his eyes. "I don't see a problem with it if it won't hurt anything." She shrugged.

Darien smiled at her innocence. He could think of a lot of things that wouldn't hurt or cross Vicky's sense of decency, but would be very unwelcome. "So trusting." He kissed her on the side of the head. Darien turned his attention back to Lady Aine. "You price is within reason, and your help would be much obliged. What do you need from us?"

"A dram of blood from each of you, to be used for this one enchantment alone."

Darien paused for a moment, considering her demands. A tracking spell should only require a few drops of blood. Why would she want a full vile from each of them? "And what happens to the leftover blood?" he asked.

"Any extra will remain with me, not to be used in any magical context," she reassured him.

Darien studied her for a moment, trying to think of what she might do with the blood outside of a magical spell. He shuddered at the possibilities but could see no harm in letting her have a little blood. He had taken a lot more than that in his lifetime. Looking down at Vicky, he made sure she was okay with it.

She nodded her agreement.

"Deal," Darien agreed.

Vicky looked down at the red line on her hand as she leaned back in her seat. Things had happened rather quickly once Darien had agreed to Lady Aine's terms. It had taken Dakine no time to produce an ornamental dagger and two vials. Lady Aine had tried to convince them to stay for the next feast, but that was a few hours away. Darien politely bowed out, using work as his excuse.

"Will her spell really work?" Vicky wondered. She wasn't sure if she trusted the fay queen. The woman had taken an unnatural delight in Darien's troubles.

"Oh, yes," Darien answered as he moved the SUV through evening traffic. "And it better." He let out a slightly sickened laugh.

"We've just given her something she's been after for centuries."

Vicky looked confused. "What?"

"Carte blanche."

"But, she said her request wouldn't hurt anyone."

"True, but handing that woman a blank check to do with as she pleases still scares me."

Vicky looked at him, shocked. "Then you should have said something."

"I didn't have much of a choice." Darien sighed. "I probably could have worked up something to help find our man, but it would have taken time we really don't have."

Zak gurgled reassuringly at both of them.

Vicky scrubbed her fingers into his fur. "It will be all right," she stated, trying to push away the horrible feeling that they had just done something terribly wrong. Lady Aine had promised her request wouldn't hurt anyone, so it had to be okay… right?

"Yes." Darien reached over and took a hold of her hand. "Dakine will get us the spell later this week, and everything will be okay." Now, he just had to make himself believe those words.

12

"I CAN'T WEAR THAT." VICKY TOOK THE NEGLIGEE FROM VANESSA AND PUT IT BACK on the rack. The garment was more sheer than there. "I might as well not wear anything at all."

"That's the point." Vanessa pulled another one out and held it up to Vicky. "How about this?" This one looked like someone took scraps of lace and cobbled them together for strategic cover.

"I could fit this in a sandwich bag." Vicky took the hanger away from Vanessa and held it up to look at the skimpy outfit. "With room to spare." She tucked it back on the rack. "How about this?" Taking out another hanger, she held up a white, lace corset with matching thong.

"Egads! *No!*" Vanessa took the bridal set away from her friend and shoved it back to the rack. "I'm sure your baby wants something more interesting than that." She walked across the room and picked another set off the wall. "Like this."

Vicky cocked her head as she looked at the strips of red satin. "What is this?" she asked as she pulled on the inch-wide straps. There were definitely cups for a bra and bits that looked like a thong, but it was hard to tell what the jumble of straps should be.

"Oh, that's the newest in our bondage line," the helpful sales clerk chirped as she closed on them. "Here." She stretched the straps, showing them how the outfit would look when worn.

"I think *Master* Darien would love it!" Vanessa squealed.

"No." Vicky shook her head. There was no way they were going to get her into a strap harness with a bow at her neck.

"We'll take it." Vanessa pushed the harness into the saleswoman's hands. "And this," she said, handing over the blue lace bra and matching thong she was holding. Pointing to something mounted on the wall, she added, "And one of those."

Vicky turned around as the clerk took the selection to the counter and fished something out from under the counter. Her eyes widened as she saw what Vanessa had requested. "No." Vicky shook her head at the suede flogger. "I am *not* taking that home!"

The clerk paused, waiting for the girls to decide if they wanted it or not.

"Yes. You are," Vanessa said pointedly. "Wrap it up," she told the clerk.

The woman added it to the pieces she had already placed in the bag.

"Vanessa," Vicky complained, "no."

"If you don't take it, I'll just give it to Darien at the wedding." Vanessa grinned at her evilly. "...Along with a pair of handcuffs and possibly a few other items requiring batteries."

A smile slipped across the clerk's face as Vicky turned bright red.

"You are evil," Vicky huffed as Vanessa paid for the indecent purchase.

Vanessa took the bag and held it out to Vicky. "Oh, you'll love it."

Vicky just looked at her.

"Take them, or they and a few other choice items will decorate the groom's cake."

Vicky growled and snatched the bag away from her friend. She stormed out of the lingerie store to sound of the clerk snickering. "I hate you," Vicky growled at Vanessa.

"No, you don't," Vanessa purred back. "You love me."

Vicky crunched the top of the bag shut so no one passing could see inside it. "I'll get you for this." This was the last stop before they were supposed to meet up with Darien and Elliot for dinner. Those two had been sticking pretty close together since Darien had come back from New Orleans.

"I would expect nothing less," Vanessa chirped cheerfully.

Vicky let out an exasperated sigh. "What else is left to do?" she asked, changing the subject.

"Oh, lots!" Vanessa grinned. "Elliot and I fought about the flowers for a long time, but we finally decided on white and red roses. Simple, yet elegant. But there are still the decorations and invitations. You know, you still haven't given me colors."

Vicky pondered this for a moment. She had asked Darien what colors he wanted, but he claimed not to care. "How about green and black?" Vicky offered. That would cover both of her boys.

"Eww." Vanessa shook her head, disgusted. "Too dark."

"How about emerald green?" Vicky suggested again.

"That I'll give you," Vanessa conceded, "but not the black. Pick another color."

Vicky looked around at the shops for some inspiration. The mall was decked out in festive Christmas decorations, and her eyes were drawn to a catching display. "How about red?"

"Mmmm..." Vanessa made a negative note. "Too Christmasy. We could do red and blue."

"I'm not marrying Superman." Vicky looked at the movie poster that had drawn Vanessa's eye. "How about blue and green?" she countered.

"Not enough contrast."

Vicky stopped at a shop showing amazing, hand-blown, glass ornaments. "How about green and gold?"

"That's..." Vanessa stopped to consider the combination. "...Perfect! And we can use these to decorate the tables." She pulled Vicky into the shop to look at the glass spires.

"How many tables will there be?" Vicky asked. Other than her few friends and her mother, she had no idea who was on the guest list.

"Mmmm..." Vanessa made another unhappy noise. "I'm not sure." She looked at the bobbles again. "Let's just get one of each and the artist's name. Then, we can commission as many as we need.

Vicky agreed, and they left with several bags of carefully wrapped glass.

"Now that we have colors, we should start to think about dresses." Vanessa went back to her planning. "I saw the perfect dress for you over at this new bridal shop."

"Let's check with Elliot first," Vicky suggested, unsure if there was something special that she should be wearing. She kind of wanted to wear that white spider-silk dress from Halloween.

Vanessa gave her a cross look.

"What?" Vicky asked, slightly offended. "You've insisted on his opinion on everything else."

"That's because Darien refuses to give me one," Vanessa huffed.

"Darien gave you his opinion on the cake, yet you still insisted on force-feeding it to Elliot." That had been quite the experience. Vicky had tried to convince Vanessa that Elliot wasn't needed for the tasting, but Elliot wouldn't let Darien out of his sight. Therefore, they both got to eat cake. Vicky gave Elliot an apologetic look as Vanessa practically shoved the bites down his throat. For a moment, she thought he was going to enthrall her to get out of it, but there were nearly a dozen people milling around the cake shop. Reluctantly, he submitted to the redhead's whims. Hopefully, his system could handle a few bites of cake.

"Yeah." Vanessa walked a little while in thought. "Have you noticed anything funny about Elliot?"

Vicky drew in a slow breath to keep from showing anything. "No. Why?"

"Something about him just doesn't sit right with me." A crease formed in Vanessa's brow. "I mean, he's sweet and fun to be around, but there's just something about him."

"Like what?" Vicky asked as nonchalantly as she could.

"He's polite," Vanessa pointed out.

"Isn't that good?"

"Yes, but he's too polite." This earned Vanessa a sideways glance from Vicky. "He opens doors, pulls out chairs, carries everything, and insists on paying for dinner even if he doesn't eat it. Which is most of the time."

"Doesn't eat it?" Vicky had known that Elliot and Vanessa were meeting, but not that he had been taking her out to dinner.

"I've never seen a man worry his food as much as Elliot does." Vanessa's face scrunched up in thought as remembered the time she had spent with Elliot. "He mashes it up and pushes it around, but I can't recall him actually eating any of it."

"Oh, I'm sure it's just your imagination." Vicky shrugged it off. "Maybe he has a sensitive stomach."

"Maybe," Vanessa agreed reluctantly.

Vicky made a mental note to let Elliot know about Vanessa's worries. The two women walked on through the lower levels of the mall towards the parking garage where the men were supposed to have taken the rest of the shopping.

"What have we here?" A male voice behind Vicky startled a squeak from her. Both she and Vanessa spun around to face a man who was much too close to them. The girls retreated a step.

"Can I help you?" Vicky looked around at the empty hall. They had left most of the shops behind. She relaxed the tension from her shoulders, preparing for action. Her two, rather-full bags would be perfect to swing at the man.

The man ran his eyes up and down Vicky. "I just came for a good look." He made a noise that raised the short hairs on the back of Vicky's neck. "Aren't you a precious little thing?"

Vicky rotated in place as the lean man started to circle them.

There was something familiar about his chocolate brown hair and hawk-like features.

"Did you enjoy my flowers?" He gave Vicky a toothy grin.

"What flowers?" Vicky asked.

The man raised a hand to his heart as if her words wounded him. "How could you forget my roses, Victoria?"

Vicky just stared at him, openmouthed. This was the person responsible for the roses sent to her office. "Who are you?" She could not remember meeting him before.

Quick steps brought the man up to Vicky. His arm snaked out, pulling her against him. "I'm the one who's going to destroy you, sweetheart," he whispered, looking into her eyes.

A tingle of power rose between them, leaving Vicky shocked. She recognized the feeling, but it was coming from the wrong man! "*You!*" Vicky pushed out of his arms and stepped back. "You're the one who stole Darien's powers."

The man laughed and bowed to her. "And, oh, what a shock that was." Grinning, he bared fangs at her. "But, I intend to take much more than that from him, my sweet." He advanced on Vicky, making her step back.

Vanessa dropped her bags and threw herself at the man. "You leave her alone!"

He twisted around with inhuman speed and grabbed her up from her attack. Vanessa screeched as he sunk his fangs into her neck.

"*No!*" Vicky shrieked as she dropped her bags. She aimed a good, old-fashioned punch at his face—a move he hadn't expected from her. It connected, knocking him backwards. His fangs popped out of Vanessa's neck spraying blood across the front of Vicky's shirt. Vicky slapped her hand over the torn skin and pulled Vanessa away from the rogue vampire.

The vampire pressed his hand up to stop the blood pouring from his busted nose. "The kitten has claws."

Panicked, Vicky pressed on her connection with Darien and Elliot for help.

The mystery man stood up and laughed at her. "I can feel your terror." His voice was rich with enjoyment.

Vicky dragged Vanessa farther away from him. The boys would be there soon. She just had to find a way to delay the man coming after them. Casting her eyes around, she looked for something to help.

The man held his arms wide to the empty area. "There's nowhere to hide!"

Where did everyone go? A flash of metal on the floor caught Vicky's attention, and she pulled Vanessa along faster. The floors in this part of the mall had been designed by local artists. Each design was laid out in brightly colored tiles surrounded by brass edging. Vicky had no idea if her plan would work, but she had to do something. The crazed vampire stalked after her as she dragged Vanessa across the points of a compass rose.

"Giving up?" He grinned as Vicky settled Vanessa into the center of the design.

Vicky glared at him as she stretched her senses out and pointed them down. "Not hardly." She had to search hard, but she finally reached a small pocket of coolness. Drawing hard on the magic, she dumped it into the brass ring surrounding the center of the compass rose. The magic hissed as it ran along the unusual metal, but Vicky willed the barrier up, and the air solidified just in time for the rogue vampire to walk right into it.

"What the hell?" he cursed as he stumbled back from the magical wall.

"Stick that in your pipe and smoke it!" Vicky snapped before she turned to Vanessa. The skin on her neck had started to heal under Vicky's touch, but there was still blood spilling out. "Hold still." Vicky dropped to the floor and pulled Vanessa up against her. She placed her hand over the wound and opened herself to Darien's power.

The vampire outside the shield stood with his hands rubbing the solid air. "Fascinating." He walked the edge of the circle, pushing on the hardened air. Stopping in front of the woman, he smiled down at them. "You may be safe in there, but your friend is going to bleed out. Oh, the irony," he chuckled.

"Not likely." Vicky pulled on Darien's powers as hard as she could, making the vampire stumble back as if he'd been sucker-punched.

Wrapping his arms around his middle, he dropped to squat on the floor. He looked up just in time to see Vicky drop her hand away from Vanessa's fully healed throat. "What the hell *are* you?" the vampire growled.

Vicky stood up to face him. "That's none of your damn business, asshole," she snapped.

Surprise stole over the vampire's face.

Vicky glared at him through the invisible barrier. If she could just keep him here a few minutes longer, Elliot and Darien had to be close.

"Interesting." The man stood up and looked Vicky over again. "I was just going to kill you, but I think it would be more entertaining to bend you to my will." He gave her an intense look. "Lower these shields."

Vicky could feel the power in his suggestion, but it was obvious he hadn't used the ability much. "Go suck eggs." She glared back at him, shaking off his hold. The rapping of feet on tile echoed through the hall. Her heart lifted; help was coming.

The vampire looked from Vicky to the corridor leading to the parking garage. He backed up from her a few steps. "This will have to wait until next time." Turning, the rogue raced down the hall towards the more populated areas of the mall.

"Come back here, coward!" Vicky yelled as Darien and Elliot turned the corner. She spun to look at them, dropping the shield away.

Darien stopped just short of plowing into Vicky and pulled her into his arms. "What happened?"

Relief coursed through her as she leaned into him. "He bit Vanessa!" Vicky's voice shook with the anger she still felt.

Elliot paused a moment to look at the two women before

turning and racing after their assailant.

"Are you all right?" Darien pushed Vicky back to look at her. She was covered in blood and seemed a little woozy.

"I'm fine." Vicky pushed his hands away and turned to her friend lying on the floor. "It's Vanessa."

Darien took one more look at Vicky before turning to check on Vanessa. "She's lost a lot of blood." There was a real mess on the front of her shirt. Gripping her shoulder, he tried to sense the extent of her injuries but growled in frustration. "I can't tell anything." He placed his fingers on her neck to feel her pulse. "Everything looks healed, and her heartbeat is strong."

Vanessa groaned and rolled into Darien. "What the hell?" She grabbed at her head as the world spun.

Darien carefully helped her into a sitting position. "Easy."

Vanessa drew in a noisy breath through her mouth. "I think I'm going to be sick."

Darien pushed her forwards, lowering her head.

"He's gone." Elliot jogged back up and looked over the scene. Vicky has sat down and bent her head forwards trying to fend off the wooziness from the magic, while Darien supported Vanessa. "What happened?"

"He bit her," Vicky answered.

Elliot looked over at the discarded bags and pools of blood. It wouldn't be long until someone came through here. "We need to get out of here." Grabbing up the girl's shopping, he came over and lifted Vicky to her feet. "Now."

Darien nodded and wrapped Vanessa's arm over his shoulder.

"Whoa!" Vanessa cried as Darien stood up with her. Her other arm waved around, nearly knocking them both off balance, before latching on to him.

He pulled her in against him, pausing until she was steady. "I've got you."

"Good." Elliot settled his grip on Vicky and hurried her along. "Let's go."

Darien matched Elliot's fast pace.

Vicky closed her eyes and hung on for dear life.

"Keys," Elliot called.

Vicky heard the beep of the unlocking SUV right before Elliot reached it.

Leaning her against the side of the vehicle, he opened the door and tossed the bags over the back of the seat. Carefully, he lifted Vicky into the back. "Just relax." He rubbed her arm soothingly before shutting the door.

Vicky nodded as she heard the door on the other side open. She cracked her eyes and watched Darien lifted Vanessa into the other seat.

"Everything's going to be okay," Darien soothed Vanessa as he shut the door and got in the front.

"Go," Elliot urged Darien from the passenger seat.

Darien took a calming breath, carefully pulled the SUV out of the parking place, and casually drove it around the garage.

Vicky's brow furrowed as they eased out into evening traffic. "I thought we were in a hurry."

"We are," Darien explained. "But, we'll be in real trouble if we get caught speeding away. Police don't look kindly on blood-covered women." He looked at her in the rearview mirror. "We'll pick up speed once we reach the highway."

Elliot turned around in his seat to look at the two women. "What happened?"

Vicky looked at him and let out a deep sigh before telling him everything.

Vanessa watched her in disbelief from where she leaned on the seat.

"Who was he?" Elliot asked.

"I don't know." Vicky shifted in her seat; she was starting to feel better. "I think I've seen him before, but I don't know where."

"Wait a second." Vanessa finally found the will to speak. "I don't think I understood you." She raised her hand up to her neck, feeling the healed skin. "What happened?"

Vicky looked at Elliot, then to Darien, and back to Vanessa.

"You were bitten." She tried to sound soothing.

"Oh, I definitely remember that." Vanessa shuddered at the memory. "It's the rest of it that I didn't understand."

Darien shoved the car into park and killed the engine. "Let's go inside, and we'll explain."

Vanessa sat up, feeling for the door handle. "I don't think so."

"Vanessa." Vicky grabbed her friend's hand, preventing her from bolting from the SUV. "How long have we been friends?"

Vanessa stopped and looked at Vicky. She looked at the two men watching her. "A while now."

"And have I ever hurt you in any way?" Vicky pushed.

Vanessa studied her for a moment. "No."

"Then trust me," Vicky begged. "There is an explanation, if you will just sit down and listen."

Vanessa teetered on the edge of running for a moment before nodding her head. "Only 'cause I love you, girl," she agreed.

Carefully, Darien opened Vanessa's door. "Let me help you." He held out his hand for her.

She gave him an unsure look before sighing and letting him help her from the car.

Vicky was feeling somewhat better, so she waved Elliot's help away and went to gather packages from the back hatch.

Elliot joined her, unloading the bags. "I can get these."

"But, we can get them in faster if we both carry." Vicky pulled out some more packages.

"You should go in and rest." Elliot slid the rest of the sacks away from Vicky's hands and slipped his arm through the handles.

Vicky shook her head and gathered up the few bags she had been able to grab. "All right." She turned to follow Darien and Vanessa.

Elliot snickered and shut the back hatch. He quickly dealt with Ethan before the man could get out from behind his desk. They really needed to do something about that poor man before all the suggestions messed with his mind. For now, they just needed to get Vanessa through the rest of the night without hysterics.

"So, you're telling me that you're all vampires." Vanessa had sat through Vicky's rough explanation of the last few months of her life.

"No," Vicky said. "I'm not a vampire."

"But you have a vampire's soul."

"Only a piece," Vicky explained again. "Darien gave me a piece of his after your Halloween party."

"When he failed to mark you properly."

Darien cringed again as he was reminded of his error.

"Yes." Vicky nodded.

"And what were you doing biting her at my party?" Vanessa shot him an accusing look.

Darien sighed.

"It was Beth's fault," Vicky added before Darien could say anything.

Vanessa gave Vicky a sarcastic look. "Right."

"Come on." Vicky's voice held a note of exasperation. "You can't tell me he wasn't just a little bit smashed."

Vanessa looked up at Darien. Darien had found something rather interesting in the carpet to study. "I'll give you that," Vanessa relented. There was no way anyone could say Darien hadn't been incapacitated when they practically carried him out of the house.

"So you're not a vampire," Vanessa went on, trying to wrap her mind around Vicky's story, "but Darien is."

Both Darien and Vicky nodded.

"But, he's not right now because some fairy put an enchantment on you that stole his powers and gave them to that jerk that bit me."

Vicky nodded her head.

"Do you know how ridiculous that sounds?"

Vicky let out a deep sigh. "Yes."

"Vicks, if I didn't know you better, I would think you're trying to put one over on me." Vanessa looked over at Elliot leaning against the wall with his arms crossed over his chest. "But you're not, are you?"

Vicky shook her head.

"They both really are vampires?"

Elliot smiled, flashing fangs.

Vicky nodded her head. "Yes."

"What else haven't you been telling me?"

Vicky looked up at Darien for help, but he just shrugged.

"There's a whole society of creatures who are not human."

"I kind of figured that," Vanessa sassed.

Vicky went on to explain about the werewolves and the fay.

"Wait." Vanessa held up her hand to stop Vicky. "The girl who makes your coffee is a werewolf?"

"Yes. Sue." Vicky nodded. "She's in the other room if you want to meet her."

"Wait. There's a werewolf in your other room?"

"Two, actually." Elliot shot her an award-winning smile.

Vanessa drew in a deep breath and held it as she worked out what to say in response.

"They really are nice people." Vicky grabbed onto Vanessa's arm, drawing her back from the scathing comment she could see forming. "You've kind of already met Sue. She was the wolf that was here when you first brought over the wedding boxes."

A shocked expression filled Vanessa's face. "You mean…?" She pointed to the area in front of the fireplace where Sue and Zak had been curled up.

Vicky nodded.

"But, you said she belonged to someone else."

"Not exactly untrue," Darien added in Vicky's defense.

"And the other?" Vanessa looked between the two.

"That's Karl." Vicky smiled. "He's a RN over at the hospital."

"A nurse!" Vanessa said, shocked. "The hospital has a

werewolf nurse?"

"They have a few." Vicky nodded. "Do you want me to go get him?"

Vanessa shook her head. "That's okay." She was sure she had seen the man herd the wolf out when they had first come in.

Vanessa closed her eyes, steeling herself for more weirdness. "What else?"

"Are you sure you want to go on?" Vicky asked. "We've already gone over quite a bit."

Vanessa opened her eyes and pinned Vicky. "What else."

Vicky fidgeted in her seat. "There's Zak."

Vanessa looked over to the cute, little dog that had curled up by Elliot's feet. "Please don't tell me he's a werewolf, too." She couldn't handle him being a person. There had been numerous times she had played with him. She had even let the little guy eat from her plate on several occasions.

"No." Vicky took a deep breath before going on. "He's fay."

"So he's not a Shih Tzu."

"No." Vicky turned to look at him. "Come here, Zak."

Zak wiggled over and jumped up into Vicky's lap.

"Are you sure about this?" Vicky rubbed Zak soothingly.

Vanessa took a deep breath to center herself and nodded her head. "Yes."

Zak shook out of his fur and wiggled his tentacles.

"*Holy crap*!" Vanessa fell off the couch as she tried to scoot away from the horror in Vicky's lap.

Vicky rubbed Zak as he whimpered.

Darien's chuckling earned him a glare from Vanessa. Reaching his hand down, he offered to help her back up. "That was pretty much the same reaction that Victoria had when she first met Zak," he explained with a grin.

Ignoring Darien's hand, she watched as Zak wiggled about in Vicky's lap. "Does he bite?" Vanessa tucked her feet under her so she was kneeling a little closer to Vicky and Zak.

"Oh yes." Darien chuckled. "Do you want to see my scar?"

"Darien!" Vicky snapped at him. "He only bites if there's good reason." She gave Vanessa a pleading look. "This is Zak. The same little mutt that chews on anything he can get his teeth on, but he won't hurt you."

Vanessa scooted a little closer.

Zak stretched his ends out so they were just inches away from Vanessa but not touching her.

"It's okay," Vicky reassured her.

Carefully, Vanessa reached out and felt the soft feelers. They were almost velvety to the touch. A few wrapped around her fingers as she played with them. "He's kind of cute, in a mind-numbing sort of way." Vanessa finally pulled herself up from the floor. She reclaimed her seat on the couch just a little farther away from where she had been.

Vicky kissed Zak on his top and pushed him off to the floor. "Let her be for a bit," she said, warning the fay away from Vanessa.

Zak looked up at her before sneezing and wiggling back over to Elliot.

Vanessa watched him move across the floor, intrigued. "And you let him sleep with you?"

"There is no 'let' to it," Darien growled. "Zak does as he pleases."

Zak gurgled a happy note as he pulled one of Elliot's shoestrings into his mouth.

Elliot lifted his foot up, trying to stop the fay.

Zak just stretched up, holding on.

Giving up, Elliot put his foot back down and let Zak chomp away on the aglet.

"Okay." Vanessa held out her hands as she collected her thoughts. "So you live with two vampires, two werewolves, and a tentacle thing."

"Elliot doesn't really live here." Vicky looked up at the blond vampire. "He's staying to help until we can get Darien's powers back. And Sue and Karl are only staying because Sue is pregnant."

Vanessa gave Vicky a disbelieving look.

"Long story there. And Zak," Vicky looked over at the fay, "he's just a sweetheart."

Zak gurgled and rolled around in pleasure.

"And you think this is normal?"

"Of course it's not normal," Vicky scoffed. "If this were normal, I would have told you about it months ago when Michael bit me."

Vanessa looked shocked.

Vicky drew in a calming breath and smiled at her best friend. "You were the one who thought my ex was cursing people with chickens. Turns out, you were right."

"Yeah," Vanessa almost laughed. She looked over to Zak pulling on Elliot's shoelace. "I guess the world is full of odd things." She looked back at Vicky. "So how many vampires are there?"

"Lots," Darien answered from where he stood at the far end of the couch.

Vanessa gave him a concerned look.

"But, you don't have to worry about them," Vicky tried to soothe her nervous friend. "Darien's already taken care of that."

Darien nodded his head in agreement. "As long as you're in this city, you're safe."

"But, what if I go someplace else?"

"Have you ever had problems with vampires before?" Elliot asked.

Vanessa gave him a puzzled look. "No."

"Then there's no reason to think they should bother you now," Elliot replied.

"What about the one that bit me?" Vanessa pointed out.

"He was after Victoria. You just happened to be with her." Elliot shrugged. "Unfortunately, since Darien's claimed her, you're probably going to run into a lot more vampires."

Vanessa shot Vicky an accusing look. "And, when were you going to tell me this?"

"I wasn't planning on it," Vicky said sheepishly.

"And, if it hadn't been for this rogue, you would never have known," Elliot added. "We've had years of practice hiding what we are."

"I bet." Vanessa laughed and turned her attention back to Vicky. "I can see why you kept this from us, but I really think we should tell the rest of the girls about it."

Vicky gave Vanessa a doubtful look.

"I think Maggie might already know, and Beth will just get a kick out of it."

"Maggie?" Vicky asked.

"You know she's been into those alternative religions for a while now."

"True." Vicky nodded.

"She keeps showing me weird stuff." Vanessa looked over at Zak wiggling on the floor. "Not *this* weird, but I think you should talk to her."

Darien and Elliot looked at each other, concerned.

"All right," Vicky agreed. If Vanessa thought Maggie could handle this, then she probably could. And it was probably a good idea to let the girls know that something was going on. If the rogue came after Vicky, anyone near Darien or her could be in danger.

"Well," Vanessa broke the silence that was settling into the room, "it's late, and I have to work in the morning."

"Yes." Vicky stood up and hurried to the shopping bags to separate out Vanessa's things.

Vanessa came over to help. "Here."

"I'm sorry, Vanessa." Vicky sighed as they worked.

"It's all right, Vicks." Vanessa smiled at her. "I still love you." Grabbing up the bottom corner of a crumpled bag, Vanessa stood up with her purchases. She shook the crushed bag, letting the red satin harness and flogger spilled out near Darien's feet.

"*Vanessa!*" Vicky snapped from where she stood holding the rest of the bags.

"And that's for getting me bitten." Vanessa shot Vicky an evil grin and left for the elevator before Vicky could sling anything at her friend's head. "Have fun!" she called back from a safe distance.

Elliot looked over at the spilt bag. "Well," he cleared his throat, "I should probably see her home." Trying to hide his grin, he followed Vanessa to the foyer.

Darien grinned as he reached for the spilled items. "What's this?" His hand closed on them before Vicky could get free of her bags.

"*Nothing!*" Vicky squeaked as she untangled herself from her shopping and came for the outfit.

Darien raised it out of her reach. "Really?" He swung the flogger around so the soft ends lashed gently across the backs of Vicky's legs, surprising another squeak from her.

Vicky's fingers finally caught on one of the satin straps, pulling it from Darien's hand. "Really!" The red on her skin shone brightly as she turned away and balled the embarrassing item up.

The soft tails of the flogger trailed up her arm as Darien wrapped himself around her. "I didn't know you liked such things," he purred in her ear, making her fidget in his grasp.

"It was Vanessa's idea," Vicky mumbled as she leaned back into Darien's warm embrace.

"So are you going to model it for me?" Darien pulled the lingerie from Vicky's hands and held it out in front of her. "I think you'll look very nice in it," he coaxed as he nuzzled the hair at the side of her head. Slipping a kiss to the sensitive skin just below Vicky's ear, he weakened her objections. *"Please."* He breathed the word across her skin, sending shivers of promised pleasure rippling down her back.

Vicky waffled for a moment before snatching the harness from Darien's hands and heading to the bedroom.

Darien smiled at her retreating form. He swung the leather flogger around his legs, testing the feel as he followed her at a more leisurely pace. It had been years since he had used a cat o' nine tails, and that had been under less-than-pleasant circumstances. The opportunity to play with one in a more enjoyable setting intrigued him. Seeing how the wicked device could be used in a gentler way was going to make for a very entertaining evening. His initial opinion of Vanessa as a troublemaker was definitely correct, but he was learning to appreciate the fun she brought to Vicky's life.

13

Vicky rocked the little vial back and forth, watching the way the violet liquid coated the inside of the glass. "So, what do we do with it?"

"Drink it," Dakine answered, taking the bottle back. He shook it hard, mixing the contents until they glowed brightly.

Darien held his hand out for the bottle. "All right."

"Not you." Dakine ignored Darien and held the bottle out to Vicky. "Her."

Vicky looked at the glowing vial. "*Me?*"

Darien wrapped an arm around Vicky, pulling her into a protective hold. "No." Lady Aine had already taken too much of an interest in Vicky. Darien didn't like that she had made this potion for Vicky. He should have been more specific when requesting the fairy queen's assistance.

Zak wrapped a tentacle around her ankle, gurgling his agreement.

"It has to be her, Kian." Dakine held the bottle towards them. "This will follow the line of your powers, and you don't have much of a connection with them anymore. Since the spell is anchored in cailín, she has the best chance of finding your rogue."

Darien held out his hand for the bottle. "I'll take my chances."

Vicky looked at it, considering their options. "I'll take it." She reached out and pulled the small vial from Dakine's hand before Darien could.

Darien squeezed her so her back pressed harder into his chest. "You don't have to do this." He really didn't like the idea of her taking something the queen had given her.

"It's the best chance we have." Vicky pulled the stopper from the bottle and dumped it into her mouth. She could feel the thick liquid coat the inside of her throat as she swallowed. It bottomed out in her stomach, making her shudder.

Darien held her, waiting for the spell to kick in.

After a few seconds of nothing, Vicky recapped the bottle. "That wasn't so bad." She handed the vial back to Dakine. He just smiled as he slipped the bottle into his sleeve. A sudden spasm clenched Vicky's stomach, making her double over.

Darien sighed. "You had to say it."

Vicky gasped as waves of power pulsated from the lump in her stomach. Shivers racked her frame as her internal temperature dropped to arctic levels before shooting back up. Darien held her tight as her muscles clenched and darkness ate at the edges of her vision. After a few moments of her system going haywire, things finally calmed down, leaving her hanging limply in Darien's arms.

Drawing in shallow breaths, Vicky waited for the feeling to return to her extremities. That hadn't really hurt, but it was not something she wanted to do again. She opened her eyes and worked to stand on her own feet. Slowly, she felt something pulling at her. It was warm and soft, like feathers brushing against her mind.

"I feel it." Vicky closed her eyes and followed the familiar feeling out. The further along the line of power she got, the more twisted and sinister it became. Pulling back, she opened her eyes. "I don't know where he is, but I think I can find him."

Elliot stood up from where he was leaning on the counter watching. "Then what are we waiting for?" He turned his attention to the elf lord standing in the kitchen. "Are you coming?"

Dakine considered for a minute before shaking his head.

"There are other things I must attend to." He sighed as if he regretted the answer.

Elliot nodded in reply and headed towards the door to the foyer.

"Do you need to feed before we get started?" Darien asked Elliot before he could get through the door. Elliot had moved into Vicky's room, but he hadn't invited any of his menagerie over as Darien had suggested. The younger vampire had argued that keeping Darien's lack of power secret was more important than his need for fresh blood.

"I'm fine," Elliot answered before heading out to the elevators and leaving Darien and Vicky to finish with Dakine. He hadn't had anything that evening, but he was finding that he didn't need as much blood recently. The drawn blood Darien kept was more than enough to quench his thirst, which worried Elliot. He had survived on drawn blood before, but it always left him feeling weak, as if it were lacking something. But now, even after almost a full day without blood, he felt fine.

"If you'll excuse us." Darien bid Dakine good evening and helped Vicky out to where Elliot had started pulling coats out of the closet.

"Do you want our help?" Karl stood next to Sue in the doorway to the bedroom they had claimed.

"No." Darien shook his head as he helped Vicky into her coat. "Sue won't be safe on the street right now."

"I could come," Karl offered as Sue whined reinforcing his offer.

Darien shook his head again. "Sue needs you here in case there's an issue." Darien tugged his coat on. "Besides, we have Zak."

The fay gurgled his agreement, wiggling over and wrapping a feeler around Darien's leg.

Darien looked down at the protective hold the fay had on him. "If you're coming, you need to get changed, too." He pulled a leash out of his coat pocket.

Zak growled at the offensive object.

Darien snickered at him. "It's not my idea."

Vicky leaned over and held her arms out for the little horror. "Come here, Zak."

Zak scampered over and jumped into her arms.

Vicky cuddled and petted him until he shook into fur. "I know you don't like it, but we can't take you out without it."

Zak growled but let Vicky attach the collar around his neck. As soon as Darien clipped the lead to the collar, the fay got the leather strip into his mouth and started chewing.

Darien tucked the leash into Vicky's hands as they headed out. "It's just for a while."

As soon as the elevator doors fully closed, Karl looked over at the serious elf lord. "Do you think they'll be okay?"

"One can only hope," Dakine said. "If you'll excuse me." He bowed to the werewolves and headed back into the kitchen. There was something he needed to discuss with Darien's fay housekeeper.

Elliot looked out of the window at the bustling coffee shop. "Are you sure?"

"Oh, he's in there all right." Vicky nodded as she tried to see through the flyers taped to the window. "And he knows we're here."

"How can you tell?" Darien looked at her, concerned. Once they had loaded into Darien's SUV, Vicky had lead them straight to this little hole-in-the-wall place.

"I can feel him in there. Waiting." Vicky explained as best she could.

"Then what are we waiting for?" Elliot reached out to open his door, but Vicky grabbed his arm, stopping him.

"Wait." She looked at the storefront and the number of people passing. "We can't just go in there and drag him out."

The two men turned to look at her. "For one thing, Darien has a reputation to uphold."

"She does have a point there." Darien sighed. Sometimes being a pillar of the community sucked.

Elliot eased back into his seat. "Then what do you suggest?"

Vicky chewed her lip as she thought. "Let me go in and talk to him," she suggested. "Maybe this whole thing is a huge misunderstanding and he'll come along quietly."

"And maybe I should take up sunbathing," Elliot scoffed. "He's not going to come along quietly."

Vicky held an exasperated hand out towards the building. "And he's not going to attack in the middle of a coffee shop."

"I don't like it," Darien grumbled. "If he knew we were coming, why would he pick such a place for a meeting?"

"Maybe he just wants to talk," Vicky offered.

"And maybe he wants to take as many people with him as he can," Elliot countered.

"Enough," Darien snapped as he put his head down on the steering wheel to think. Someone needed to go in there and find out what was up with this guy. But, if Vicky's feelings were right, there was a good chance the guy would disappear if they all went in. The logical choice was to send Vicky in to get him out. She had seen him up close, and there was less of a possibility of a public confrontation if she went in alone.

Darien sat up and looked at Elliot in the rearview mirror. Something was up with his friend. He had been acting oddly for a while now, but Darien couldn't tell what was wrong. Clenching his jaw, he leaned back and made a decision. "Victoria." He turned to look at her. "Take Zak in and find out what's up with this guy."

Zak barked his agreement.

Elliot gave Darien a sharp look.

"We will wait here in case there's trouble." It wasn't the most desirable answer to the situation, but it was the best they could do at the moment.

Vicky opened the door and slid from the car. "Come on, Zak."

Darien and Elliot watched as she led the small fay across the street.

"Are you sure about this?" Elliot asked.

Darien let out a long sigh. "As sure as I can be." He hoped this was the right thing to do.

Vicky looked around the little café as she held the door open for Zak. The place was bustling with tired holiday shoppers. She shouldn't have been surprised; Christmas was just around the corner, and this shop was nestled between two long rows of stores. Vicky paused for a moment as the thought of Christmas rushed through her head. She still wasn't sure what one should get a billionaire vampire.

Shaking away the stray thought, Vicky's eyes quickly found who she was looking for. The rogue vampire had claimed one of the booths in the back of the shop. She carefully slid into the empty seat across from him.

Zak jumped up into her lap and growled at the man across the table.

The vampire raised an eyebrow at the little dog and pushed a large cup across the table towards Vicky. "Caramel macchiato." He smiled at her.

Vicky looked at the cup warily.

"Don't worry. I haven't done anything to it."

Sliding the cup over, Vicky popped the top off. She let Zak sniff at it. The little fay lapped at the whipped cream happily for a moment before Vicky took it back and sipped the coffee. "Thank you." Vicky set the cup down and rested her hands on Zak.

"You're welcome." The vampire smiled and leaned back in his seat to look around the room. "I used to love coming here. They have the best chicken salad sandwiches. Unfortunately, they don't agree with me now."

"What do you want?" Vicky cut into the man's reminiscing.

He stopped and looked at Vicky for a moment. Pinning her with angry eyes, he replied, "Justice."

She gave him a confused look.

"I want Darien Ritter to pay for what he's done."

"And, what did he do?" Vicky asked.

The man slammed his fist into the table and yelled. "He ruined my life!" The room went quiet as heads swung to take in the sudden outburst. The only sound was a steady growl from Zak. The vampire took a ragged breath and rubbed his hands through his hair. Slowly, activity started back up in the room. "It seems you don't even know the man you intend to marry." The vampire smiled at Vicky as he eased back into his seat.

"Then, tell me." Vicky rubbed her fingers into Zak's fur, soothing the tension from the little fay. He was ready to eat this rogue.

"Gladly. My name is Travis Darecy, and I am really not a bad person."

Vicky raised a questioning eyebrow at this, but the man was deep in his own thoughts and missed it.

"My father, William Darecy, use to drive a semi for Ritter Enterprises. Two years ago, he was killed when his truck hit a school bus."

Vicky's jaw dropped. She remembered that accident. It had been on the front page of every newspaper in the area. The driver of a tanker truck had lost control and nailed a school bus. The trailer flipped over, spilling out ammonia gas and causing an area-wide evacuation. Vicky closed her mouth and listened as Travis went on.

"Darien took my father away from me and then had the nerve to visit each of those families and pay them off."

Vicky shook her head, trying to wrap her mind around Travis' story. The papers had told how Darien had visited the children from the bus with an apology and a $50,000 trust towards their college education. She could see how that might be viewed as paying them off, but how had Darien been responsible for the truck driver's death?

"Wait." She held her hand up, stopping Travis from continuing. "How is Darien responsible for your father's death? Didn't the autopsy show that the driver was drunk at the time?" An in-depth investigation revealed that William Darecy's blood-alcohol levels were more than twice the legal limit at the time of the accident.

"*My father was not drunk!*" Travis slammed his hand into the table, making the room go quiet again. He took a deep breath, composing himself. "He spent years in AA meetings and had just gotten his five-year coin. He was so damn proud of that thing that he had it mounted on a chain so he could wear it. There's no way he would have been drinking. There had to have been something wrong with that damn truck. Darien must have paid the coroner off to cover it up. Better a drunken employee than failure on maintenance."

Vicky shook her head. "Darien wouldn't do that." She had seen Darien do horrible things, but he always stood up and took responsibility for them. He would never blame another for an error in his business.

"He did," Travis snapped at her angrily. "Two days after the accident, he had all the trucks in his lines pulled for full inspections and service. Why else would he do that unless he was guilty of neglect?"

Vicky didn't have an answer.

Zak just growled at Travis.

"So, you blame Darien for losing your father, but how did that ruin your life?" Vicky pressed. She had lost a father, but she had managed to get through it.

Travis narrowed his eyes at her. "Because the autopsy came back saying he was drunk, Dad's life insurance refused to pay out for his death. Apparently, they had taken his alcoholism into consideration when writing the claim. Mom and I struggled to get Dad the burial he deserved. And, while Darien was out flaunting his money to those kids, he never once lifted a finger to help us."

The bitterness in his voice made Vicky's heart hurt.

"A few months later, Mom was diagnosed with terminal cancer and took her own life. That bastard then had the nerve to show up at her funeral—after he wouldn't do a God damned thing to help us!"

Vicky could feel the waves of hate rolling off Travis.

"I swore he would pay for that. I was going to take away everything he loved. Crush his life as he'd done mine, no matter what it took."

"So you stole his powers."

This comment shocked Travis out of his rant. "I asked those things for Darien Ritter's power, but I never expected this." He held his arms out, looking at his hands, seeing the changes in his body. "To think, he's been cheating his way to the top for all these years. He probably didn't even pay the coroner off, just mesmerized him into lying on the forms."

"Darien would never do that," Vicky snapped.

Zak growled his agreement.

"Yeah, right," Travis scoffed. He leaned forwards to place his elbows on the table. "What I want to know is how he gets past the daylight thing."

Vicky cocked her head in confusion. "What do you mean?"

"How does he function during the day?" Travis asked. "When the sun comes up, I'm out like a light until night. He's got to have some secret to staying awake during the day."

Vicky smiled sweetly. "He's just outside if you want to go ask him." Maybe she could talk him into coming out to the SUV. "It's not like he's much of a danger to you. You've got his powers."

"Oh, no." Travis laughed. "I've seen that other vampire that he keeps as a pet. I don't know how he keeps it under control without his powers."

Vicky raised an eyebrow. Was he referring to Elliot? Hadn't

this guy ever had *friends*? "You have to leave some time." She leaned back in her seat, willing to wait him out. Travis would have to seek shelter before dawn.

"Sure." Travis grinned at her evilly. "But you're going to be long gone before I leave."

Vicky petted Zak. "And what makes you say that?"

"This." Travis pulled some kind of switch from his pocket and flipped it open.

"What is it?" Vicky asked cautiously. It looked like something she had seen on a cop drama somewhere.

"It's a dead-man switch." Before Vicky could do anything, Travis pushed a button and squeezed the trigger. "There is a box truck parked just behind the Boys and Girls Club, filled with ammonia nitrate and nitro methane. Oh, did I happen to mention there's a Christmas party going on over there this evening?"

Zak growled in anger.

Vicky glared at him. "You're lying."

"Do you really think so?" Travis started to loosen his grip on the device. Vicky gasped and moved to grab it, but Travis pulled it out of her reach and squeezed back down on the thing.

"What do you want?" Vicky asked in a defeated voice. She didn't know if the man had really set up a bomb behind the club, but she wasn't about to take the chance with children's lives. The man was just crazy enough to do it.

"Take your dog and your vampire, and leave." Travis leaned back in his chair and smiled at her. "And, just so you know—whatever you did, I can feel when you're near."

Vicky felt him push on their connection. She clenched her jaw and clamped the link down as tight as she could.

Surprise filtered across Travis's face.

"Fine." Vicky scooped Zak up and stood up from the booth. "But, you know we will be back for you."

"Oh, I am looking forward to it." Travis smiled. "It will be fun to kill Darien using his own powers."

Zak barked at Travis as Vicky placed him on her shoulder and stormed out of the shop. She was glad when the door swung shut, cutting off the evil man's laughter.

"And?" Darien asked as Vicky threw herself into the SUV and slammed the door angrily.

"Drive," she snapped. Both Elliot and Darien stared at her in shock.

"Where?" Elliot asked.

Vicky buried her fingers into Zak's fur as she stared straight out the front window. "The Boys and Girls Club." She had to know if Travis was bluffing or not.

Darien exchanged a look with Elliot before starting the car and pulling out into holiday traffic.

If there was a truck there, Vicky was going to make Travis pay for endangering innocent kids.

Vicky dropped herself on the couch, exhausted. There had been a box truck parked behind the Boys and Girls Club. Darien had called the police to report the potential hazard, but it turned out that the truck belonged to the club. Yes, it did have fertilizer in it—three bags that the kids were going to use in potted flowers for the local nursing homes. Travis had played her like a fool. He was so going to pay for that.

"You did the right thing," Elliot tried to soothe her.

Vicky rocked her head over and gave him an irritated glare. She had spent the rest of the embarrassing ride home telling them about Travis Darecy and his troubled past.

Darien fell into the seat next to Vicky. "I just can't believe he would go this far."

Vicky sighed, and she leaned her head over onto his shoulder. "He thinks you killed his father."

"The investigation *did* find something wrong with the truck. That's why I had the rest of the trucks serviced," Darien said, defending himself for the second time. "But I didn't do anything to the man's autopsy. And I certainly didn't bribe the coroner to cover anything up."

Vicky petted his arm soothingly. "I know."

Zak wiggled up into their laps and cooed his support.

Darien absentmindedly scrubbed his fingers into the fay's tentacles. Leaning his head over, he rested it on top of Vicky's. "I *did* try to help them," he said again. "I went to see Mrs. Darecy shortly after the accident to offer help, but she turned me away. I could tell she was ill, so I extended her medical coverage. I didn't know about her suicide until I saw the funeral announcement in the paper."

Vicky patted Darien again. "It's all right." This subject was obviously bothering him.

Darien drew in a deep breath and let it out.

"So what do we do now?" Elliot asked from where he had stretched out on the other couch. He folded his hands neatly over his chest and stared at the ceiling, thinking.

"We're going to have to take this to the Council this weekend," Darien said, unhappily. "If he's got my full powers, there's no way they could stand against him if they went after him."

Elliot rolled his head to look at Darien. "Do you think you could defeat the whole Council?"

Darien lifted his head up and gave his friend a stoic look.

Elliot looked back up at the ceiling. "So, we have to warn Clara, but do you think it's a wise idea to take this problem to the Council?"

"Why not?" Darien asked.

"In light of recent events, do you think it's wise to show them any weakness?" Elliot glanced at the vampire-turned-human.

"I appreciate what you've done in keeping my troubles from the Council, but I can't think of anything else." Darien paused, considering his options again. He came up sadly short. "The Council has to be warned away from a hunt. Vicky can track him, but he's going to know that we're coming. We can't do this by ourselves."

"True." Elliot sat up and turned to face Darien. "But, you're not alone anymore. You have people here to help you."

Darien straightened up. He had only thought about the three of them going out to hunt this man. It hadn't occurred to him that he now had a whole menagerie to call on for help. "What do you suggest?"

Elliot gave him a grin that spoke of mischief and trouble. "I have an idea."

14

"We don't have to do this," Darien said again as Elliot pulled the sword out of the back of the SUV.

"The other option is to admit to the Council that you've lost your powers and beg them for help," Elliot pointed out as he strapped on the sword. "At other times, I would have even encouraged that path; but with Lillian's betrayal, I don't think you should take the chance. What if someone else is gunning for you, too?" He paused and looked at Darien. "I know you don't like to play these games, but others do. Many of the masters have friends outside the city, and they would see this as a prime opportunity to make a move on Clara."

Darien brushed the threat away. "Clara can handle herself."

"Yes, Clara can handle herself, as we have recently seen," Elliot agreed, "but say someone stronger had tried for the city. Would you have stood by and watched them come in, kill her, and take over?"

Darien paused to think. "No." The word slipped out in a soft breath. He had confidence that Clara could take care of any challenge to her position, but he would have stepped in if she had needed it. After years of denial, it hurt to admit this really was *his* city. If he were truly honest with himself, he had allowed Clara to run the Council unchallenged because she held its members to the rules he'd originally set for her. Had she been looser with the rules or a poor leader, he would have taken over when he originally arrived. As it was, he moved to Brenton because she was such a good leader and he didn't have to play stupid vampire games with her.

Elliot rested his hand on Darien's upper arm, trying to reassure him that this choice was right. "She'll understand."

Darien let out a long sigh. "I hope you're right." He turned towards the large manor house where the Council members should have already gathered. Taking a deep breath, Darien pulled himself up straight. He had seen many master vampires do what he was about to attempt. Some had more success than others, but all had had the power to back it up. As it was, he was going to rely on Vicky, Zak, and Elliot, and pray that Clara would understand and let the bluff slide.

"Let's go." Darien tucked Vicky to his side and let Zak lead the way to the door.

Elliot fell into step just behind them.

Hank opened the door and bowed to the master vampire as he always did. "Good evening, Master Darien." The old man raised an eyebrow at the entourage. "The Council is already in chambers."

"Thank you." Darien escorted Vicky up the steps and stopped just outside the door so they could prepare for their entrance. "Remember what you need to do?" he asked as Vicky swallowed back her anxiety.

"Easy." She gave Darien an encouraging smile. "I do this every day at work." She smoothed down her long, red gown, checking to make sure it hung properly. The cut of the dress was a little revealing, but Darien had explained that this was all for show. As it was, he and Elliot were dressed in impeccable suits. The only thing that marred their look was the silver sword strapped to Elliot's waist.

"All right." Darien tugged on his jacket to make sure it was straight and nodded for Elliot to open the door. It was show time.

The Council chamber doors actually creaked as Elliot pushed them open, clipping off the conversation in the room. Silence fell as Elliot stepped in and bowed Darien through.

Darien could feel the questioning eyes of the Council as he escorted Vicky to his seat at one end of the table. Pausing there, he waited for Elliot to close the door and bring her a chair before settling her down and claiming his own.

Vicky rested her hand on the arm of his chair as Zak jumped up into her lap.

Surprise flashed on Clara's face as Elliot took his place just behind Darien. Laying one hand on the back of the chair and the other on the hilt of his sword, he took up a stance that Clara had never seen in this room. "Good evening, Master Darien." She greeted her sire, but ignored the others. She ran a tight ship, but she didn't stand on formalities. As long as there were no issues, Clara treated all the masters as equals. Elliot's stance labeled him as a servant to a greater vampire. Clara's eyes jumped to Vicky, taking in the bowed head and silky, red dress that marked her as a blood slave, not the inamorata Clara knew the girl to be. Something was up.

"Good evening, Grand Master Clara." Darien nodded his head respectfully, setting off all Clara's warning lights. Something was *most definitely* up. For a moment, their eyes met. She could see a plea in his gaze before their stoicism returned.

"And what can the Grand Council of Brenton do for you this evening?" she asked, using the group's formal name.

A hint of amusement flickered across Darien's eyes. "I have come to speak of matters most dire," he stated.

The Council sat up a little taller.

"Although I stand outside this Council, it has come to my attention that a rogue has been wreaking havoc in this fine city."

Anger licked at Clara, but she pushed it back before answering. She didn't know what he was doing, but she would play his game. "We, of the Council, have gathered this night to discuss that very matter," she answered. "Would you care to join us in this debate?"

"No. I have come to tell you what you will do." Darien's answer shocked the group.

Clara's eyes narrowed slightly. "And what is that, My Lord?"

"Nothing."

A cry of outrage sounded around the table, but Clara banged on the wood until the room fell silent again. She considered Darien for a moment. There was something off about him—other than the fact he was playing games—but she couldn't tell what. His eyes were penetrating, and she could feel him willing her to accept his word unquestioned. "And you expect us to just leave this vampire unpunished?" Clara asked, unable to let this act slide.

"No." Darien shook his head. "This man had slighted me, and I claim the right to punish him, myself." This statement had the rest of the Council exchanging curious glances.

"And what has he done to one so great?" Rachel asked. Had anyone else brought up the question, Clara would have squashed it, but the raven-haired beauty was the voice of reason on the Council. Even Darien listened to her when she spoke.

"This man has found a way to tap into my powers," Darien explained.

Suddenly, Darien's actions were making more sense to Clara. If this vampire had managed to get ahold of Darien's full power, then there was no way the Council would be able to stop him. "And what will you do?" Clara asked. She was dying to know how this man had gotten access to Darien's power. It was a feat she had never before heard of.

"Me and mine will go after this threat. And, once we catch him, he will pay dearly."

"Will you desire help from the Grand Council of Brenton?" Clara offered.

"No." Darien shook his head. "Your assistance is not required. In fact, the Grand Council of Brenton will stay out of this matter completely." He held Clara's gaze. This was the moment of truth.

As Grand Master of the Council, it was Clara's job to keep the city safe. This included going after rogues who entered her region. Darien was treading a fine line here by demanding that the Council stay out of this.

Clara weighed her options carefully. Either she could agree to Darien's declaration and sit back to let him deal with this problem, or she could challenge him.

Challenging Darien would be a huge mistake. He didn't wield it often, but he had more power than she had ever seen in any master. Their fight would wound him greatly, but it would end in her death. Clara looked around at the faces of the Council. Some showed outrage, some held agreement, and still others were blank. If she let him go and he failed, it could undermine her position as head of the Council. It was Elliot's willingness to lower himself to servant that made up her mind. If he believed in Darien that much, she would, too. But, when this was all over, she was going to corner Darien and demand the explanation she couldn't ask for now.

"Very well." Clara leaned back and crossed her hands over her chest. "The Council and I will do as you ask and remain here while you deal with this issue." More protests sounded around the table. Clara raised her hands to quiet them again. She pinned Darien with a pointed look. "I am still Grand Master of this City, unless you're challenging?"

Darien shook his head no.

"Then you have until Monday to solve this issue. Monday night, if this rogue is still free, we will hunt him."

Darien's eyes narrowed as he took in Clara's decision. "Agreed." He stood up from his chair. "Then I will bid you good night."

Zak jumped down as Vicky stood up and wrapped her hand around his arm.

"Good hunting," Clara called as Darien escorted Vicky from the room. He raised a hand in answer but said nothing. The click of the closing door echoed around the shocked Council members. They had never seen Darien posturing. He didn't play high and mighty.

"What the hell?" Michael voiced the thought that had passed through all of them. Of all the times he had seen Darien make a statement, Michael had never seen him draw on his status as an Ancient before.

"I agree." Clara drew the masters' attention back from the closed door. "Something is up." She looked at each of Council member.

"Rachel," Clara turned to the timid master, "your kiss is closest to Elliot's. What can you tell us?"

Rachel sorted through her thoughts for a moment before beginning. "I've learned many things." The woman sighed. "Elliot has been essential in Darien's takeover of Lillian's kiss. He has eased a lot of stress that Darien never knew about. Recently, Elliot has been acting weird. For the last week, he's been staying at Darien's penthouse full time, and he refuses to let any of his people over to visit."

Clara made a disturbed noise in her throat.

"There've been two wolves staying with him," Daniel added. "I got it from Mitzy that Sue attacked a wolf from a visiting pack and nearly killed him. She's disappeared, and rumor has it that she won't shift back to human and explain herself. The pack got together to go get her from Darien's, but he turned them away. Rupert refuses to answer any questions on the subject.'

"That's another thing," Clara pointed out. "Has anyone noticed an increase in wolf activity?" Several of the Council members nodded their heads.

"Last Saturday night, I was out at the club," Vincent started. "There were at least three wolves there, getting into it. Thankfully, Phelan showed up and dragged them out before someone could call the police." He shuddered at the memory. "If I didn't know better, I would have said it was the night before the full moon. Tensions were that high."

"I saw something like that, too," William added. "It felt like they were just going to shift right there in the street and eat each other. That time, Rupert showed up to knock some sense into them."

"Wow." Clara rubbed her hand over her face. "He usually has a better handle on his pack than that. But, could that have something to do with Darien's odd behavior?"

"I don't think so." Daniel shook his head. "Things were strange before this stuff with the pack."

"Like what?"

"I had a long conversation with Allen. There was something wrong with his bond with Darien."

"How so?" Clara asked.

"He was worried about Darien being strong enough to support Lillian's kiss."

Clara made a dismissive noise at this.

"That was my thought, too, but I tested his link to be sure," Daniel went on. "It was extremely weak. I suggested that he say something to Darien, or even Elliot, but the power stabilized before he could bring it up."

"Okay." Clara gathered her thoughts together and laid what she had learned out to better understand the problems. "So, Elliot's acting weird, and Darien's power is unstable. If a strange vampire were tapping into his power base, then the instability could be explained. But, why would they hide this from us?"

"They're scared," Rachel answered.

"Of what?" Clara asked, shocked.

Rachel turned her dark eyes to Clara. "Us."

"We would *never* do anything to hurt Darien," Clara growled, angry that anyone would even suggest that.

"Would you have said that same thing two months ago?" Rachel asked with just a hint of accusation on her face.

Clara clenched her jaw shut on the scathing remark she wanted to make, but couldn't. Lillian's betrayal had taken them all by surprise.

Rachel turned to take each master in. "We all have our

reasons for moving to Brenton." She looked back up to Clara. "And you have welcomed us each as equals. You do have some rather peculiar rules for vampires, but you don't lord over us or push etiquette as some in other places do. If there is an issue, we can bring it here and discuss it in ways no other Council would allow. Personally, I find it refreshing, but we all have kith or kin outside the city that we talk to. If it got out that Darien's power was failing him, there are those out there who would see this as a perfect opportunity to move on him." Heads nodded around the table.

"I see," Clara said stiffly.

"Clara," Rachel smiled to take the sting out of her next words, "you do a wonderful job as Grand Master of the city, but we all know who really holds the power here." A murmur of agreement circled the table, leaving Clara sighing in defeat.

"You're right." Clara hung her head as she gave in to the truth. "If it ever came down to a fight, he would win." She shook her head. "But, he doesn't want the head Council seat."

"And, we wouldn't want him to have it," Daniel chuckled. "That man's too busy to give the Council the attention it deserves. He's stretched too thin as it is." More agreement sounded from the Council members.

Clara chuckled. "Thankfully, Elliot is there to help him."

"Can he be trusted?" Michael asked, surprising them all.

"Elliot is loyal to Darien." Clara nodded. "He would give up his life before he betrayed his Master." The Council members exchanged another series of looks. Clara rapped her knuckle on the table drawling their attention back to her. "All other things aside, we still need to decide what to do about Darien and this rogue."

"You've tied our hands with that," William pointed out. "We can't do anything until Monday."

"Not exactly." Clara smiled defiantly. "I agreed that the *Grand Council* of Brenton will stay out of this until Monday, but I never said anything about our kisses." Amusement circled the table.

Daniel leaned forward and rested his elbows on the table. "So what do you have in mind?"

"If it were up to Darien, he would probably try to go after the rogue by himself." Distress sounded in the Council, but Clara raised her hands to calm them. "Elliot won't let him. He'll insist they find help. And, if they don't trust us, they won't trust anyone else."

"So, where will they go?" Michael asked.

"Darien's kiss." Understanding spread across the faces of the Council as Clara laid out her plans and gave orders. They couldn't help in this fight, but they would make sure Darien had cover if he needed it.

"Do you think they bought it?" Darien asked as they pulled away from Clara's estate.

"Absolutely not." Elliot sighed as he leaned back in the front seat. Vicky and Zak were curled on the back seat of the SUV. He had insisted they lay down for some rest. It was late, and they were still in for a long drive. "But, it bought us a little time to work."

Darien nodded his head in agreement.

"So, what now?" Vicky asked as she drew the blanket Elliot had packed closer around her shoulders. She hadn't had a chance to change out of the blood-red, silk dress.

"Well, now we head over to the kiss." Elliot looked back at Vicky. "We gather anyone willing to help and see about hunting Mr. Darecy down."

"You know," Vicky said as she thought about what they had just done, "this whole thing confuses me. I get that you didn't want the Council involved, but I'm still not sure why."

"If Darecy has access to my full power, then they stand no chance against him," Darien explained.

Elliot looked worried. "Do you think he's figured them out?"

"No, but I don't want to take that chance," Darien said with a sigh.

"Do you really think he could stop the full Council?" Vicky asked.

Darien gave her a sad-eyed look in the rearview mirror but didn't say anything.

"You know what Darien's special talent is," Elliot replied, speaking for his friend.

"Yes, healing," Vicky answered.

"Not exactly," Darien said softly, but he refused to look at Vicky in the mirror.

"Darien has the ability to manipulate living tissue," Elliot explained, "be it healing or bursting every cell in the body."

Vicky's mouth dropped open in shock. "You mean..." She looked at Darien's profile, but he was intently watching the road.

"If Darecy has figured this out, he could kill them all with a single, focused thought," finished Elliot, voicing Darien's deepest fear.

15

"WE'RE HERE." DARIEN SPOKE SOFTLY AS HE PATTED VICKY FROM HER SLEEP.

Nodding her head, she sat up. After Elliot had revealed the true extent of Darien's powers, she had curled up on the seat with Zak to think about it. She was having a hard time coming to terms with the fact that Darien had such a frightening ability. She always thought his special power was healing. Elliot knew he could use it to hurt, though, which meant Darien had used it that way before. What was even scarier was the fact that she had used Darien's power without realizing it. If she could use it to heal, did that mean she could use it to kill, too? Shuddering, she collected her bag from the floorboard and followed Zak out of the backseat.

"He would never use it," Elliot said, standing close behind her.

Startled, she turned to look at him.

Elliot was watching Darien open the back hatch, but when she moved, he looked down at her. "I can only remember once when he used his power against someone. A mob had Clara trapped, and they were just about to set her on fire. He let go and dropped the entire crowd where they stood. Pop. Out like a light. Killing them would have made our lives much easier, but he made us check every single one of those villagers to make sure he hadn't hurt them permanently."

"That just makes me worry more." Vicky pulled her blanket

tighter around her. "I've used Darien's powers," she admitted.

Elliot just smiled. "You have nothing to worry about, My Lady." He placed his hand on her shoulder and guided her to the back of the car. "It may not take much to hurt someone, but it does take intent. If you were capable of that type of cruelty, Darien wouldn't love you the way he does."

Vicky drew in a long breath as she thought about his words. "What about Darecy?"

Elliot licked his lips as he chose his words. "Vampires don't start out knowing how to use their powers," he explained. "It can take a while for them to learn about them."

"Or a very stressful situation," Darien added as they approached. "I don't think he knows yet." Taking a heavy bundle out of the back of the car, he handed it over to Elliot.

"What makes you think that?" Vicky asked.

Darien stopped and looked at her. "He would have cut a path across Brenton if he had." He shut the door and hefted up their suitcase. "Let's go get this over with." Darien held out his free arm, and Vicky slipped in against his side.

The house that held Darien's kiss was magnificent. A long, stone driveway led up to a two-story, stucco house with a red tile roof. Darien knocked on the dark wood of the front door.

Elliot chuckled as he held out the key. "This *is* your place."

"Maybe." Darien pushed the offering back at Elliot. "But, it's *their* home."

Elliot shrugged and put the keys back in his pocket. Darien had to knock a second time before someone came to open the door.

"Master!" Allen was surprised to see the group standing there. He held the door wide for them to come in. "What are you doing out here? Come in."

Elliot grinned as they entered.

Darien felt a little foolish stepping into the circular foyer. "Sorry for stopping by so late."

Vicky looked around. She had only been there once before,

but it still amazed her. The light of a crystal chandelier glimmered off the cream stone walls, while a single staircase curved up to a balcony on the second floor. The place was steeped in old-world grace.

Allen took the suitcase from Darien and set it on the inlaid-stone floor. "You're always welcome here." He looked at the bag and the bundle Elliot dropped next to it. "Will you be staying with us for a while?"

Vicky added her bag to the pile.

"Not really." Darien followed as Allen led them through a door into a great room. The dark floor of the two-story room dropped a few feet into a sunken sitting room that was overlooked by another second-floor balcony. The huge windows were covered with heavy curtains to keep the warmth of the fire from getting out. Two of Darien's new kiss looked up as they entered.

"Master Darien!" Rose cried. At only twenty years old, she was the youngest of the vampires. Just looking at her, Darien could see why Lillian had brought her over. She had the same curly, red hair Lillian had. The two could have been sisters in both looks and personality. Shortly after Darien's takeover, Rose had chopped her hair into a cute bob. The young man who sat on the couch, Harold, had been one of Christian's members. Darien had decided to spare him when the young man had showed them pity while Christian had held them captive. The pair started to stand up.

"Relax," Darien tried to soothe them as he and Vicky came down the two steps to the sitting area.

Elliot grinned and slipped past Darien. He plopped himself down in one of the empty armchairs to watch. The tension in the air was thick as Darien settled Vicky on the second couch and sat next her.

"So." Allen broke the uneasy silence as he reclaimed his seat. "What brings you to visit?" He looked over Darien's outfit. Both Darien and Elliot had taken off the suit jackets and ties, but

Vicky's red gown peeked out from under the fleece blanket she was still wrapped in.

Zak wiggled up into her lap and looked out at the room.

Darien let out a deep sigh; it would probably be best to get right to the point. "I came to ask for help," he admitted. "Where is everyone?" It was only a little after one—prime time for vampires to be up.

"Out," Rose answered. "It's Friday."

"Ahh," Darien answered. Of course they would be out living it up.

"Most of them should be back around three," Allen added.

"Good." Darien looked around the room, uncertain what to do or say. He was responsible for these people, but how was he supposed to relate to them? He didn't know them very well, and they had watched him kill someone they loved dearly. What was he supposed to say after that?

Seeing the tension settling into the room, Vicky turned to Rose and smiled. "I love what you've done with your hair."

"Thanks." Rose smiled back and fluffed her curls a little. "I didn't realize that short hair needed so much tending."

Darien listened as Vicky eased the discomfort in the room with small talk. He could have kissed her for it. Give him a roomful of executives or auditors and he was fine, but in this intimate setting he was lost. How had he gotten so out of practice socializing?

Rose pointed to the red silk sticking out of the bottom of the blanket. "I want to see your dress."

Vicky shifted Zak off her lap and stood up. She let the blanket fall away from her shoulders to show off the flimsy gown.

Allen sat up in his chair, surprised. "Wow!" He had been to other cities with Lillian and knew what the clingy garment meant.

Rose got up to take a look at the dress. "I like it!" The only thing that held the flowing material up was a thin collar wrapped around Vicky's neck. The red silk that flowed from the band barely covered Vicky's chest as it dropped to the floor, wrapped around her waist, and came back up to overlap a little in the front. Some double-sided tape was the only thing holding the edges in place so they wouldn't slide forwards exposing her. The wrap left a massive amount of skin on her back exposed, and the front was in danger of gaping open if she moved wrong.

"Where did you get it?" Rose asked as she came over and touched the golden cuff on Vicky's upper arm.

"Darien," Vicky answered as she turned to show it off. It was a little rumpled from where she had been wrapped in the blanket.

"I want one."

"No, you don't," Elliot added from where he lounged in his chair. He stood up and came over to pick up the blanket. "This is the dress traditionally used to mark someone as a blood slave." He wrapped the blanket back around Vicky, covering the dress up. "It's worn when a woman is given to an Ancient to feed, usually from the neck."

Rose cocked her head and visualized the dress again as Vicky sank back to the couch. "But how would they feed at the neck?" she asked. "The collar is in the way; they'd have to take it off to..." Rose stood there with wide eyes as the truth sank in.

"Exactly," Elliot chuckled as he retook his seat.

Rose glared at Darien and sat back down.

Darien sighed as Vicky leaned into him. "It's not what you think." He wrapped his arm around her protectively. "We had to go talk with the Council tonight."

"And you made her wear *that?*" Allen snapped.

"It wasn't his idea," Elliot added as he settled in to explain. "Something's come up, and we needed to make a statement to the Council. Sometimes playing dress-up and flaunting your power a little can get you places faster than words can."

"What's up?" Allen looked over to Elliot.

Elliot just nodded his head towards Darien.

Darien drew in a calming breath before looking up at the

three people waiting for him to explain. "We know who the rogue vampire is."

"Who?" Harold asked. Everyone had been out looking for this illusive man since Halloween.

"His name is Travis Darecy, and he's a very disturbed individual," Vicky answered.

Zak gurgled his agreement.

"Unfortunately, he's found a way to tap into my powers," Darien admitted.

"What?" Allen asked, shocked. "When?" He looked from Darien to Elliot and back.

"Shortly before the hunt this summer."

Allen was shocked by Darien's answer. "Well," he said, leaning back in his chair, "that explains a few things."

"Like what?" Elliot asked.

"Fluctuations in my powers," Darien offered, recalling the conversation Vicky had with Jakob.

"That and why no one's been able to find out who's been attacking people," Allen added. "There's been a lot of speculation."

"Most everyone thinks it's someone in Michael's kiss," Rose offered.

"Figures." Elliot chuckled.

"So what do you need from us?" Allen asked.

Darien sat up taller. "Help taking Darecy down."

"We are at your call, Master." A male voice rang out across the room, drawing everyone's attention.

Darien turned in his chair to see Josh coming through the doorway. His brother was only a step behind.

"I don't have full control over my powers at the moment." Darien stood up as he addressed the new vampires. "What I ask of you could be dangerous."

"We know," Josh answered as he leaned his hip against the railing that divided the room. "We were wondering when you were going to bring this problem to us."

"Yes." Jakob continued down the steps towards Darien. "A

few of us have felt the subtle shift in power." He stopped to look Darien over. "How much of your power do you have left?"

Darien tensed at the question. "Practically none," he admitted. If he wanted help, he was going to have to be up front and honest with these people.

An evil glint flickered in Jakob's eyes as he stepped around the end of the couch.

Darien turned to face him.

"So, I could bleed you out, and there'd be nothing you could do about it?" A hint of fangs slipped past Jakob's lip as he spoke. The cocky smile vanished from his face as Elliot's hand closed around his neck.

Vicky blinked in surprise. She hadn't even seen him move.

Darien smiled at him. "Yes," he admitted. "You could bleed me dry right now, and there would be nothing I could do about it." He looked pointedly at Elliot's hand, pressed into Jakob's throat. "If you managed to survive the night, my death would leave you tied to this inexperienced rogue. And, if he isn't stopped, the Council will hunt him. They now know he has my powers, and Clara will stop at nothing to destroy him, leaving this kiss masterless." Reaching out, Darien drew Elliot's hand away from the stunned vampire. "Who do you think will take you in, then?"

Understanding flickered in Jakob's eyes. Hurting Darien would be a death sentence for all of them. "Forgive me, My Master." Jakob dropped to a knee in front of Darien. He raised his hand to his heart and bowed his head.

Darien reached out and touched him on the shoulder. "Remember this."

Jakob looked up as Darien spoke.

"Just because someone is down, doesn't mean they don't have unseen strength." He patted Elliot on the arm in thanks.

Elliot nodded his head and went back to lounging in his chair.

"Yes, My Lord." Jakob stood up and fell as he tried to step back from Darien. His legs were tangled in blackish-green tentacles.

Zak gurgled a warning before releasing his hold on the vampire. No one had noticed the fay's silent shift during the exchange.

"He won't do it again," Josh promised as he came down the steps and ruffled Zak's feelers. "Sometimes, my brother likes to push things."

"I know." Darien sat back down on the couch next to Vicky.

Zak wiggled into his lap protectively.

"So, how can we help?" Josh asked as he found a seat on the couch next to Rose.

"Vicky has the ability to track Darecy." Darien patted Vicky on the leg.

She smiled at him reassuringly.

"But, the man is clever. He got away from us once."

"He threatened to bomb the Boys and Girls Club," Vicky explained.

Zak grumbled and writhed in Darien's lap.

Allen and Josh exchanged a worried look.

"This man is dangerous," Darien said gravely. "I want as few people around him as possible, so Elliot and I will take him on." He nodded to his friend.

Elliot nodded back.

"So what do you need us for?" Jakob asked as he claimed the chair next to Elliot.

Darien smiled at the crafty twin. "Verification."

16

VICKY LOOKED OVER HER SHOULDER AT THE TWO VAMPIRES SITTING IN THE BACK of Darien's SUV. "Are you sure this is going to work?"

"Of course." Josh smiled at her. "We've been tracking the sights where Darecy has been attacking people in hopes of finding him. If he stays true to his habits, we'll only have to cover the center of the city." The younger vampire looked over to Elliot sitting next to him. "With all the kisses spread around, we should be able to verify a bomb if he tries that again."

"Yeah," Darien growled. "I don't like the fact that so many people just happened to show up at the house and volunteer to help."

Elliot chuckled. When they had woken up in the afternoon, the living room was bustling with activity. There was at least one person from each kiss hanging out. When Darien questioned them, they all claimed to be there for game day—a tradition that had many of Darien's people confused.

Grinning, Elliot leaned back in the seat next to Josh. "Clara found a way around our plan."

"I will not have them endangered in this," Darien grumbled.

Josh smiled. "We've already got that covered."

Vicky looked back at the powder-blue Prius following them. "I still don't understand how this is all going to work out." She had fallen asleep while plans were being laid.

"I'll relay the information to Jakob, and he will call it out," Josh explained.

"But, will that work?" Vicky still didn't understand.

"My brother may be an insensitive bastard at times," Josh let out a deep sigh, "but he wouldn't be foolish enough to endanger our new master by neglecting this."

Vicky gave Elliot a worried look before turning back to Josh. "That's not what I meant." She shook her head. "I know you and your brother are linked, but how does it work?" Pausing, she tried to form her question more clearly. "I mean, I can feel things through Darien's marks, but all I get are flashes of feelings and abstract thoughts. Sometimes I can pick up images if I concentrate hard enough, but how do you send specific information across that link? And won't Darecy pick it up?"

Josh chuckled at her. "Our connection is different than what we share with Darien. We are linked directly and are always in each other's minds." He looked back over his shoulder at the car following him.

Vicky wiggled in her seat. "Well, that's got to be uncomfortable at times." She could think of many times she wouldn't want anyone in her head.

Josh laughed at her. "It can be, but we've learned to handle it." He shrugged. "We can close off the link if we want to. It's how I know Jakob is getting into mischief." Josh let out a snort of laughter.

"What?" Vicky asked.

"Nothing." Josh shook his head. "My brother just made some choice comments that I will beat him for later."

Vicky raised an eyebrow at this and turned back around in her seat. She wasn't sure she wanted to know what had passed through Jakob's mind.

Pointing her thoughts inward, she felt along the lines that linked her to the vampires. Since Darien's power had been stolen, she had started to feel those pathways more clearly. Before, she had to reach for Darien before touching the others. Now, it was like a buffer had been pulled away. Each line had a different feel, almost a flavor she could feel on the back of her tongue. Each responded to her touch, some more energetically than others, but all seemed to be waiting for her call.

Touching a power that was cool and green like dappled sunlight, Vicky recognized Elliot, but there was something different about his power. It was warmer than the last time she encountered it. Turning, she looked at him. Elliot held her eyes for a moment. She thought about asking him what had changed, but a slight shake of his head derailed her question.

"So." Elliot broke into her contemplation. "Where are we going?"

Shaking her head, she pulled herself away from the vampires. She would ask Elliot about the change in his power later. Vicky focused her thoughts on the one line she should be following. "Downtown." The line was steadily growing stronger as they drove closer to the center of the city. "He knows we're coming."

Darien nodded his head. "We knew he would."

"He's confident about this fight." Vicky pressed at the connection as much as she dared. "More so than the last time we saw him."

Darien nodded. "He's up to something."

"I think so." Vicky sighed.

Darien took a deep breath and kept on driving. They had done everything they could think of to cover any plans Darcey could have made. They had people spread out to deal with any diversions the man could come up with, and Darien was still a formidable magician, even without his vampire abilities. Plus, they had weapons, both hand to hand and long range. It didn't matter what Darcey was planning; they would take him down one way or another.

"There." Vicky pointed to a building off in the distance. "He's there."

Darien nodded as he pointed his SUV towards the parking garage.

Vicky squinted as she looked at the building."About halfway up."

"Jakob is clearing the area," Josh added from his spot in the back."Are you sure you just want us to go in?" Several brave people had offered to go into the fight, but Darien had limited the group to just the five who had to be there. He would have loved to keep Vicky out of it, but she was the only one that could find where Darecy was hiding.

"No." Darien shook his head. "I have to take him down myself." Having a large group to help him with this would have been preferable, but Dakine had been very clear on this point. If Darien wanted his powers back, he had to be the one to kill Darcey.And it would have to be up close and personal. If Darecy died without Darien there to take back his powers, there was no telling where the loose energy would go.

Vicky rubbed him on the arm reassuringly.

Darien caught her hand and kissed the back of it.

It only took them a few minutes to get to the concrete structure in the business end of town. It actually wasn't too far from Darien's main office. He found a few open spots on the lowest level and pulled in. Allen's powder-blue Prius pulled in right next to them.

"Shouldn't we go higher?" Josh asked as they all piled out of the SUV.

Darien shook his head."He may know we're coming, but I want to take him by as much surprise as I can." He opened the back door of the SUV. Pulling out two swords, he handed one to Elliot.The other he strapped to his waist.

Vicky recognized the dark sword that had given Darien his fay name.

"Do I get one, too?" Jakob jeered as he climbed out of Allen's car.

Darien shot him a withering look."Do you know how to use one?"

Jakob shook his head and took up a protected spot behind

his brother.

"Then don't ask stupid questions," Elliot chided as he pulled his belt tight. He tested the draw of his sword and adjusted it.

"Here." Darien held a gun wrapped in a leather harness out to Josh. "I trust you know how to use this."

Josh nodded and took the gun.

Darien pinned the more responsible twin with a sharp look. "Don't use it unless you absolutely have to, and aim for low center mass or legs if you do."

Josh slipped out of his coat and into the leather shoulder strap. "Yes, Master." He checked the gun over before stowing it away under his jacket again.

Darien nodded his approval and handed a second gun to Elliot.

This one Elliot fed into a holster he had already placed on his belt.

Taking one more sword out of the SUV, Darien closed the hatch and turned towards the group gathered around. "Now, everyone understands that I have to take him down, correct?" He got a mutter of understanding from the group. "Good. Let's go."

The group turned as a whole and started towards the ramp that would lead them up to the next level.

Darien slid in close to Vicky and wrapped her hand around his arm as they walked.

She took a quick glance back at the people following them. They must have been an interesting sight as they walked. Vicky and Darien led the way, with Zak weaving around their feet. Josh and Elliot stood at their backs with hands already on their weapons. Jakob and Allen followed up a few steps behind them. The sound of their footsteps was the only thing that broke through the frosty air.

"How far?" Darien asked.

Vicky turned her attention to the link she has with Darecy. She could feel him above them, waiting. "Two floors," she guessed.

"Then shut it down," Darien directed.

Vicky clamped her connection with Darecy down as tightly as she could. She was starting to get good at this control thing. Nodding, she signaled that she was as disconnected from Darecy as she could get.

Darien stopped and turned to the four men following them. "Allen, Jakob, take the stairs up but stay out of sight." They both nodded and headed towards the concrete steps in the corner of the building. Darien looked back at the three people waiting with him. "Let's go." He turned and hooked Vicky's arm again.

Zak barked his agreement and scampered off up the ramp.

Elliot fell into step next to Darien, while Josh took the side next to Vicky.

Vicky took a deep breath and let Darien lead them up the ramp to whatever Darecy had planned.

17

The cold December air rustled through the garage. Cars of those working late and holiday shoppers filled the lower two levels, but the third level was mostly empty. A few cars were clustered near the corner with the steps, and one lone van sat parked in the center of the floor. Travis Darecy leaned against the van, watching as Darien and his entourage made their way up the ramp.

"I see you found me." Travis smiled and stood up as they approached. "That's close enough," he called. Darien's group stopped near enough to talk but well outside any type of engaging range.

"I want my powers back," Darien called.

"And I want you dead," Travis replied.

"Well, it looks like only one of us can have what we want." Darien tossed the loose sword at Travis so that it slid to a stop by his feet. "I challenge you." Tugging off his coat, he handed it to Vicky and drew out his sword.

Travis looked down at the hunk of metal lying at his feet and back up to Darien. "You have got to be kidding me." He laughed. "This isn't the Dark Ages." Travis kicked the sword away and pulled a gun from his pocket. He fired a shot, hitting Darien in the shoulder.

"Darien!" Vicky screamed as things whirled into action.

Dropping his sword with a loud clang, Darien spun around from the impact and straight into Elliot's grasp.

Zak let out a roar that didn't fit his cute dog disguise.

Darien hissed as the pain from the bullet registered.

Vicky dropped Darien's coat and rushed to check on him, while Travis laughed at the flurry of activity.

"Swords are for relics." Travis waved his gun around at them. "Your time is over."

Darien twisted in the grip of his friends to glare at Travis. He pushed Vicky's probing fingers back from his mostly healed wound and stood up away from Elliot. "I may be a relic, but at least I have the decency to face my foe honestly." Slipping a small vial from his sleeve, Darien shook his hands next to his side, readying himself for the next attack. "Sneak attacks are for cowards."

"That may be true, but I'm going to win." Travis raised the gun to point at Darien's chest.

Vicky stepped back as she felt Darien pull energy from the world around him.

As Travis pulled the trigger again, Darien threw his hands up, flinging the contents of the bottle out in front of him. He barked a word of command and the air hardened, catching the bullet in its flight. The projectile hung between them for a moment before Darien lowered his hands and the lead lump clattered to the concrete floor.

Travis just stared at the bullet in shock.

"It would be wise if you just surrendered," Darien offered. "We could go back to the fay and have them undo whatever it was that they did."

Vicky turned and looked at Darien, confused. She was sure that Dakine had said the only way to break the spell was to destroy the anchor. She opened her mouth to say something but a quick shake of Elliot's head shut her up.

Travis had lowered his gun as he considered the impossibility of stopping a flying bullet.

Darien took a slow step towards the bewildered man.

Drawn by the movement, Travis shook his shock away and raised the gun again.

Twisting his hands around in the air Darien pulled more magic from the world and channeled it into the gun with another word of power.

Travis let out a squeal as he dropped the weapon; the metal around the grip started to glow.

Elliot pulled Vicky back as the first of the bullets exploded in the heat.

Travis danced backwards as the gun jumped around from the popping of the shells.

Darien stepped back to stand next to where Elliot was protecting Vicky from potential shrapnel.

"Smart move," Elliot sassed as he released Vicky.

"Had to be done." Darien shrugged. "I was out of iron filings." He turned his attention to Vicky. "Are you okay?"

She nodded her head and looked at where the damaged gun had come to rest.

"What the hell *are* you?" Travis screamed.

Darien looked back at the ruffled man. "I thought you knew." He smiled at Travis. Once he was sure Vicky was okay, he turned to face Travis again. Tapping into the magic once more, Darien readied himself for a third attack.

Seeing Darien's unusual stance, Travis held out his cell phone. "Do it and they die!" He held his finger over the button.

Darien paused. "Who dies?"

Travis inched his finger closer to his phone. "Everyone!"

Darien slowly raised his hands; he wasn't about to make a move until they knew if Travis really had set up a bomb.

Vicky did her best to open herself up and listen to Travis' thoughts. Maybe she could catch something about his target.

Darien took a step closer to Travis. "What do you want?"

"I want you to know the pain I've had to suffer!" Travis screamed at him.

"I know that pain." Darien's voice dropped. "I've known suffering for hundreds of years. The loss of loved ones. The empty holes they leave in your world. I've had to live with the agony of taking the life of the one closest to me."

Vicky stiffened as she listened to him. She felt Elliot's power brush against her mind reassuringly. Turning, she caught the sad smile he gave her. She pushed the thoughts away and turned back to the standoff. Darien had stopped just a few steps in front of her.

"I understand your pain, but that is no reason to take it out on others."

"You have no idea how I feel!" Travis screamed. "*You killed my father!*"

"Luke, I am your father!" Josh whispered next to Vicky while breathing heavily.

She tried to hold in the mirth, but the inappropriateness of the comment mixed with the tension of the situation drove a snort of laughter out.

Travis turned his eyes to Vicky. "You think this is *funny?*" he screamed at her.

Vicky shook her head and tried to wipe the smile off her face. "No." She tucked her hands deep inside her pockets. Anger washed out through their link, coloring the edges of her mind.

Travis waved the phone around. "Damn right, bitch. People's lives are at stake, here."

A flash of an image crossed into Vicky's head, making her gasp. "You wouldn't blow up the Christmas Village!" She took a step forwards in shock. With it this close to Christmas, there had to be hundreds of people wandering around the city's largest light display.

"Get the hell out of my head, bitch!"

Vicky staggered back from the force Travis threw down their connection.

Josh caught her before she could fall. The line between them clamped down, but Vicky caught the location of the bomb.

"The main tree," she whispered to Josh.

He nodded and looked back towards Darien and Travis. His eyes slid past them to the stairwell where his brother was hiding. "Stall for time," he muttered as he set her back up on her feet.

Vicky nodded and faced Travis. "Why would you endanger the lives of children like that?" She put a hurt note into her words; maybe she could play to his sympathy, if he had any. "Do you really want to put innocent people through the same kind of suffering you've had to endure?"

Travis paused and looked at her, confused.

Vicky took a step forwards pushing compassion against the link Travis had closed off. "All of this was to make Darien pay for the wrongs he's caused you, but how does blowing up innocent people accomplish that? If you do this, you're no better than he is." She waved her hand towards Darien, standing silently between her and Travis. Attacking Darien's character hurt her, but it was the only way she could think of to get through to Travis.

"You're right." Travis lowered the phone. "That does bring me down to his level." He waffled for a few minutes as he studied Vicky. "But, I'm a vampire now, so that makes me evil." To her horror, Travis pressed the button on the phone.

"*No!*" Vicky lunged forwards as if to stop the electronic signal, but Darien turned and grabbed her before she could get past him.

Darien pulled Vicky in against him as she sobbed. "Being a vampire doesn't make you evil." He looked up at Travis. "Acts like that do." Turning, he walked Vicky back over to Elliot and Josh.

Zak rubbed up against her leg before growling at Travis.

"Now what are you going to do?" Darien glared as he moved to face Travis again. "You're down a gun, and you've used your bomb. What other tricks are you going to pull?"

Travis actually smiled at him. "You know, I've discovered something."

Vicky felt him open their connection back up.

Travis looked straight at her as he poured malice and hate into her. "Kill him."

Vicky let out a scream and doubled over, holding her head. Images of Darien lying dead by her hands rushed through her mind, and she felt the urge to strangle him. "*No!*" she screamed and wrapped her arms around her middle. Dropping to her knees, she fought with the compulsion. Darien's hands touched her, but she flinched away from them.

He pulled back, not sure what was wrong.

Zak whimpered at her and pressed his face into her chest.

Vicky wrapped her arms around him and buried her face in his fur as he chased the magic from her mind. The desire to hurt Darien slipped away from her.

Darien stood back up and turned to face Vicki's attacker.

"Bitch!" Travis screamed at her. "*Kill him!*"

Shaking her head again, she felt him shift his attention to another.

Josh shuddered next to her and took a step forwards.

Vicky looked up to find Josh advancing on Darien.

Darien's attention was back on Travis, and he didn't see the other vampire moving.

"No." Vicky reached out and grabbed at Josh's ankle. His shuffling steps stopped as she searched through her mind and found Darien's mark on him. Travis had shoved his hate into Josh, washing out the man's own feelings. Vicky shoved Zak out of her lap and struggled to her feet. Grabbing Josh's face, she turned it to her. Josh's eyes were empty as if his soul had been plucked out.

"Josh." Vicky patted him on the cheek. His body tried to move towards Darien, but Vicky held him fast. His eyes shifted, but she pulled him back to look at her. "No, Josh." Zak gurgled from behind Vicky, but she ignored him as she tried to break the hold Travis had on the lesser vampire. "*Josh!*" she yelled and slapped him hard.

Josh blinked and stared at her in confusion.

Vicky sighed in relief; life had come back to his eyes. A growl grabbed Vicky's attention, and she turned to look at Darien, standing behind her. Concern colored his face, but it was the sight behind him that terrified Vicky. Elliot's eyes were as empty as Josh's had been. "*No!*" Vicky yelled just as Elliot's arms wrapped around Darien, pulling him back.

Darien grunted in surprise as the air was crushed from his lungs.

"*Kill him!*" Travis' voice washed over them again.

Vicky felt the power in the compulsion. Had she not spent hours fighting Darien's power, learning about suggestion, she would have fallen under the pull. She staggered under the press but shook it off just in time to see Elliot tip Darien's head over and drive his fangs deep into the exposed skin.

"*Elliot!*" Vicky screamed as Zak roared behind the attacking vampire. Since the move had worked once with Vanessa, Vicky threw a punch straight at his face.

Elliot's head jerked back, tearing his fangs through Darien's neck, but he held on tight, sucking away Darien's life.

"*No!*" Vicky rammed the palm of her hand into Elliot's nose and pushed, trying to pry him off.

A growl rose from the vampire's throat as he clamped tighter to Darien.

Darien gasped for air.

"*Stop!*" Vicky shoved all the power she could get her hands on into the suggestion and rammed it into Elliot.

Life flickered in his eyes, and his mouth released Darien's neck.

Tentacles wrapped around Elliot from behind and ripped him away.

Vicky reached for Darien and tried to support him, but they both fell to the floor under his limp weight. "Please. Please," she begged as she covered the gushing wound with her hand. Opening herself to Darien's power, she urged the flesh to knit back together.

He drew in a trembling breath as she cried.

"Oh no!" Travis yelled. "He will die!" He turned his attention to Josh. "Kill them both!"

Josh trembled as he fought the suggestion, but it was too strong. The life washed out of his eyes again, and he bent to pull Vicky up. She swatted at him, and he hissed, showing his fangs.

"Josh!" Vicky tried to get through to him as she scooted backwards across the floor. Her hand fell on something hard, and she grabbed the handle of Darien's sword. She swung it around hopping to discourage Josh's attack, but the man lunged impaling himself on the sword.

"*Nooo!*" The scream echoed from across the parking area as Jakob felt his brother's life flicker out.

Travis turned to look at the two men tearing across the floor. "Stop!" He held out his hand and forced his will into the two men.

Allen's feet faltered slightly, but Jakob bowled over the suggestion and plowed straight into Travis.

Vicky pushed Josh's limp body off and pulled Darien's sword free from the vampire's stomach, shocked. That hit might have killed a normal man, but she thought vampires could suffer more damage. Tears welled up in her eyes as she took in the mess around her. Darien lay limp on the floor, covered in blood. Elliot was still and wrapped in a writhing mass of tentacles. She couldn't bring herself to look at the Josh's lifeless face, so she concentrated on the action next to the van.

Jakob and Travis rolled about on the floor exchanging punches and snapping at each other while Allen tried to find an opening.

Vicky felt the subtle shift in Travis's power as he poured it into Jakob.

Jakob let out a scream of agony as his flesh started to bubble.

"*No!* " Vicky screamed. Darien's worst fears were being realized as she watched. Lifting up Darien's sword, she raced over to the struggling pair.

As Jakob rolled away from the source of his pain, Allen took the opening to drop a knee into Travis' gut. Travis' hands landed on Allen's leg, and Allen screamed in pain as Darien's power raced through him, destroying tissue.

While the two men were distracted, Vicky took the end of the dark sword and rammed it into Travis's chest.

His grip on Allen loosened, and the injured man fell away. Travis's eyes widened as he looked up at the woman holding the sword.

"*No more!*" Vicky screamed and pulled the sword out. Ramming it home again, she crushed Travis' heart. She didn't care what Dakine had said. There was no way she could sit there and watch as this twisted soul destroyed her friends.

Pain raced across Travis' face as he reached up to try to remove the sword, but the life flickered from him before he could budge it.

Dropping to her knees, Vicky wailed in anguish. How could things have gone so wrong? Hands pulled on her upper arms, and she spun around to find Darien kneeling behind her. He was pale and coved in blood, but she didn't care—he was alive. Burying her face in his chest, she let out another bout of frame-wracking sobs.

"It's all right." He drew her into his lap as he shifted to sit on the cold concrete.

Vicky balled her hands up in his shirt and held on for dear life. After a while, his soft petting and reassuring noises calmed her hysteria. She drew in a lungful of his spicy scent. Even with the sharp tang of his spilt blood, she loved the way he smelled. Burying her face deeper into him, she pulled his scent in again. A sharp pain hit Vicky in the stomach, making her curl up. She gasped as she felt the power Travis had stolen let loose of his body. It slithered up their connection and slammed into her with enough force to drive her breath from her. "Darien!" Vicky gasped as the power burned through her veins. She trembled as her world swam in and out of focus. Closing her eyes, she tried not to be sick.

Darien slid his hand up into her hair, turning her head to rest on his shoulder. "I've got you."

The smell of his blood hit her hard, making her stomach cramp. She felt movement in her mouth and ran her tongue over her teeth. Two sharp fangs had slid down replacing her rounded canines. Popping her eyes open, Vicky stared straight into the slightly bloody crook of his neck. The urge to sink her new fangs into that soft skin stabbed through her. "*No!*" She twisted away from him, denying the hunger rising in her. Wrapping her arms around herself, she breathed slowly, trying to find something to think about that would get her mind off the emptiness gnawing at her insides.

Darien sat there for a moment, studying the lines on the back of Vicky's jacket. With his powers settling inside her, they were going to have some really big problems very soon. He had seen the fangs poking out of Vicky's mouth as she turned away from him. It had been a long time since he was driven by hunger, but he knew how potent is could be. He was going to need to find Vicky fresh blood, or she was going to completely lose it.

"We'll figure this out." Darien leaned forwards and wrapped his arms over hers, pulling her back into his lap. "Together." His hands slid over her fists.

Vicky nodded her head but kept it down. Her hands loosened just enough for him to weave his fingers together with hers, right to right and left to left.

"No matter what happens, I will always love you." He kissed the back of her neck softly and squeezed her. Warmth radiated up Darien's left arm, and he could suddenly feel the anguish and fear coursing through Vicky.

Astonished, he raised his hand up away from hers and looked at it. The green ribbon that Dakine had set into their skin at their handfasting glowed brightly. The power running along it started to fade as he held his hand up, staring. Had Lady Aine known this was going to happen? Darien dropped his hand back down to Vicky's. Once again, his power started to flow through the ribbon that bound them together. It didn't matter if the queen knew or not, this could be their life-saving ticket.

Holding her left hand tightly, Darien placed a kiss on the side of her neck, driving a gasp from Vicky. With his right hand, he turned her head and shifted so he could place a kiss on her lips.

Vicky tried to pull away from him, fighting the need for blood. "No."

"It's okay," Darien reassured her and shifted her back so he could kiss her.

The kisses started out soft and light, but when the tip of Vicky's fang clipped Darien's lip, releasing a few drops of blood, she moaned and leaned into him, deepening the kiss.

Darien turned her in his arms to get a better angle. As passion rose between them, he could feel his power swirling between them. He explored every crevice of her mouth as his free hand slipped under her coat and ran down her body. Hunger rose in him, and he pulled back from their kiss, gasping for breath.

Fangs still hung in Vicky's mouth, but Darien could feel his power returning to him through their binding. Even though her eyes were slightly glazed, he couldn't help but think she was the most beautiful thing he had ever seen.

Vicky's breathing slowed just slightly, and she tipped her head back in a silent invitation.

Need slammed into Darien, tilting him towards the soft skin of her throat. "I love you," he whispered against her skin and kissed her pulse before driving his fangs deep into her neck. Vicky gasped as he began to drink. Her blood was fire, the sweetest candy, and the most delicate wine all rolled together. Darien moaned in ecstasy, and he gripped her harder.

Vicky's fingers laced through his hair as she returned his moan of pleasure.

They clung together for what felt like forever as he pulled

his power from her. Slowly, he withdrew his fangs and licked her wound closed. The feel of feathers shifted around inside them both as his powers worked to heal them. He held her close for a moment more before sitting up and staring down into her face. The paleness of her skin was exaggerated by the bright blood on her lips, but the fangs were gone. Kissing her once again, he licked their mingled blood from her mouth. "Better?" he asked as he pulled away.

Vicky studied him with glassy eyes before nodding numbly.

"Good." He sat her up and held her for a minute longer. Some of his power was still swirling inside her, but retrieving it would have to wait. There were other things that needed to be taken care of. "Come on." Darien slipped her from his lap and stood up without releasing her left hand. Power slowly trickled down the line connecting them.

18

It was hard to decide where to start. Now that he had his powers back, he could feel the worry from his kiss. He washed their connections over with reassurance before turning to the matters at hand. His people would be coming soon to help.

Darien looked down at Travis' still body. The loss of life pained him. Why couldn't the dead man have used that wish for a more meaningful purpose?

"I'm sorry." Vicky's voice trembled with unfallen tears.

Darien rolled her into his side, holding her. "It's not your fault," he reassured her. Reaching out, Darien grabbed his sword and yanked it out of the dead man's chest. Power coursed up his arm from the relic, and he smiled. If nothing else, the sword was happy that it had been used again.

"Come on." Darien steered Vicky around Travis' body to where Allen was leaning against the tire of the van, holding his leg. Darien released Vicky and knelt down next to the injured man.

"Let me see." Reaching out, he grabbed ahold of Allen's pant leg and sliced the hem with his sword. Dropping the large blade to the floor, Darien ripped up the side of Allen's jeans.

Vicky gagged as she turned away from the ruined mess that was Allen's leg. The skin had sloughed off, and the muscle was starting to melt away from the bone.

Darien poked at the flesh, making Allen hiss in pain. "I'm sorry," he said as he placed his hands against the massive wound.

Allen tried to smile through the pain. "Just another day at the park."

Darien chuckled at the attempt to lighten the moment. He opened himself to his power and poured it into Allen's leg.

The man let out a groan of relief as the pain stopped and the flesh slowly started to knit back together.

Concentrating on setting the cells to regenerate, he pulled his hands back and watched for a moment to make sure the healing process continued before looking up at Allen's face. "Give it a few minutes to heal." He patted the man on the shoulder.

Allen nodded and leaned his head back against the tire to wait.

Darien picked up his sword and stood up. There were still more who needed his help. "Thank you for stopping him." He leaned into Vicky and kissed the side of her head.

Vicky shrugged and leaned into his comforting warmth.

Darien led them over to where Jakob was wrapped around his brother's body. The surviving twin had pulled his limp brother up into his lap and rocked him.

Jakob looked up when Darien approached. "Please, Master," he begged, "save him!" Tears streamed down Jakob's face.

Darien squatted next to them and reached out to touch Josh's body. Closing his eyes, he let out a forlorn sigh and shook his head. There was no life left in the man's body.

Jakob reached out and grabbed onto Darien's arm before he could pull it back. "Please, Master. *Please!*"

Darien looked down to the blistered hand of the desperate brother before looking back up into his face.

Jakob could see the hopelessness in Darien's eyes. "*PLEASE!*" He clutched at his master's arm.

Darien nodded. "I'll see what I can do." He pulled free of Jakob's fingers and stood up.

"Can you save him?" Vicky asked as Jakob wrapped himself

around his twin again. She wiped at a tear rolling down her cheek.

"How'd he die?" Darien asked as he looked over the pair folded together. Josh had already been down when he had come to.

"I didn't mean to," Vicky hiccupped. "He lunged at me and kind of fell on your sword."

Darien looked at her, shocked. "My sword?" He looked down at the bloody metal in his hand.

Vicky nodded. "It was the first thing I could lay my hands on." She sniffed back her anguish. "I didn't mean to hurt him."

Darien threw his head back and laughed. Sighing in joy, he looked over at the shocked look on Vicky's face. Reaching out, he wrapped his hand around the back of her neck and pulled her close. He kissed her softly and looked into her confused eyes. "I love you." Releasing her, Darien turned towards the last problem.

The tip of his sword tinked loudly as it hit the ground in front of the mass of greenish-black tentacles. Leaning on the weapon, Darien studied the hellhound and his captive. He couldn't make out where the center of Zak was, but the tips of the tentacles wiggled, waiting for Darien's word. "Down, Zak," Darien said softly.

The mass of ends wiggled and unfurled, leaving Elliot limp on the floor. Zak had ahold of the back of his coat. He shook it furiously with a growl before releasing the vampire and wobbling over to rub against Darien's leg.

Darien reached down and ruffled the fay lightly before Zak wiggled off to check on Vicky.

"Are you alive?" Darien asked his unmoving friend.

Elliot's eyes cracked open.

They glowed gold with a power Darien didn't remember seeing in his friend before. He pondered it as he leaned on his sword, waiting for Elliot to sit up and take stock of his faculties.

Elliot leaned forwards to rest against one bent-up knee

while the other leg stretched out in front of him. He looked a little mauled, but seemed to be in one piece. "My life, My Lord." Elliot hung his head.

Darien let out a long sigh. Proper etiquette required payment for Elliot's attack on his master. Darien pushed up from leaning on his sword. "Stand up, my friend." He held his hand down to Elliot.

Elliot looked up at him in disbelief.

"We both know you were not in control."

Regret washed across Elliot's face.

"Besides, we have work to do."

Elliot's eyes flashed to Josh and Jakob, then back up to Darien.

Darien nodded.

Elliot took Darien's hand and let the greater vampire pull him to his feet. "My Lord." He hung his head in shame as he held on to Darien's arm.

"Stop it," Darien snapped as he pulled his hand back from Elliot. "We can talk about it later if you want, but there are other things needed now." Turning, Darien knelt down next to Jakob. "I need you to let him go." He touched Jakob's shoulder, drawing him away from his brother.

Jakob clutched at the lifeless form for a moment before letting Darien separate them.

Vicky's hands pulled him up and away.

Darien caught Vicky's eye as she helped Jakob up. A moment of gratitude and silent understanding passed between them.

Vicky turned Jakob into her, and he buried his face in her shoulder, wrapping his arms around her. She returned his embrace, giving him as much comfort as she could.

Elliot and Darien straightened Josh's body out to look at it. Elliot touched the cold skin and grimaced. He shot Darien a sickened look. "How did he die?" he asked, looking at the single wound in his stomach.

"My sword," Darien said softly.

Shock raced over Elliot's face as he looked up at Vicky holding

Jakob. The vampire was peeking out, watching them work.

"A single thrust, here?" Elliot asked, pointing to the wound.

Vicky nodded.

Darien pulled up his shirt to look at it. "From an upward angle," he said, imagining how the sword would have slid in. Mimicking the movement needed to make the wound made Jakob squeeze Vicky tighter.

Vicky nodded and patted the upset man. "I didn't think it would kill him." Her voice cracked with sorrow.

"Normally it wouldn't." Elliot sat Josh up and looked at the exit wound. "But Darien's sword is special."

Both Jakob and Vicky looked at the bloody blade next to Darien.

Elliot stripped the coat and shoulder harness from Josh's body.

"The fay enchanted the blade long ago to help in one of their battles," Darien explained. "It's how it got its name. It doesn't matter what the creature is, a mortal wound from this blade will pull the life from them."

Vicky pulled back from Jakob as she thought. "But, I had to stab Darecy twice to kill him."

"How long did you leave it in him before you pulled it out?" Darien asked, looking up at her.

"A few seconds," Vicky answered. It had seemed like an eternity, but it had only been a moment before she pulled it out and rammed it into his heart.

Darien turned his attention back to where Elliot was lying Josh back down. "It takes a moment for the blade to work."

Elliot tucked the coat in under the still man's head.

"Plus, it had already eaten once."

"*Eaten!*" Jakob shrieked as he turned from Vicky. He looked down at the wicked blade and to his brother. "Can you save him?"

"We will try," Darien promised.

Vicky placed a hand on Jakob's shoulder as he sunk to the

floor in despair.

Zak gurgled and rubbed up against him. The fay turned to watch as the two vampires prepared Josh's body.

Darien and Elliot exchanged glances; the chances of this actually working were slim, and they both knew it.

"My blood would be better," Darien said from where he knelt near Josh's feet.

"*I'll* do it," Elliot cut Darien off before he could continue. He knew Darien was low on blood at the moment. He wasn't sure how much he had taken, but Elliot could feel the power from Darien's blood coursing through his veins. Hopefully, it would be enough.

Darien nodded and stood up. He picked up the sword and looked over at Vicky and Jakob. "You may not want to watch this," he warned.

Jakob nodded and wrapped his arm between Vicky's legs and round her calf.

Vicky reached out and caught his other hand. She held it tightly and nodded.

Darien shrugged and turned towards Elliot. "Are you ready?"

Elliot nodded as he took up his position above Josh's head. Pulling his sleeve back, he held his wrist out to Darien.

Grabbing it, Darien slid the sharp edge of the Damascus steel across Elliot's skin. A line of blood ran down and dribbled across Josh as Elliot pulled it back and pressed the wound into the dead man's mouth. Darien took up a stance straddling Josh about the knees. "Here goes nothing." Darien slid his thumb down the blade, slicing it open. He pulled more magic from the world and ran the wounded down the fuller of the sword. "Dubhlainn..." he breathed the name of the sword.

The runes etched into the groove glowed with power, making Darien smile. He aimed the sword at Josh's wound and carefully slid the sharp blade back into the cut. "Return what you have taken!" he ordered. The sword warmed in his hand but did nothing. "*Ar ais an méid atá tógtha agat!*" he tried again in

Gaelic. This time, the swirls in the blade shone with light. "Please work." Darien prayed as light shimmered down the sword and into the wound. He carefully pulled the sword out and dropped it to the floor. Covering the wound with his hand, Darien willed the flesh to heal. He looked up at Elliot and pulled his hand back from the sealed wound.

Elliot pulled his wrist from Josh's mouth, but Josh didn't move.

"*No!*" Jakob screamed as he turned his face into Vicky's legs.

Darien crouched down, looking over his fallen friend. He placed his hand on his chest and opened himself up to check him. Power was swirling inside Josh, but it hadn't yet found where it was supposed to go.

"You could try CPR," Vicky suggested.

Darien looked up at her, confused.

"It's worth a shot." She shrugged.

Darien looked over at Elliot. The man had backed up from Josh's head, holding his still-bleeding wrist.

"Here," Vicky huffed, untangling herself from the distressed vampire wrapped around her leg. "Do the chest compressions, and I'll do the breaths."

Darien chuckled as he repositioned himself. "I know how to do CPR." He placed his hands above Josh's sternum and waited for Vicky to start.

She tipped Josh's head back and pulled down his chin. Blood poured out from where it had pooled in his mouth. Vicky wrinkled her nose at the mess but sealed her lips over his and blew, filling Josh's lungs with blood and air.

He coughed harshly and gasped as life flooded back into him.

Vicky jerked back as blood flew up and splashed across her face.

Josh's eyes popped open, and he looked around, bewildered.

"*Josh!*" Jakob leaped to his brother's side.

Darien just managed to get out of the way before Jakob lay across his brother in a crushing hug.

Shock rode Josh's face as he wrapped his arms up around his tormented brother. He looked up at Vicky for an explanation.

"I'm so sorry." Tears of joy spilled down her face as she wiped the blood droplets away.

He turned confused eyes to Darien.

"You just spent the last few minutes dead." Darien smiled at him and patted his brother on the back. "Up," he ordered.

Jakob slowly relinquished his hold on Josh's body but claimed his hand, unwilling to let him go completely.

"Josh?" Darien asked.

"Master," Josh answered him.

Darien placed his fingers on Josh's chest and probed him. Everything seemed to be in the right place, but only time would tell if there was lasting damage or side effects. Getting a soul out of the sword was easy, but Darien had never succeeded in putting it back into its owner before. Someone must be smiling down on them today. The thought of God helping vampires made Darien's lips curl in irony. "Come on." Darien slid a hand in behind Josh and helped the confused vampire to sit up.

Jakob grabbed onto him and pulled him into a crushing hold.

Darien looked over them and sighed. He reached out and touched Jakob on the neck, opening his power back up to heal the wounds Travis had caused. After a few moments, he pulled back and stood up. Vicky caught hold of him as he staggered, lightheaded. He had used way too much of his power on top of the blood loss. They were all going to be in need of a good feeding soon.

"My life, My Lady." Jakob reached out and wrapped his hand around Vicky's ankle.

She looked down at him, confused.

"And mine," Josh added.

Vicky could see that the confused man really didn't understand what was going on, but if his brother was pledging to someone, he would, too. "Umm..." She stood there, shocked, unsure what they were doing.

"We will talk about this later." Darien stood up looking around at the bloody mess around them. They were going to need to get out of here before some innocent bystander came in and found them. Bending over, Darien caught up his mostly clean coat and pulled it on over his ruined shirt.

"Master!" A call and the sounds of footsteps echoed up from the ramp.

Darien turned to see half a dozen people running towards them. He let out a relieved sigh and smiled at them. The cavalry had finally arrived with Harold leading the group.

"Thank God." Darien sighed, looking over the mix of his and Elliot's people. "Thanks for coming." Moving to meet the incoming people, he held out his hand to Walter. Walter was the oldest vampire Darien had acquired and was nearly a master himself. Darien hadn't expected the rugged man to join in on this fight.

"All you needed to do was ask, My Lord." Walter bowed to Darien.

Darien smiled at him. "Thank you, my friend." He looked over the faces in the group. "Thank you all." A murmur of welcome came back to him.

"What would you have of us?" Walter asked as he surveyed the aftermath of the battle.

Darien turned to the depressing scene. "We need to get out of here." He looked back to the group. "Go get whatever vehicles you brought. Allen, Josh, and Jakob are all going to need help out of here and a good supply of blood." Several heads nodded and turned back towards the ramp to the lower levels. "Harold," Darien called to the young man.

Harold stepped out of the group. "Yes, Master?"

"Do you remember the church where we first met?" Darien asked.

The young man nodded his head.

"Good. Take someone and load up Darecy's body in his van. Drive it out to that church, and drag him to the center of the cemetery behind the church. Don't worry about burying him. Beckett," Darien looked at the only other male vampire in his kiss. Beckett was barely old enough to be called a man, despite the fact that he had been a vampire for nearly eighty years. "Go with them in case they run into trouble."

Beckett nodded.

Harold grabbed Billy, a younger man from Elliot's group, and the three went to deal with the dead man.

"And don't linger in the graveyard!" Darien yelled after them.

Harold raised his hand in acknowledgement.

"You're just going to dump him?" Walter asked, shocked.

Darien shot him a devious grin. "I have a friend out there who will take care of him for me."

Walter's mouth opened to ask, but he thought better and shut it.

Darien turned to look at what was left. Elliot had gathered up the loose swords and stood quietly waiting for Darien to finish. "Thank you." Darien took his sword and wiped the blood off on his pants before sliding it back in the scabbard. He was really going to need to clean it well when they got home. The sound of cars drew his attention back to the ramp, and three vehicles pulled up and surrounded them.

"Let's get the hell out of here." Darien turned to collect Vicky and Zak. Weariness had started to creep into his bones, and he just wanted to find a nice, warm place to rest for a while.

19

"IN OTHER NEWS, A BOMB WAS DISCOVERED AT THE CHRISTMAS VILLAGE IN HYDE Park last night. Two good Samaritans, who wish to remain anonymous, found the improvised device and pulled it apart mere seconds before it was remotely activated. Police have traced the number and are currently looking for this man—" A picture of a familiar face popped up on the television screen. "—Travis Darecy. He's been linked to a few other attacks in the downtown area and should be considered armed and dangerous. If you have any information on his whereabouts, please call the tip hotline."

Vicky turned to look at Rose curled up in one of the upstairs entertainment room's armchairs in the menagerie's home as they watched the early morning news. "I wouldn't know how to pull a bomb apart."

"It was easy." Rose waved the amazing feat away. "I just yanked the wires out of the brick of C-4. It wasn't made very well."

"Well, thank you anyway." Vicky smiled at the other woman. "I can't believe the audacity of that man!" she huffed.

Rose let out a sigh. "What happened to him, anyway?" she asked. The police had detained her all night getting her statement and asking questions. She had just barely gotten home before dawn.

"He's been dealt with," Darien growled from where he sat

on the far end of the couch. He stretched, tired from the long night.

Getting everyone settled had taken a lot more effort than Darien had thought possible. Once the call had gone out that Darecy had been stopped, everyone involved in the hunt descended on Lillian's old home. Darien's group had arrived to find over two dozen people ready to help with the injured.

The flourish of activity had woken Erin and Bridget, and Mary had encouraged the two little girls to visit. Once they had gotten over their shyness, the little girls raced around the house, squealing with delight. There were more than a few souls willing to play chase with them.

Overall, the night had gone pretty well. Allen and Jakob were both fully healed and fed. Josh was having a hard time dealing with the idea that he had spent part of the night truly dead, but his brother was staying close to him. The two men had, once again, offered Vicky their lives and followed her around making sure she wanted for nothing. Darien had finally gotten upset with them for being underfoot and had sent them to bed. They only agreed to leave after he promised that he and Vicky would remain there until the brothers rose again.

Darien had a shadow of his own throughout the night. Elliot was making sure Darien didn't have anything to do. Every time Darien went to deal with something, the younger vampire was already handling it. He'd made sure everyone was fed, instructed Harold as to where to stow Darecy's van until he could arrange for its disposal, and even managed sleeping arrangements for the oodles of people who were remaining for the day. Darien was truly grateful for Elliot's help, but the stiff formality that had slipped into his demeanor was starting to grate on Darien's nerves. He was going to have to sit the younger vampire down and have a long talk with him soon, but that could wait until he had rested.

"Are you ready for bed?" Darien looked over to where Vicky sat on the couch. After a long night of playing, Zak, Erin, and

Bridget had all curled up in Vicky's lap and were snoring away softly.

Vicky rubbed the blonde curls on the younger one's head lovingly. "Yes." She smiled up at Darien. "But I'm going to need some help here."

Darien chuckled and stood up from his end of the couch. He scooped up the larger of the girls and let Rose claim the younger.

Bridget wrapped an arm around Darien's neck and snuggled into him.

He rubbed her back soothingly as he followed Rose to the girls' room. Pulling back the covers, he tucked the little girl in before turning to check on Rose tucking Erin in.

Rose checked on Darien's work before following him out of the room. "You would make a good father."

Vicky smiled at him from where she waited in the hall with Zak in her arms. "That he would."

Darien wrapped an arm around her and kissed the side of her head. "Vampires can't have children." He gave Vicky a sad smile. "Besides, I wouldn't know the first thing about children."

"You'd figure it out fast." Rose smiled at them. "The only difference between kids and pets is the ability to talk back." She scratched her fingers into Zak's fur.

"Then I should be well on my way." Darien laughed and rubbed Zak's head.

The small fay gurgled at him.

"Come on." Darien slid his hand down Vicky's back and turned her towards the bedroom Elliot had arranged for them. "It's well past time for bed."

"Good night, Master." Rose waved goodbye and headed back into the den to sit for a while longer. Dawn was just starting to break, but the vampires in Darien's kiss were in no danger of being pulled in by the power of the sun. Darien had opened all their connections up so they could draw on his strength freely. He found it odd having so many pressing on his mind, but after a few days, he would get used to it. It had been foolish to hold them at arm's length when he had first acquired them. Had he not been so standoffish, one of them might have been more comfortable coming to him when they were having issues with the connection early on. Just that hint would have been enough to set Darien looking for the problem. They would have been able to find Darecy long before he finished stealing Darien's power, avoiding this whole ordeal.

"Good night," Darien called after her and led Vicky down the hall to their room. He shut the door behind him and turned the lock on the door. "Finally alone." He leaned forwards and kissed Vicky on the lips. A gurgle rose up between them, pushing a chuckle from Darien. "Well," he ruffled Zak still held in Vicky's arms, "mostly alone."

Zak sneezed his displeasure and leapt down from Vicky's arms. Finding a chair, he shook out of his dog disguise and jumped up in it.

"You're probably going to lose another pair of pants tonight." Vicky smiled as she pulled the hem of Darien's shirt from his waistband.

He let out a long-suffering sigh and pulled her into his arms. "Que será, será." He smiled down at her. "I have others." Vicky laughed as he leaned forwards and pressed a kiss to her lips. Darien was ready to push the rest of the world away for now. His powers were back and his people were once again secure. There was still much that needed to be addressed, but right now, he was just interested in the warmth of the woman in his arms. They could figure everything else out later. What would be... would be.

Epilogue

"YOUR PLAN DIDN'T WORK. HE'S STILL ALIVE." A WARM VOICE CUT THROUGH THE cold morning air. Two figures stood at the edge of the tree line, watching the lights going out in the house.

"How many of your plans have failed over the hundreds of years you've followed him?" A second voice crackled in scorn.

"You have a point." The first one sighed.

"Fear not, I have other things set in motion."

"Good." The taller of the two figures turned to look at his companion. "I've tired of this world."

"Soon you will get to go back." The darker of the two growled in disgust. "But, remember our deal."

"Of course." The first voice sneered. "Everything had been arranged, just make sure he dies." A flurry of feathers rustled out as the tallest of the pair shot into the air and disappeared into the growing dawn.

"Foul creature." The second figure growled. He studied the quiet house for a minute thinking of its contents. Usually, he liked vampires, but this group was proving to be more of a pain than others.

"You're end will come soon." The dark shape stepped back and melted into the shadows without a sound. Dead leaves skittered across the cold ground wiping away all traces that the pair had ever been there.

About the Author

Originally from Ohio, Julie always dreamed of a job in science. Either shooting for the stars or delving into the mysteries of volcanoes. But, life never leads where you expect. In 2007, she moved to Mississippi to be with her significant other.

Now a mother of a hyperactive red headed boy, what time she's not chasing down dirty socks and unsticking toys from the ceiling is spent crafting worlds readers can get lost it. Julie is a self-proclaimed bibliophile and lover of big words. She likes hiking, frogs, interesting earrings, and a plethora of other fun things.

Acknowledgements

WELL, HERE WE ARE AT THE END OF ANOTHER BOOK. I HOPE EVERYONE ENJOYED it as much as I enjoyed bringing it to you. I'm still beside myself about this whole publishing thing. In the past, there were times when I fantasized about being a writer, but it was a passing fancy and never a real goal. At one time I had this great detective story I was all gung-ho about, but it never made it out of my head. It boggles my mind to think that this is my fourth published book. I pray every day that I don't lose whatever I've found that leads me to these great stories.

But, of course, these stories would never happen without a whole lot of people behind me. The ladies at CTP are my heroes. They have supported and encouraged me every step of the way. They have dealt with my tantrums and demands with grace and help to bring these books together. There is also my family. I know we have argued over things involving the books, but thank you all for being there for me.

The last group I need to thank are my friends. The staff at HobbytownUSA, the racer guys from FRC, and all the people that have sat down and listened to me rattle on or complain about bookish things. Without your ear to bend, I probably would have exploded from frustration and excitement. Thank you.

Now if you will excuse me, I need to go back to my box so

I can get the next novel ready. Thank you all for coming on this amazing ride with me!